BUTTERFLY JAR

A novel by
Jalondra A. Davis

www.JalondraADavis.com

Butterfly Jar

Dancingquills Industries

103 S. Locust St.

Inglewood, CA

ISBN-13: 978-0615627649

ISBN-10: 0615627641

Cover design by Ljliljana Kovacevic.

www.jalondraadavis.com

This book is dedicated to my family
and especially to the memory of Gregory Davis Jr.

Acknowledgments

Thanks first and foremost to my Creator, my ancestors, and the divine source of all life and creativity. I would like to acknowledge all of the family, friends, students, colleagues, and associates who have supported my various endeavors tirelessly through the years and who have helped to keep me accountable to fulfilling this goal. To the Davis family, who have always been my cheerleaders, my confidantes, heroes, and greatest inspiration, thank you for always loving me and rushing to my rescue. I want to especially thank the women in my family for providing such examples of strength and such incredible capacity for fiercely protective, unconditional love. To my loving partner Lorenzo, the Brown family, and my best friends Sandra and Buffany, thank you for always advising me, looking out for me, and being there. To my colleagues, mentors, friends, family, and students at CSU Dominguez Hills and Precision Dance Company, thank you for your support, and for patiently sharing me with this project. Thank you to Michael Datcher, my ongoing mentor and the first to believe in my writing career and to Nicole Sconiers for the attention, inspiration, and support. To my prior-release readers, thank you for your honest and helpful feedback. Thank you to Ljiljana Kovacevic and Joanne Asala for the impeccable editing and design work. Thank you to my teachers, mentors and friends at Loyola Marymount University, the Master of Professional Writing Program at the University of Southern California, Lula Washington Dance Theatre, the Anansi Writer's Workshop at the World Stage Arts Gallery, and the LA poetry community. Thank you to everyone that I didn't mention who has encouraged me throughout the years. I am because you all are.

Jalondra A. Davis

Chapter One

I was in the fifth grade when the light-skinned and dark-skinned girls started to form distinct banana and chocolate puddles on the yard. I was ten years old when the boys shifted from tormenting us all to targeting those with the symmetry and curves of their liking. A fat wadded note or a snapped training bra strap meant the same thing, and I was the object of neither. When I was ten years old, the mirror became more than something I looked into when my mother made me brush my teeth; it glared at me with grasshopper bulb eyes with not even a light color to redeem them, with muddy brown skin sprouting white-tipped spikes, and one overbiting front tooth overlapping the other like a big brother blocking a punch.

I knew my mother didn't like me much. It was in the way she studied me, the way she snatched the comb through my hair with no mercy. It was in the rough way she scrubbed my face and the aggression of how she drove on those repeated trips to the orthodontist. My mother was light boned with praline-candy skin so soft it looked like you could put your fingers through it. It looked like someone, maybe God, had reached in and set her bubble-plump mouth, her hairbrush-thick eyelashes, the single mole on her temple right in place. My godmother Trish always said that one day I'd straighten out to be a fine young lady, but I doubted her. I could tell from sepia-toned photos in Grandmere's house that my mother had been beautiful on every day of her life. I covered my mouth every time I smiled.

It was my father who first noticed that I hid my teeth. We were playing tickle monster, one of those games we made up just for an excuse to bump and shriek on the carpet. My father's skin was rough and hairy, and I had seen him slice himself with a handsaw and barely flinch when my mother poured hydrogen peroxide over the wound. He was ticklish only on the very bottoms of his feet. I would sneak up on him and snatch off his ratty, funky house shoes, unless he caught me up and got me first. I loved it, the thrill of creeping up as he nodded off in front of the TV, the gleeful panic of being snatched into his arms, his growling in my ears, his musky scent in my nose, his leathery fingers grazing my waist and shoving beneath my arms as I kicked and thrashed in his strong grip.

We were playing tickle monster one night in November, the month I started wearing my old Tinker Bell sweatshirt around the house so we could save on the gas bill. I had ambushed my father as he watched a *Cosby* rerun on our fuzzy twenty-seven-inch screen. Before I got one of his beat-down Dearfoams off, he grabbed me and drum-thumped beats on my neck until I screamed. I was vaguely conscious of how long my legs had gotten, kicking the side of his leaning recliner instead of the air like they used to, of how I had to balance on his lap to not fall. My mother shouted from the kitchen for us to shut up, and his grip loosened. I wriggled away, rolling across the floor, my hands going to my mouth to cover my laughter.

"C'mere, Tanis," he said, beckoning with his finger. His voice had changed suddenly, sounding like it did the time I soaked his Camels in the sink. I walked up to him in my slouchy, slew-footed way, my pudgy belly hanging over the glittery belt on my jeans.

"How old is you, ten? Ain't that old to still be losing teeth?"

"I have all my teeth."

"Then why you keep covering your mouth up like that?"

"I don't know."

"You shouldn't be doing nothing if you don't know why you're doing it. You smarter than that."

"I don't want people looking at my teeth," I whispered, cupping my hands around my mouth.

"I ain't people. I'm your daddy. What's wrong with your teeth?"

"They stick out. They don't look right."

"Who told you that?"

"People at school say so."

"What I tell you about listening to people? People just jealous. People ain't nobody in this house."

"Mommy says so, too." I shouldn't have said that and knew it. I watched my father's eyebrows clench in tighter.

"Becky!" he barked. His voice shook the house, but we heard nothing from the kitchen but the ringing of plates and rush of running water.

"Becky!" He rose from his recliner, unrolling like a six-five, 300-pound Tootsie Roll. My mother still didn't answer, but the cymbal clash of the plates got louder.

"Rebecca, don't act like you don't hear me!" We heard a plate slam down so hard I wondered if it had cracked.

My mother appeared in the doorway, her reddish-brown hair pulled into a knot on top of her head, gripping the dishtowel on her hip with dark-red nails. I expected her to yell back, but she leaned against the flaking paint of the doorjamb and spoke softly. "Did you want something, baby?" she asked. Something in her tone, something hard and sarcastic, took away from the uneasy, giggly warmth I usually felt when my parents called each other baby. My father sat back down, his chair screeching out in protest. He took his Dearfoam out of my hand and stuffed it on his big, cracking foot.

"What you been telling this girl about her teeth?"

"I haven't been telling her anything. Anybody can see her teeth aren't straight."

"Ain't nothing wrong with her mouth. She fine."

"You only saying that 'cause she got those messed-up Sutton teeth. You know all those messed-up teeth run all through your side of the family."

"Can't nothing be worse than that evil running all through yours."

"Evil?" My mother stood up straight from the doorjamb. "At least they have something. My grandmere's people got big houses down in the Bayou. Businesses, good jobs. You don't even know my people like that to be—"

"Here we go with that shit. You such a princess, take your ass back to your grandma, leave my baby with me. Leave her to you, you'll have her all fucked up in the head like your fake French grandma did you."

"Please," my mother laughed. "Yeah, I'll leave her with you. You gonna comb hair every day, you gonna drive back and forth to school every day, you gonna buy clothes she grow out of every week, you gonna pay for braces. Three-thousand dollars, Tannah, that's what they cost. You got that? People talking about her at school, pictures looking like I don't know what."

"Becky, go on with that shit; I don't want to hear all that shit."

"Yeah, I didn't think you did. Wasn't anybody bothering you." She swung her hips back into the kitchen, muttering to herself, and my father sank back into his chair, heavily. He took his cigarette pack out of his pocket and shook one out.

"Daddy." I tugged his sweatpants leg.

"Yeah?"

"We're doing the DARE program at school."

"What's that about? Daring people to do things or something?" he asked absently.

"No, Daddy," I said solemnly. "It's about learning how to say no to drugs and alcohol and tobacco products." I stood up, broke into the song and dance we were learning for the commencement of the DARE program.

DARE! To keep a kid off drugs.

DARE! To keep a kid off dope.

DARE! To give a kid some help.

DARE! To give a kid some hope.

I spun around and started in on the ad libs, which only the kid who got picked for the solo did when we practiced at school, with me mouthing along in the back. I tended not to get picked for things like that.

Weeeee, we real-ly need your help, oh yeah, we need your help—

"Okay, okay, baby," my dad broke in. "You sound really nice, you have a pretty voice. I didn't know they talked about all that type of stuff in fifth grade."

"Oh, yeah. I'm learning a lot. About how marijuana is a gateway drug and how tobacco products cause lung cancer and emphysema and even..." I dropped my voice to a whisper. "Even death."

My dad took out his royal blue plastic lighter. "Is that so?"

"And black gums."

"Really?"

"And stinky breath."

"Ain't that something." He lit the cigarette and deeply inhaled.

"And," I ripped off his house shoe. "Stinky tickle monster toes!" I squealed, reaching for his feet.

"That's enough, Tanis." He took his floppy shoe back. It was so old the wooly cushion was almost black, and the sole had split almost completely from the rest of it. "Daddy tired now."

I scooted closer to his leg. He took another drag and stared at the TV, where Bill and Clair Huxtable were ballroom dancing in the foyer. He took a sip of the beer from the folding table by his chair.

"Daddy—"

"Tanis, go on now," he repeated without looking my way, his voice weary but firm.

I crawled up off our dark-brown carpet and walked through our tiny dining area to the kitchen. I picked off flakes of peeling pea-green paint from the doorsill with my nails as I watched my mother wash dishes. I could see my mother anywhere in the world and know her from the back alone. She sweated easily, and her fine, Creole-silk hair always curled, moist and lazy, against the nape of her neck. Her back was small and slender, and her shoulder blades stood out in a back that looked like it should only be touched with fingertips. Her sides arced down into a small waist and back out into a high-mounted, plum-shaped butt my father said you couldn't miss from a block away. Her torso was short, and the rest of her length was all slim bowlegs covered by her bleach-stained, around-the-house leggings. She never looked down when she washed the dishes, just out through the window over the sink, even when it was dark outside.

"Is your homework done?" she asked abruptly without turning around. Never in my life was I ever able to sneak up on my mother, to watch her without her sensing it, to get close without her knowing.

"Not quite completely."

"Not quite completely, my ass. It's either done or it's not. You better get in there and make that not quite completely quite complete."

"I am. Mommy?"

"What, girl?"

"I didn't mean to get you in trouble with Daddy," I said, even though maybe I had. She turned and looked at me with exasperation. "Girl, get on out of my face. And wash your hands. I don't know why you like to set there and play with people's feet, especially your daddy's nasty feet. You're getting too old for stuff like that."

"Yeah, Mommy."

"Yeah or yes?"

"Yes, Mommy." She nodded and turned back to the sink. She turned back half towards me, her face and voice a little softer. "Go on, I'll come in and help you, later."

"I can do it by myself," I said, dropping paint flakes into the trash.

My teeth continued to be one of many volatile topics in my family that we jumped over like the broken step of the back porch. My mother shook her head at my school pictures, the ones before I started hiding my teeth and the ones with my lips so tightly closed you could see the tension in my face and a frightening wildness in my already big eyes. "Lord, have mercy," my mother would say, holding up a picture. "And I was going to give one of these to Grandmere. Why'd you have to smile like that?" My father continued to tape my pictures all over his dashboard and tell me there was nothing wrong with me. But the more I got clowned on at school, the more I suspected that my mother's assessment was closer to the truth.

I was tight with a boy in my fifth-grade class named Yosi. When the other girls played double-dutch, which I wasn't that great at, and the boys played basketball, which Yosi wasn't that great at, we spent recess and lunch together catching insects in jars. I'd finish off the jelly or pickles in jars at home, rinse loose their labels under the hot water faucet, get my father to drill holes in their tops for air, and sneak them to school in my back-pack. There was a spot along the back gate of our school facing a quiet block of small, worn Spanish-style houses. Here, deep-green bushes climbed the chain-link metal and grew thick as my hair, sprouting small red flowers and dripping spit puddles of sugary sap on the asphalt. The bushes created a dark, cool space hidden from the rest of the campus by nearby handball courts. This was the place where girls told secrets and sixth graders played Hide and Go Get It and Truth and Dare, where the truth was always "do you like so-and-so?" and the dare was always to kiss with tongue.

For Yosi and me, this was the butterfly place. We caught the tiny brownish-orange kind, pinching their coarse, powdery wings between our thumbs and forefingers as they landed on a flower and stuck long black tongues into its center. I had never been graceful, never been patient, and never been able to be quiet for too long. But somehow, when it came to catching butterflies, I was silent and soft-footed, I moved slowly and did not speak, I stood next to Yosi with my breath held and my own heartbeat in my ears and waited for that perfect moment. We swept them into our jars, where we had put small flowers and tiny red tomatoes we found growing in the kindergarten yard. This was their food, though they still always died after a few weeks. I had about fifteen living butterflies in my jar then, but Yosi had twenty-three.

The other kids in class said that Yosi and I would grow up to get married and do the nasty; they liked to say that when we got married and did the nasty our babies would have six legs and wings. I hated this and responded with screeching and fists, leaving Yosi to hunt alone while I spent recess or lunch on punishment inside. He never protested much when we were teased in this way, so I shouldn't have been surprised that he turned out to be the first boy who ever liked me.

This first relationship began in a classroom that stank of must and chalk and saliva, of the droppings from the class guinea pig and the vague fishy smell coming from Mrs. Ackerson-Smith's Tupperware. One Friday, I raised my desktop to find an envelope taped around my bug jar with butterflies and hearts and stars drawn all over it, looping along an intertwined Y and T. I checked that my teacher, Mrs. Ackerson-Smith, was occupied and opened it.

Dear Tannis,

You are my best friend. I like talking about Power Rangers with you and catching butterflies. You never make fun of me when I stutter. Your hair smells like cocoa butter and grass. Will you go with me and be my girl?

Then, further down:

Check Yes __ No __ Maybe__

My stomach burned on the inside. I knew my mother's opinion of kids "going together" at our age. "Go where?" she'd say. "Where can ten year olds go, except behind the bungalows to do something nasty? Stay out of these boys' faces, Tanis, only fast-tailed little girls get up in boys' faces, and you already know what fast-tailed little girls grow up to be." She had pointed out to me what fast-tailed girls grew up to be when I asked about the ladies in heels and skirts riding up their thighs who tottered up and down Figueroa, ratty duffels or just plain grocery bags clutched in one hand. I knew I didn't want to be that as much as I knew I wanted to be liked, even if it was just by Yosi.

I slipped a look at him as Mrs. Ackerson-Smith (whom we liked to call Ms. Ass-Lick on the yard) crackled on about constitutional amendments. Yosi was as bony as I was chunky, with big lips that didn't help his stutter and black licorice-colored skin. He always smelled puppy-musty, but then, so did most of the boys in school. I thought his profile was dignified as he took diligent notes I would copy later. I admired his focus, whether it was on catching a butterfly, diagramming a sentence, or chasing one of my ribbons that came loose. I checked "yes" on the note and wrote across the bottom in my scrawled printing:

What does your girl have to do? I'm not going behind the bungalows.

On the pretense of sharpening my pencil, I got up and crossed the room, dropping the note on Yosi's desk on my way.

"Tanis Victoria Sutton." I jumped at the sound of Mrs. Ackerson-Smith's gravelly voice. "We ask permission to leave our seats in this classroom."

"I'm sorry," I said. "My pencil broke, and I was eager to sharpen it so that I wouldn't miss any notes about our nation's Constitution." I had learned at some point that using words like "eager" and "speaking" in an exaggeratedly proper way confused and infuriated teachers. They sensed that you were making fun of them somehow but couldn't identify a punishable offense. As she glared at me, I hurried back to my seat, feeling Yosi's eyes on my back. I felt conscious of everything: my big tee shirt gripping my butt and thighs where I had pulled it to the side over my cotton leggings and secured it with a hot pink scrunchy; my different-colored, Punky Brewster stacked slouch socks rubbing against my shins; the hard plastic points of my barrettes knocking against my neck. I wondered what my mother would do to me if she found out, and how the other kids in class would look at me if I became one of the first girls to have a boyfriend. The girls would envy me and welcome me into double-dutch games. The boys would cease calling me Chipmunk and see me as desirable. Focusing was impossible, so I stared at Mrs. Ackerson-Smith with wide, intrigued eyes, knowing that, in her daily need to humiliate, she only called on kids who looked like they weren't paying attention.

A few minutes after I had delivered my reply, Tia Nichols tapped me on the shoulder and handed me a folded-up wad of notebook paper. I unfolded it in my lap.

*What's behind the bungalows? We can just do the stuff we always
do. You can come over to my house to watch the Power Rangers*

finale if your mom will let you. I think the green one is going to die. And you have to eat lunch with me every day because my papi eats with my mama every night.

"Tanis Victoria, do you have something you would like to share with the class?" Ms. Ass-Lick's voice interrupted my thoughts. I snatched my head up in a rush of clattering barrettes.

"Yes," I said quickly.

"Yes?" She raised her skinny, drawn-on eyebrows.

"I would like to share my love for our nation's Constitution. Our nation's founders were brilliant men."

A few coughs of quickly aborted giggles cut the air in the room. Mrs. Ackerson-Smith studied me suspiciously, twisting her pointer stick. As my mother would say, I was on Ms. Ass-Lick's "shit list." It was a perpetual existence.

Bringing your lunch to school was a sign of prestige. School lunch was a lunch ticket or eighty-five cents. No one wanted to be seen using a lunch ticket; that was for the poor kids. (Most of us qualified for them, of course, but would hide them in our fists until we got to the front of the line.) The lines were long and slow, and if you had one of those teachers who didn't let you out early you often barely made it to the table with your lunch before the bell rang, leaving no time to play. Of course, Ms. Ass-Lick was one of these teachers. When I started going with Yosi, I made sure to always bring my lunch and so avoid him until it was too late to eat together. For an entire week since we started going together, I had managed to escape that consummation of our relationship.

Yosi was disgusting when he ate. He always bought the school lunch in the molded Styrofoam trays, and he would mix things together that didn't go together, like applesauce and refried beans. He'd fold up his entire hamburger and stuff it all at once into his mouth, which always stayed open when he chewed. The sight made me feel like I had the one time my father took me fishing, when he slid a knife down the fish's belly and glimmering, reeking flakes of guts and scales popped onto my hair. Yosi was my friend, but before we went together, I always sat as far away from him as I could at lunch and turned my face towards the wall.

Table manners were important in my house. My mother taught me the right forks to use and tied my shoulders to my chair with a scarf to break my habit of leaning low over my food. She got on my dad so hard about smacking loudly and swirling his bread around in the gravy to sop up all the juice that he never ate with us anymore; he took his plate to the living room and chomped his food in peace on his fold-up table in front of the TV. I was not allowed to follow.

"Let him be a heathen," she'd say, wiping up the table where he had been sitting. "I'm raising you to be something better."

So I didn't know what to do about Yosi. The more I avoided him, the more he chased after me, until one day when I had to buy my lunch because my parents had argued the night before. My father had stormed out, and my mother had spent the night on the phone crying and relating the fight to my godmother Trish, blow by blow. I had made myself a bowl of cereal and there were no dinner leftovers to pack up, no bread and cheese to go with the lonely pack of old baloney in the fridge. Ms. Ass-Lick had kept me in to have a talk about my attitude. By the time I made it to my class's table with my tray, the only seat left was the one Yosi had saved next to him.

"Come over here, Tanis," he said, grinning at me. I could see crushed up hamburger mixed with some kind of cranberry dessert inside his mouth. "What?" he asked me as I stared at him in disgust. My parents' fight, my empty fridge, the red lipstick on Mrs. Ackerson-Smith's cocky teeth fizzed up like a warm soda inside me.

"Close your mouth when you eat!" I shrieked. "You're so nasty. Why do you have to be such a heathen?"

A quiet smothered the lunch table, followed by a series of snickers, children laughing in that full-throated, rocking back and forth, *keep laughing at him and not me* way. Yosi jumped up, his eyes hot and watery. "At least my teeth don't look like they trying to break out of jail!" A long, heavy ooooohhh coursedthrough the table, spurring him on. "I don't know why I wanted to be your boyfriend, anyway, with you looking like a chipmunk on crack." The laughter at the table soared.

"Well, I never wanted to be your girlfriend, stupid," I said with as much dignity as I could gather, spinning on my heel, which caused the edge of a barrette to catch me in the eye and my applesauce and boxed orange juice, the only parts of school lunch that I liked, to fly off of my tray.

I tasted salt and snot on my breath all day from holding in my tears. My mother worked odd hours as a cashier at Robinsons-May, and I was often the only kid left in aftercare until past six, with the supervisor tapping her heels and cutting her eyes at me until my mother honked from the curb. Thankfully, today was not one of those. I sat near the gate, and when I saw my mother's small white car, I ran for it, the tears pressing down like urine did the closer you got to the bathroom. I let it all go as soon as the door of the car closed, sobbing as if someone had died.

"What's wrong with you?" my mother cried with alarm. I liked the concerned look on my mother's face, seeing her attention so focused on me without her criticizing or adjusting or polishing me up in some way. I cranked up my wails.

"Lord have mercy. Did somebody do something to you? Did somebody touch you? Tell Mommy the truth." She grabbed my arm, her nails digging in, and looked so wild-eyed that I decided not to draw it out any longer.

"Yosi talked about my teeth. He said—he said I look like a chipmunk on crack." I snorted. "Yosi was my best friend!"

"Lord, child." My mother sat back, looking relieved, and started the car. "Fix your face. Girl, there is no such thing as a real forever friend. Definitely not in a woman, and especially not in a man. You look out for yourself in this world. You are all you have." She pulled away from the curb and turned a corner that would take us away from our house.

"Where are we going, Mommy?" I whimpered, trying literally to "fix my face" by pushing my cheeks up with my hands.

"Back to that orthodontist. If we have to take my bill money, if we have to get a loan on that raggedy-ass house, you're getting those braces now."

I did get braces a few weeks later, after a few orthodontist visits and several of my mother's elegantly written post-dated checks. But though, in a sense, the incident with Yosi had helped me to get my way, I never forgot the way my chest felt when he turned on me, like that hollow chlorine pain that comes from staying in the pool too long. The next day that he was home sick, I took his butterfly jar from his cubby and opened the top in the kindergarten yard. I had expected a breathtaking rush of wings, but only a few of them flew up and away when I shoved the jar into the sky and shook it. The others fell softly to the ground and limped across the chalked hopscotch lines.

Chapter Two

My father called it nigga-rigging when something around the house broke down and you fixed it so that it would work, but not so that it was really fixed forever. Most people I knew had houses that were nigga-rigged. The faucet you had to turn around twice then spin the other way real quick to get the hot water running, the screen door with the hole in it you had to reach through to get to the handle that had fallen off on one side, the windows covered with bed sheets instead of curtains. In my bedroom, it was my mirror that had fallen from where it had been mounted on my wall that now sat tilting dangerously on my once-white dresser. My father kept saying he would put it back up but always forgot or didn't have the tools he needed. I pushed the bottom of the mirror in towards the wall and climbed on my bed to observe myself full length. The hot-pink sweatpants my mother had bought for me to wear to cheerleading practice only a few months before were already flooding well above my ankles. My parents' voices came clear from the kitchen, which was just on the other side of my pink bedroom wall.

"I need some money around this house," I heard my mother say.

"I just gave you a hundred," my father grumbled back.

"What do you think that did? We have groceries, light, gas, telephone, cheerleading shoes, all this shit around here. And did you pay the insurance? They steady sending letters."

"Ima pay the balance in the grace period, don't worry about it."

"Guess I better not get in no accident, huh?"

"Guess you better be careful."

They could have been in the room with me. In my mind, I pushed them out and slammed my bedroom door, the door I was never allowed to close in my mother's house. I inched my sweats down until the hems touched the top of my sneakers, leaving the top of my Tweety Bird printed panties exposed. I changed my tee shirt for one that would come to my thighs.

"I told you we couldn't afford that second mortgage," my father was grumbling.

"Well, I had bills to catch up, car note, braces. Maybe if you hadn't smoked your way out of a job with benefits, that wouldn't be an issue. What did you do with your money, go get loaded?"

Every time my mother talked about my father getting loaded, I thought about Melanie Stewart. Melanie was a girl in my second-grade classroom with pollen-seed spotted skin and bean-pie-colored curls who wore sweetheart-collared blouses under sweaters the texture of cotton candy. She was the kind of girl who everyone wanted to be partnered with when we paired up to walk out to the yard, and one day I'd gotten the courage to ask her to come over and play. I hadn't been aware of any deficiencies in my neighborhood or home back then. I didn't understand why Mrs. Stewart gripped Melanie's shoulders so tightly as she took in the shirtless guys hanging out on the porch next door or the graffiti on the wall of the storefront church down the street. I was proud to show Melanie my block, my room, my extensive Barbie collection. I was squeezing fluorescent miniskirts over flat rubber behinds and happily anticipating Melanie Stewart telling everyone on Monday that she had been over to my house when we heard the screaming. It was a man's screaming, rougher, more alien, and much more frightening than a woman's, and my father's voice was swallowed up deep inside it. The entire house seemed to rumble, and I heard the specific sound of flesh and muscle ramming into walls, the full thud of stomach and thigh, the sharpness of elbows and fists cracking plaster. The sounds came closer and closer. My mother ducked into my room, breathless. Without a word to us, she pulled shut my door, though not before Melanie and I got a glimpse of my father tearing his shirt off in the hallway. His face gleamed with sweat, as if his head had been dipped in baby oil. His bare chest was a stocky mix of muscle and fat clustered in black pearls. Blue cotton, limp and defeated, hung in his big hands. Mrs. Stewart had to wade through ambulance and police cars when she picked her daughter up in her luxury sedan that evening. Even then, I admired how Melanie's hair flew out behind her as her mother yanked her down our driveway. Neither she nor anyone else at school ever came over to my house again.

"Why you gotta say some shit like that, Becky? You know I left that shit alone. Why you always have to bring that up? And you know damn well I had to pay TJ's football fees and uniform and stuff."

"Hmmmph," was my mother's response to that.

"I gotta take care of my son, too, Rebecca." I could hear the refrigerator door opening and closing, my parents' footsteps crossing each other on the linoleum, my father's heavy work boots and my mother's heeled mules she wore even in the house.

TJ was my father's son that he had with someone else the same year my parents got married. TJ's mother infuriated mine by naming him Tannah Junior. When I was born, my mother named me Tanis, anyway, saying that I was my daddy's first real child. I wondered if that would have been my name if TJ never existed, if my mother hadn't felt she needed to make a point.

"You know, he doesn't look anything like you," she said. My father didn't dispute her. TJ was long and slender and light brown, my father molasses-thick and dark.

"Well, I stop taking care of business, she'll put child support on me, and they'll take what little I do make off the top and you wouldn't like that at all, would you?"

"If she did that, you all would have to take a blood test, and we could find out for sure."

"He's fourteen; what's the mutherfuckin' point now? That's the only son I'm ever gonna have, and you know that." Uncharacteristically, my mother didn't answer right away. "All right then," she finally said in a quieter voice. "I guess the one daughter I gave you isn't enough."

I fixed my ponytails, trying to weigh them down with heavy barrettes. I had a lot of hair then, but my ponytails were so thick and fluffy that they always puffed up close to my head instead of hanging to my back. They looked like birthday balloons after you've had them in the house a couple of weeks, when most of the air is gone and only that little fat ball at the end of the knot is left. I switched the barrettes for heavy balls that would stretch the twists out even though they would also slam into my face at practice. That was all I could do. The eyes popping out of my face from behind thick glasses, the metal-covered teeth, the fat nose and spiky acne would all stay exactly where they were. When I hadn't heard my parents raised voices for several minutes, I grabbed my pink nylon shoulder bag and walked in my slew-footed, waddling way into the kitchen.

"Mommy, Daddy, can I get a perm?" I asked.

"What?" they asked in unison, turning towards me.

"Lisa at school has a perm and that's why her hair hangs down straight. It wouldn't take so long to comb my hair in the morning."

"You're too young now. Maybe when you're older," my mother said, handing our thermoses to my father, who stuck them into his old dark green duffel bag.

"I don't want no chemicals in her hair," he said firmly.

"What do you know about girls' hair? Tanis, tuck in that shirt, you look sloppy."

I tried to tuck in the shirt while leaving the pants low on my body. My mother peered at me.

"Why's your crotch down all low like that? Lord." She reached out and yanked up my pants so hard my underwear stuffed themselves into all my spaces. "T, she done outgrown these pants already. I just bought these! She needs new clothes. You see what I mean? It's always something around here."

My father looked tired. "Tanis, it's time to go." He put his hand on my head to steer me and opened the side door. My mother leaned out the door and called after us as we clumped down the flaking side porch steps.

"Here," she said stiffly, holding out a third tall thermos to my father. "For that boy. I know they work those boys hard out there." She looked at him with her large, catlike brown eyes, and their fingers touched as he took the thermos from her hand. Even standing above us on the porch steps, she was about my father's height and not that much taller than me. Somehow, though, she always felt big.

We walked down the cracked pavement of our driveway, me swinging my bag by my side. My father opened the passenger side of his big green Ford pickup and gave me a boost into the seat. The cab smelled like tobacco ashes, Old Spice, and sweat. My father got in the car, started it, and pulled away from the curb.

"You got your seatbelt on?"

"It hurts my stomach, Daddy."

"Put your seatbelt on." His voice had that "don't make me tell you again" tone, so I did as I was told. He turned off our street, took out a cigarette, and lit it.

"Daddy, secondhand smoke can cause bronchitis, asthma, lung disease, and death." He rolled down all of the windows and continued to smoke. We rode in quiet most of the way to Vermont and Adams where Charlotte, my brother's mother, lived, walking distance from the bricked campus of USC.

"I don't want you to worry about none of the stuff you hear me and your mama discussing," my father said suddenly. "It don't got nothing to do with you."

"I'm not worried."

"I got a test for the city next Saturday. I did my program, my community service. Ima get a better job. You don't have to worry about no uniforms, no braces, no nothing, you hear me?"

"I hear you."

"We gon' get you some new pants, too." He grinned at me, one front tooth crossing over the other. "You don't have to walk around saggin' like TJ no more." I couldn't help but giggle.

We drove through a neighborhood of big but run-down old homes. Next to these houses, with their large wooden porches and jutting dormer windows and low-hanging eaves, our neighborhood seemed like a hasty collection of stucco boxes. "These are real houses," my father always said when we drove through the older parts of LA, not seeming to mind that these houses were often squeezed between gas stations, fast food restaurants, and graffiti-scrawled strip malls. "Wood floors, real shingles, wood-burning fireplaces. Them pretty windows like the ones in church. Handmade, hand-carved shit. These houses got soul. People mess 'em up, breakin' 'em into apartments and stuff, but you can't kill soul. They don't look like much now, but fixed up nice...that's the kind of house I wanna have someday." I heard the wistfulness in my father's voice but couldn't help wondering where my mother would live if he ever got a house like that. Her tastes, from the way she slowed down and softened her voice when we drove through certain areas and the pages she dog-eared in her home decorating magazines, ran towards the modern, the flashy, towards lots of clear glass and open space and straight lines.

"I'm going to buy you a house like that, Daddy."

"Is that so?"

"Yup. When I grow up and go to college and get a lot of money."

"Well, that sure sounds good, baby." He shook his cigarette off out the window. "But don't grow up too fast."

We pulled up to Charlotte's building and honked. She lived in the back unit of a little duplex. The paint was faded to the point that you couldn't tell what the original color was supposed to be, and it looked even smaller than it really was squeezed between the larger Craftsmans on either side. But the sandy lawn was low trimmed, no garbage leaned against the curb, and it had a metal instead of a netted screen door. I noted with satisfaction that the roses in front were slouchy and dull. My mother's flowers frothed over their stems like big bows of Easter Sunday ribbons on my hair.

TJ bounded out of the gate, long and golden, bobbing his head to his Walkman. His jump rope legs brought him to the truck in what seemed like four strides. I saw TJ rarely enough that I was always happy to see him, as eager for his presence and attention as a teenage girl with a crush. I liked when his voice charged up the air around me, when his boy smell filled the car. But since he'd turned fourteen he was, as my father said, "smelling hisself," and far above returning my excitement.

"What's up, Pops?" TJ and my father gave each other quick, Black man nods, thrusting up their chins to show their Adam's apples and bringing them back down in the exact same way.

"Hey, Tiny," TJ said, hitting the passenger door with the flat of his hand. "Shotgun. Out. Now." This was a new thing of his, talking in cocky one-word statements and expecting to be obeyed. The adoring greeting that rose up in me at the sight of him got kicked back down my throat.

"Who do you think you are, Fresh Prince of South Central?" I shot at him. I'd been saving that one all week. My father chuckled, but TJ just rolled his eyes. "Not funny," he said, so dryly and authoritatively I believed him even though it had been hilarious in my head. "Out. My. Seat."

"Go on, baby," my father said mildly. "Your brother needs more room for his legs." I looked at my father then back at TJ. I felt betrayed, but I opened the door and slid out, giving TJ a shove and knocking myself off balance as I bounced off the new hardness of his arms.

Before I made it back into the truck, Charlotte had come out of the house. She pulled her body through the yard like a wagon, rolling her huge hips over one another. She breathed hard when she moved, but her face was full and soft and her features made you think of sweet, thick things, dark licorice and maple syrup. Charlotte liked me for some reason, and I loved attention, so not liking her back was hard. For my mother's sake, I always made a concerted effort. But that day, with only one foot into the back seat and the car door still open, I had no choice but to submit to her hug.

"Look at you," she said after pressing me into her big, soft breasts. "All that silver in your mouth, you must be rich." She slipped me a five-dollar bill. "I heard you been doing real good in school, so add this to it."

"Thank you," I mumbled, wondering how she knew about my grades. My mother would hate the thought of my father talking to Charlotte about anything, especially about us. I slipped the five into my pocket, climbed back up into the truck's cab, and folded my pudginess into the narrow area behind the front seats.

"You still gon' come move TJ's stuff out to my new place, right?" Charlotte turned her attention to my father, leaning her folded arms heavily on TJ's window. I watched to see if it would break under her weight.

"I don't know, I gotta see," my dad said. I knew that meant he had to get past my mother.

"I need to know if you gon' do it or not. I don't want to have to get another U-Haul if I don't have to. I'm spending enough on this move as it is."

"I don't see why you gotta move all the way out there, anyway."

"I told you, I'm tired of this neighborhood. All these loud-ass, dingy-ass college students. They goin' to that big, fancy school, you think they would have more sense. And it's too many damn

Mexicans moving in here, too." She cracked her gum, a high, hard sound.

"People gotta live somewhere," my father said mildly. "Remember when it was the white people running away from us?"

"Yeah, well, we didn't pack no chickens. Them people in front of me got a rooster that wakes me up every morning."

"Look on the bright side: you don't need no alarm clock." They laughed. Charlotte laughed real deep and loud and hoarse, with her mouth open wide, and I imagined throwing something inside her mouth that would choke her right at that moment and telling my mother about it later.

"I'm serious, though, Tannah. I'm tired of renting a little piece of something. Moving out there is the only way I can afford to buy my own house."

"Owning a house ain't all it's cracked up to be," my father said. "You gotta do everything yourself. Gotta fix the pipes, cut the grass, paint the trim, fix the roof —"

"TJ's gon' do all that, aren't you?" she punched her son lightly, but he ducked her touch and sent his eyes up to the ripped truck ceiling. She flinched as if he'd slammed her fingers in the door.

"Well, Tannah, I might have to call your black ass, then." My father laughed, and she laughed, too. There was a calm easiness between them. I sat up straighter in my little crevice in the back and narrowed my eyes.

"Well, Char, I gotta get them on to practice." My father put the truck in gear. Her hand brushed the side of the door as we pulled off.

My dad had to make a stop at an auto parts store on Crenshaw, so we drove west and then tried to take Crenshaw back towards the high school where our Pop Warner football team practiced. It was almost six p.m. and traffic dragged, packing the wide boulevard both ways. The cars were as different as the people: tricked-out low-riders bumping deep, wordless bass; stuttering buckets spewing smoke into the air; luxury sedans throwing off the sunlight like freshly pressed hair. Bumpers love-tapped and snapped at each other as their owners leaned out of windows and lay fruitlessly on their horns. The street was blocked off up ahead, and we could see police cars and black stretch limousines.

"What's going on, Daddy?" I asked.

"Look like a funeral." The way my dad's gruff voice pushed out funeral, it blurred the three syllables into two. My father turned down the nasally lullabies of The Isley Brothers, and we sat quietly, watching the police gesture, the limos turn. Cars followed, some of them full of young men hanging out of the window and waving purple bandannas. They weren't wearing nice clothes.

"Dude must have been Grape Street," TJ said, taking one of his headphones out of his ear.

"What you know about that?" my father grunted.

"Shoot, you gotta be up on this stuff, you gon' live here. I can't go to a birthday party without some niggah asking what set I claim."

"Just what set you claimin'?" He turned his furious eyebrows on TJ, who just smiled his disarming glow of a smile.

"Nothin'. Come on, Pops. Maybe some of my homies bang, but you know I don't get down like that."

"Better not," my father said. "I'd shoot your ass myself."

A rusty, low-sitting Chevy with purple bandannas fluttering out of the windows rounded the corner, right in front of the police escort. "That's ignorant," I said decidedly. "For them to act like that, waving those things."

"Well, don't you learn in school how they hold up flags when soldiers die?" TJ asked me. "What's the difference?"

"It's real different. Soldiers are good. They die fighting for our country." I was going through a very patriotic phase, being in Mrs. Ackerson-Smith's class. I hated her as much as I hated singing "America the Beautiful" and looking for crayon colors to shade in the Founding Fathers' faces; but she was still my teacher, and I believed the things she taught us.

"Fuck this country," TJ said. My father grunted but didn't get on him for cussing. "That dude died fighting for something, too."

"Not something good," I retorted.

"Maybe you right," my father said mildly. "But don't be so quick to call them boys ignorant, baby. Maybe they are, but there's different ways of cryin'."

My father turned off the main street and took a winding shortcut through Baldwin Hills. A few calm-looking black people watered their lawns and carried their groceries from gleaming cars, up smooth driveways, into neat-edged houses. I wondered if they ever had to do what my mother often did at the grocery store, tell the irritated clerk that she wasn't taking a quarter of the items in her cart after all once she saw how much everything would be, how loud it seemed when they got on the speaker and said "perishable go-backs at lane three." As we drove over these rolling streets, the truck's bass turned down, my father and brother's conversation turned to football stats, yards, weight classes, and other things I didn't understand. Their deep tones, my father's guttural and rough, my brother's hoarse and cracking slightly, blended into a rich, narcotic murmur that lulled me out of my urge to interrupt.

Once we passed up the funeral traffic, my father crossed to the other side of Crenshaw, which was like another world. There were still some nice houses, but they were packed in next to tired, faded ones with trash lining the edges of their gates. "Just don't understand people who don't sweep they yards," my father observed as he pulled up to the high school. Puffed-up bodies in crayon bright blue and yellow gear hustled back and forth behind the chain-link gate.

"I'm late." TJ jumped out before my father pulled to a complete stop and started strapping on his pads. My father and I followed him out and watched his lithe body, more like a basketball than a football player's, become thicker with each dingy rectangle of foam. He looked like a man when he was done, big and powerful and broad-shouldered.

"Here, Rebecca made this for you." My father handed TJ the thermos after he had strapped on his helmet.

"Is it poisoned?" TJ cracked in a muffled voice, his crooked grin shining through the gate-like things that covered his mouth. My mother was right; he didn't look like my father. He didn't have his color or his build, but there was still something in the smile that was exactly the same. My father slapped him upside the helmet with the heavy flat of his hand.

"Boy, you know I don't like to hear you talk like that. I don't like to hear you talking to your mama like you did today, either."

"Man, she's buggin'. I don't wanna move way out there. I don't wanna leave my friends and my block and be around a bunch of white people."

"Well, we can't always get what we want. The schools 'sposed to be better out there, might be good for you. Get you away from them hoodlums who ain't doing shit."

"How's it gon' be better when the football team at that high school is straight wack? How am I gon' get recruited out of there?"

"You should come live with us!" I piped up without thinking. Well, I was thinking, but I was thinking about how it might be to not be the only kid in the house. I was thinking about how TJ used to make me feel special, how he used to spin me around by the arms until they felt like they were coming out of the sockets. I wasn't thinking about how different things were now that he was almost grown up, and I certainly wasn't thinking about my mother.

"Damn, maybe this kid is smart," TJ said, pulling one of my ponytails until I glowed. "Maybe I could do that. I could still hit my block, see my peeps. I could go to Dorsey, like you did. They send mad people to NFL."

"Funny, I don't remember getting my ticket nowhere," my father said, looking at me out of the corner of his eye. "You go on, though, you gon' be late. You, too, Toodle Woodle." He'd called me by my pet name, so I knew he wasn't mad for what I had brought up. I took my thermos and ran over to the handball courts where the girls were already in line.

Cheerleading was one thing I was undeniably good at. Cheerleading in the South Central Pop Warner league in 1990 was not the frozen smiles, stiff angles, and choreographed acrobatics of cheerleading on ESPN. It was neck swinging and finger snapping, ass-shaking and trash-talking, stomping and clapping, hip-hop in blue pleated skirts. It was little girls playing Little Sally Walker in the schoolyard with attitude and hood-style team spirit thrown in. I knew how to come up with good rhymes and how to shake my skirt until it made a thundering sound and fanned out into a flat blue disc around my waist.

The coach frowned at me for being late, and I grinned back at her and pushed myself into a spot in the front line. We started with some stretches and jumping jacks, lunges, and offense and defense cheers. Coach Aisha must have been in a good mood because she called a one-by-one cheer before practice was half over. One-by-one cheers were our favorite because we got to show off by ourselves, and we usually only did them at the end of practice. I had a new rhyme that I had been working on all week. When my turn came, I cried out so loud my voice cracked like a boy's.

They call me Tanis!
(Hey, Hey)
And I work my magic!
(Hey, Hey)
When I shake my skirt,
(Hey, Hey)
All the boys wanna flirt.
(Hey, Hey)
My brother TJ
(Hey, Hey)
Will knock you down.
(Hey, Hey)
If you mess with us
(Hey, Hey)
Then get the hell out of town!

(Hey! Hey!)

The rhyme got the appropriate amount of approving groans and laughter. I was drinking it in, full of self-satisfaction, when I saw Coach Aisha beckoning with a red acrylic fingernail that matched her filled-out biker shorts.

"Tanis," she said my name in her serious voice.

"Yes?" I responded, pitching my voice high and sweet.

"Cheerleaders are ladies, and young ladies don't curse."

"I didn't curse. I said heck."

"That's not what I heard, Tanis."

"What did you hear? 'Cause I didn't say anything else."

"I heard hell, Tanis."

"Oooh, Miss Aisha."

"What?"

"You said a bad word." She blew air out of her mouth, making a sound that was part laugh, part frustrated groan, and gave me a little shove towards the bench. "Sit your booty down until the break. You know very well what I've told you about cursing."

I fumed on the bench until I was allowed to rejoin practice, and we reviewed the cheers we would do at that weekend's game. I peeled off from the lines when Coach Aisha released us, my hands and thighs stinging pleasantly and a wet puppy scent permeating the cloth under my arms. Two girls, the captain Taylor and her best friend Jonelle, came up to me as I gathered my jacket and thermos from the ground.

"Hey, I don't care what Miss Aisha said, that rhyme was mad tight yo," said Jonelle, a thick, red-boned girl whose family had moved to LA from New York. She blew a filmy pink gum bubble in my direction and killed it with her teeth.

"Yeah, it was cool." Taylor clicked her hot-pink nails, which had rhinestone flower designs. She was vanilla wafer-skinned, with springy brown hair swept up into a smooth ponytail on the side of her head. The wavy "baby hair" along her hairline was naturally fine and silky, not plastered down into swirling shapes with a dirty toothbrush and gel. "I like the part about your brother." She laughed sideways at Jonelle, who joined in.

"Thanks," I said, warily. Taylor was one of those girls who was always right in the middle of every routine formation, not only because she knew the dances, but because the coaches liked the way she looked there. She was one of those girls who seemed like she should be front and center before you ever saw her do a kick or hit an angle. She reminded me of Melanie in that everyone clamored to be partnered with her when we took our walks across the field to use the bathroom. But unlike Melanie, who had always made her choice with a small smile and shy pointed finger, Taylor wasn't nice about it. She held her attention out like a piece of candy that might get snatched away as soon as you reached for it, even with her friends. Just smelling her minty breath that close to me made me tense.

"Hey," Jonelle said. "Does your brother have a girlfriend?"

"He has a lot of them," I answered tersely.

"But does he have, like, one special one? 'Cause if he has a lot of them, those are just girls he's talking to, not his girlfriends."

"I don't know all that. We don't live together."

"Why not?" Taylor asked.

"None of your beeswax."

"Well, excuse me. I just wanted to know if you would give him this note for me."

She tried to hand me a piece of paper folded many times over, so if you put your fingers in it and opened and closed it, the different flaps would say different things. I folded my arms. Taylor was older than me, the oldest in our cheer division, and she already had breasts the size of the oranges on the tree in my backyard. But the thought of my brother liking her made me feel as if I'd gotten off one of those spinning metal carnival rides that pressed you back against the walls. TJ could be an asshole some-times, but he was still *my* asshole. Since my mother didn't like him around much and the inside of Charlotte's house was forbid-den ground to me, Pop Warner practice was the only time that belonged to us. Even as we practiced on opposite sides of the field, I thought I could distinguish his war cries from the other players. I imagined that he ran drills and did pushups to the rhythm of my claps and stomps. It was our thing, and here was this little yellow bowlegged heffa trying to infringe.

"My brother's in high school," I spat out. "He doesn't want that."

"I'm almost thirteen. He might," she said with a confidence that I wished I had. She tried to give the note to me again, and I took a step away. "Tanis, why are you acting like that?" she said on a laugh, using my name as if we were friends.

"Because you're a fast-tailed ho." The words escaped me be-fore I knew I had decided to say them.

Jonelle's eyes grew wide, and her mouth formed that hoop with a laugh at the corners that instigators always wore. "You heard what she said?" she taunted her friend. "You gon' take that?"

Taylor's fair skin had flushed a deep red, but she smiled calm-ly and put her hand on her hip. "You're just jealous, you mud duck. That's why your pants are flooding!" They ran away, screeching with laughter. I had no idea what a mud duck was, but the words sounded ugly and clunky, not at all something I wanted to be.

We had a quiet drive home. My father usually listened to his oldies, but that night he let the hip-hop station TJ and I liked play and kept Ice Cube's thick voice up loud enough so that there was no pressure to talk. TJ let his seat back so far it squished my legs, but for once I didn't kick him in the back or complain. When we dropped TJ off, he opened the back door and kissed me on my forehead. His lips were wet and soft on my forehead's bumps, his breath stale from the plastic mouth guard he wore all through practice. I was so surprised and grateful for that kiss that it made me angry, so I roughly pushed him away. "Your breath stinks," I cried. "Don't you ever wash that mouth thing?" He pushed me back onto the seat and stuffed my face into his armpit until I screamed.

"All right, y'all," my father called. "That's enough."

My father and I winded southward through the residential streets, watching the lawns alternate between scraggly and green, the curbs between clear and trashy as the sky darkened from purplish gray to black. Our street was quiet except for a few guys planted like palms on the porch of the green house next door, growing from the floorboards in low-slung pants and sleeveless tee shirts that showed off knotty, ink-barked arms. Their laughter was loud and hoarse as they talked shit and fed from brown paper bags. "What's up, Mr. Sutton?" they called as the truck passed the house. The guys on the block liked my father, called him OG, and always listened when he told them not to do any of their business in front of our house or leave beer cans at the curb. He held his hand up to them in response as we pulled into the driveway.

Our small stucco house hadn't been painted in so long that the once-bright peach color looked like watered-down sherbet, and no stone facade or cute shutters livened up the exterior. But our front yard looked like a woman's hands fresh from the nail shop, neatly manicured, topped off with precise strokes of bright paint, any imperfection buffed away by my mother's vigilant eye. She always directed my father from the porch as he cut the lawn with our ancient, asthmatic uncle of a mower. "Get the edges, Tannah. The same as the other side! Don't you see how that looks?" Sometimes he'd humor her, but when her nagging stopped being cute, he'd knock the mower over in frustration. "Dammit, woman, can't I just cut my grass in peace?"

"Look, you can do the back however you want to, but this is the part people see."

I wondered if my father really would go over and cut Charlotte's grass for her, if he would take off his shirt to do it the way he did at home, if she would direct him from the porch or just stand there and watch, if she'd touch his burnt-blacker back the way my mother sometimes did when he came in, even if they had fought about the straightness of his paths. I tried to shake the thoughts out of my head, knowing that as soon as my mother had me alone, she would gouge me for every detail of Daddy and Charlotte's interaction, how they looked at each other, whether they touched each other, and everything that was said.

"Baby?" My father killed the engine and turned towards me. "What we was talking about, about TJ moving or maybe staying here, we not gonna say nothing 'bout that to your mama just yet, you hear? You understand?"

"Is he going to?"

He stared at the house, not answering. "Let's just get in there." He put his hand on my hair, which had burst from my ponytails into flowering bushes around my head.

Chapter Three

My mother woke me up for Saturday's game by shoving a hot, soapy towel in my face. That was as far as she got. When I was younger, I used to wake up to her scrubbing my face, under my arms, and between my legs in vigorous swipes while I struggled to climb out of my dreams. I was a hard sleeper, but I had learned to come to life at the first touch of her towel, if not the sound of her footsteps coming into my room. "Okay, okay," I coughed through the sudsy terrycloth in my mouth. "I'm up."

"Well, if you would move when I called you," she muttered, slapping her rubber-soled house shoes across the cold wooden floor. "You know how your daddy doesn't like to be late." I dragged myself out of bed until I remembered that it was game day, not a school day, and opened my eyes a little wider. My uniform, which my mother had pressed hard enough to slice a finger on the skirt's pleats, hung on the back of the door. Below it sat my Keds tennies and ankle socks, bleached so white they hurt my eyes in the dim room. No sun came through the faded sheets hung over my windows as I stumbled to the door and pulled the uniform off the wire hangers.

"You need to eat good," my mother muttered, coming back a few minutes later with steaming oatmeal in a round blue bowl.

"Don't get anything on you." She stuffed a paper towel in the front of my vest, her robe falling open to reveal sweatpants and a black negligee that always embarrassed me when she wore it around the house. Musk rose from her breasts pulling against the soft material, her purple silk scarf still turban-wrapped her head, her face was ashen looking from the cold cream that had dried and turned to film through the night. "Mommy, aren't you going?" I asked. She turned slightly, her hand on a hip made fat by her sweatpants and robe.

"I have to think about it." This was what my mother always said when she knew she would say no but wanted to stave off appeals.

"Mommy, you have to come, it's the championship."

"All the teams playing today?" she asked warily, and I knew that she didn't want to stay to watch TJ's game, which my father would never miss.

"I don't know," I lied. "I'm not sure."

"Hmmph. You just eat all that food up." She swept her fuzzy blue bathrobe around her as if it was a queen's cloak and left the room.

Defeated, I sat down on the edge of my bed in my vest and bloomers and raised my spoon. The oats were bland on my tongue. My mother had made my oatmeal plain with no extra sugar or butter, no maple syrup. She'd been making my food that way since my last doctor's appointment revealed that I was twenty pounds overweight for my height and age. I took the bowl to the doorway, listening hard for the slap of my mother's house shoes. When the whip sounds they made on the kitchen's linoleum floor silenced over the carpet and lashed out again in my parents' bedroom, I slipped down the hall to the kitchen, going straight for the sticky, woman-shaped syrup bottle pushed into the back of the fridge.

As I held the syrup bottle high above my bowl, my father

walked in through the side door. He jerked his head back, eyes passing over my too-big behind in my too-small bloomers, my rose-printed panties hanging out the sides of them, my bare fat thighs. He turned away and then looked back at me, his face crunched in around his thick lips, his eyes narrowed. "Girl, don't you think you better put something on?" he growled. I jumped at the roughness in his voice, which he hardly ever raised at me, at him calling me girl in that way my mother did, not baby, not Toodle Woodle. My hands, still holding the syrup, clenched and squirted the cool dark liquid onto the cracked tile of our kitchen counter. I swiped at the mess with the dishtowel, tossed it in the sink, and rushed out, conscious of how my butt curved out from my hips and hung on back of me like cargo, how the heavy flesh pulled on the skin, and how naked it suddenly felt exposed to air and eyes.

My mother came into my room several minutes after I left the kitchen. I looked at her warily; I had heard my parents' voices talking uncharacteristically low in the kitchen while I finished getting dressed. I thought she would fuss, but she spoke almost nicely. "You can't be going around the house like that anymore, Tanis." She straightened the skirt I had pulled on the second I got back to my room, pinching long fingernails full of flesh along with the material. "You're getting too old for that."

"You come in my room when I'm not dressed all the time," I told her. "You even come in the bathroom when I'm in the tub."

"Yeah, but Daddy is different. Men are different. Walking around like that is not appropriate for young ladies to do around their fathers."

"Is Daddy mad at me or something?"

"No...Maybe he's a little mad you're growing up."

My mother's voice softened. I sensed that she felt for me, that she had moved into a calmer mood, one that I could take advantage of. "Please come to my game today, Mommy. It's the last game of the season."

"Girl, I got things to do in this house today. I still have to get dressed and..." She looked at my face. "All right, all right. I guess I'll put on something and go."

My father and I waited quietly in the truck, Lenny Williams wailing out of the radio. My father sang along, looking young and bright in his blue and yellow Cougars tee shirt, blue jeans, and backwards baseball cap. He couldn't hold a note or carry a tune, but his thick voice still sounded good singing those old songs. The love they sang about was loud and deep and mournful, not like the whiny crushes of the fast-dancing boy groups whose posters papered my walls. I appreciated the music not only because I loved my father's voice but because it kept us from having to talk. My father had seen me in my underwear that morning, and I was old enough to be ashamed.

"I'm 'bout to leave your mama," he finally said. "We gon' miss the damn kickoff." Just then, she came trotting out in black clunky-heeled sandals, fitted stonewash jeans, and a low-cut cranberry-colored blouse. I felt envious of how she looked.

"You gon' break your neck in those on them bleachers," he told her as she got into the car.

She shook back her hair and slid her sunglasses down over her eyes. "Don't you worry about me."

The day began as warm and bright as a game day should be,

the sky a strong unwavering blue, the sun like egg yolk in a pan, bubbling round and golden and blurring around the edges. As good as the sun felt at first was as bad as it got later for the cheerleaders shimmying in its view. It was still a California November in the middle of a California drought, and we bled sweat that turned to crusty white salt trails on our foreheads and necks. Sand from the track latched onto the sweat on our calves and made them itch, and we scratched our legs with the dusty rubber soles of our shoes. It must have been much worse for the football players, loaded up with foam padding and metal helmets in that suffocating heat, but I never thought about that then. Of course, we knew on some level that game days were about the boys, that football was what the people came to see, that we were secondary to our brothers and cousins and friends on that field. But in our minds, it was our show. The boys grabbed for our parents' attention with their tackles, catches, field goals; we fought for it with white Keds pounding into the pavement, with newly minted hips thrusting back and forth, with the shrieked rhyming couplets of a cheer.

Sunflower seed shells, balled up napkins, and cheese-soaked nacho cartons carpeted the ground and the steps of the faded, weather-beaten bleachers. Men of all ages lined up against the gate, all of them black. There were grandfathers, fathers, and uncles. There were teenagers who had aged out of the Pop Warner program and missed the stardom they'd enjoyed there, fronting to everyone that said what's up or asked after them that they were still something special. There were the requisite neighborhood bangers with bandannas in their back pockets. We were playing the LA Sheriffs, whose colors were black and crimson, so blue and red flooded the packed stands. "Lord have mercy," Trish had said when she'd come with us to another LA Sheriffs-Crenshaw District Cougars game. "Y'all can't tell me all this damn blue and red don't make y'all wanna drop and take cover." We had all been taught to fear too much of those colors gathered in one place, but Pop Warner football was a different world. Sometimes there were fights and even near riots when the older cheerleaders got too feisty with name-calling and flipping up their skirts at the other squad, or when one of the more hot-headed coaches got into it with a crooked ref, but no one ever started shooting. We fought with our cheers. Most of them were some version of rapper-influenced bravado, and the audience responded like fans at a Heavy D concert.

> *They don't want no blue and gold, they don't want none!*
> *And if you want some blue and gold, come and get some!*

The crowd responded, shaking the stands with their feet.

> *They don't want no blue and gold, they don't want none!*
> *And if you want some blue and gold, come and get some,*
> *come and get some, come and get some! Say what!*

The heat bore down worse, and my voice traveled into hoarseness as the minutes on the scoreboard ticked by. My throat began to hurt, my feet ached, and my thighs and hands burned from being slapped together to the rhythm of our songs. I loved every second of it. When I cheered, I forgot about everything I hated about myself, and I imagined that everyone else did, too. My fellow cheerleaders and I, bitter and bickering when we weren't in line, united as long as the cheer lasted. We were on the same rhythm, yelling with the same voice. When I looked into the stands and saw faces and mouths yelling back at me the things I said, I felt more powerful than I did in any other moments of my life.

I scanned the crowd for my parents. My father wasn't among the men chewing on straws and toothpicks at the gate and cussing out the coaches. He sat in the stands about halfway up, a hulking figure right in the glare of the sun, his tight, thick-lashed eyes squinting so hard that they looked completely closed. My mother sat next to him under the wide-striped picnic umbrella we only used on game days, fanning her face with a folded up magazine, leaning back on the bleacher behind her with her elbows, and staring dispassionately ahead. My mother had been athletic before she met my father; she ran track, played volleyball and softball, all things I had tried and quit quickly. She humored my cheerleading partly because it kept me out of her hair and mostly because it might combat the doctor's diagnosis about my weight.

TJ's age division played after mine. The older kids, who were supposed to be resting before their games, wandered back and forth between the snack shack and the bleachers, buying nachos and hot dogs and pickles and teasing us through the rusty chain-link fence. The smells of chili, cheese, spicy beef hot links, and pickle juice mixed into the hot air and swept right under our noses. I never had finished my oatmeal that morning. My stomach growled audibly, and I began to wish I hadn't begged my mother to come. I had wanted her to see me cheer, but with her watching my weight like Koreans watched us in liquor stores, I knew that a trip to the snack shack was not in the cards. Coach Aisha and the team manager walked between our lines every ten minutes, squirting water into our baby bird-opened mouths, but by the second quarter, my stomach felt like it was eating itself from inside.

When TJ, glowing brown-gold in the sun, first came up to the gate, I was happy. He was grinning at me and gesturing for my attention instead of ignoring me the way he usually did in front of other kids. I tossed my head as if I couldn't be bothered and looked for envy in the other girls' eyes. Having a cute older brother was almost on level with having a boyfriend in a higher grade.

"Tiny!" he hissed. I looked at him in a bored way. He pulled a wax-paper-wrapped, big dill pickle from behind his back. "I bet you want some of this." The sweet green juice ran down his forearm. He knew that was my favorite, as was the pack of red Kool-Aid he dipped the pickle into. He ate slowly, eyeing me and exaggerating every greedy bite.

"Stop it," I hissed at TJ. He took another big chunk out of the pickle and grinned at me with teeth pink-tinted from Kool-Aid. Giggles sputtered through our lines, and he laughed too as he leaned over the chain-link gate. I hadn't even known I had decided to throw my pom-pom at him before it soared from my hand. The fat ball of blue and yellow shredded plastic flew like a comet and smashed into his face with a loud, rustling thump. A gasp hopped through our lines, and I felt a small pang of remorse as TJ jumped back and rubbed his nose. Our pom-poms looked soft, but they had hard wooden handles inside them.

"Who threw that?" Coach Aisha jumped up from where she'd been leaning against the gate with her yellow baseball cap pulled down low over her eyes, the toe of one sneaker at the end of her long brown leg hooked into one of the chain-link diamonds. "Who did it?"

"Tanis!" Several voices sang out my name with no hesitation. Coach Aisha looked at me as if she were not surprised, her hands on her hips.

"Tanis, I know you know better than that," she said tiredly.

"He was messing with me first!"

"What can he do from way over there that was bad enough for you to throw that? What if you really hurt somebody, and right before the championship game, too?"

"It's all right, Miss Aisha," TJ called, dusting Kool-Aid he'd spilled off his jersey. I noticed with satisfaction that he had dropped his pickle, and that the other men on the gate were laughing.

"No, that's not all right. She shouldn't act like that, and you shouldn't be messing with my cheerleaders. Get on away from here." She tried to sound stern, but her voice carried the hint of flirtation TJ's crooked grin elicited in women of every age. Coach Aisha, while I thought of her as a grownup, was only in her late teens herself. I wanted to be like her one day, with her ponytail swinging silky out the back hole of her baseball cap, her Jordache jean shorts hugging her hips. But I couldn't stand her at that moment, the way she swung her hair and hips away from TJ to cut her eyes at me. "And Tanis," she turned back to me. "You know the rules. You go sit down with your parents for the rest of the half."

"No, Coach Aisha, please." The unjustness of the whole thing squeezed my voice into a breathy, pitiful plea. "I won't do it again."

"I know you won't because you're going to sit out this half."

"But Coach Aisha, it's the last game!" I thought of my mother in the audience. "Please." My coach's face softened, and I thought she might relent, until she looked around at the other girls watching her expectantly. Not bothering to protest again, I picked up my one remaining pom-pom and dragged my feet to the gate.

"That's what she get," I heard a voice snicker behind me. I knew before I turned around that it was Taylor Everett. She hadn't closed her mouth yet before I leapt into the front line and pushed her hard in the chest. Taylor was taller and older than me, but I was thicker, and I had been wrestling with my daddy as long as I could remember. As she stumbled backwards, the pom-poms on her designer tennis shoes shimmying, none of her friends reached to catch her. Jonelle, the closest person to her, stepped aside, and Taylor went sprawling into the sand, half sputtering, half wailing Coach Aisha's name. Then, remembering herself, she jumped up and made a half-hearted effort to step up to me. I balled my fists in preparation. Coach Aisha came between us, and Taylor looked relieved.

"Tanis, that's it!" cried Coach Aisha. "That's it, now. I won't have cheerleaders hitting each other on my field."

"What about her? Always talking about somebody."

"You need to learn about sticks and stones and not letting words get you into trouble. You won't be cheering any more today. I'm going to send you to your parents—"

"Don't worry about that," said a voice like steel. "I'm right here."

I always laughed at the parts in horror movies where the stupid girl running stops to look behind her, and when she turns back around, the monster or killer is standing right there, smiling viciously. I would never laugh at that again after the fear that struck me when I turned around and saw my mother's unsmiling face. Coach Aisha stopped talking, as did the girls who had been tittering and ooohing the whole time. Taylor, who had been fussing from the protection of Coach Aisha's back, fell silent. Even the stands seemed to go on mute during the second my mother lowered her sunglasses and held out her hand to me. When I didn't step closer right away, she snatched me by the upper arm, her red acrylic nails digging deep. I had visions of her taking me behind the bleachers to kill me, but she dragged me up the bleacher steps instead. I stumbled in my tennis shoes as I tried to keep up with her heels ringing out loudly on the wide-spaced, battered wooden risers. We reached my father, who sat with his eyes down, fiddling with the video camera.

"Time to go," my mother told him, holding me like a vice.

"You crazy? The game ain't over, and I want to see the next one."

"You saw what she did, right?" He looked at me and back at my mother.

"Yeah, I saw it." I ducked my head.

"Y'all got me out here just to embarrass the shit out of me. I'm not going to sit out here with people looking at me crazy, like I raised a heathen of a child."

"Plenty of people out here got heathen kids. Sit down."

"I'm not going to stay out here with people looking at me!"

"You steady worried about somebody lookin' at you."

"Oh, I know somebody out here who's looking at me, I know it." My father stared at her, his eyebrows grabbing each other, his thick mouth a hard dark line. "Sit your ass down, you blocking people's view." I saw my mother's face working. Normally my father could never talk to her that way and end it there, but being embarrassed by me was still not as bad as getting into it publicly with him. She sat down and placed me down tight between them. Their shoulders pressed me on both sides and my upper arm ached. When I looked at it, I saw that my mother's nails had pushed deep, clean, half-moon imprints into my skin.

I watched the game without watching it, everything a filmy blur. The cheerleaders' skirts flashed blue through the steam of my own tears and the clouds of sand lifted by their feet, and their shouts sounded like my parents' voices when I lay under the filmy surface of my bathwater to block the noise of them fighting.

"They're not even loud enough," I commented bitterly.

"Maybe they would have been, if you would have been down there with 'em," my father responded.

"Yeah, but she messed that up for herself," my mother snapped. "Hauling off and hitting some little girl like that. Now tell me, was that worth it?"

"I don't care." I hugged myself. In the shade of the picnic umbrella, between my parents, with my body not moving in the sun, the heat seemed to be gone. "People just keep messing with me."

"People like who?"

I opened my mouth, fully intending to tell TJ's part in it, but closed it at the last second. I could see him with his team filing over to the edge of the field to warm up, which meant the current game would end soon. Even with his helmet on and number not visible, I could distinguish my half-brother's long-legged gait, the almost girlish way he had of standing far back on one bow leg whenever he stood still. "That girl Taylor," I said. "I hate her."

"Don't say hate," my father grumbled. "That word got power. That thing got power. Hating somebody is like wishing them to Hell."

"But I do," I protested.

"Well, I don't see what good hating that girl is doing you," my mother said, lifting her sunglasses to examine her nails. "She's the one still out there on the field."

There was nothing to say to that, and I watched my age division's team lose 14–7 in hot-eyed silence. The game ended quietly, with the football players filing across the field to shake hands with the other team and our audience breaking into the obligatory "we are proud of you!" cheer as the boys limped, slump-shouldered, back to the stands. They were used to winning. Several of the boys were red-eyed and swiping at their noses when they took off their helmets. Fathers thumped them on the back and told them to shake it off; mothers tried to stuff them with pig-in-the-blankets and juice boxes from the bright-colored ice coolers everyone dragged to the games.

The crowd revived instantly when the oldest boys, TJ's team, rushed out onto the field, their strides long and swift and certain, their metallic gold helmets like a stampede of miniature suns. I thought of football only in the way I thought of most things: in terms of its relationship to me. I saw the events of games through the lens of whether we were on offense or defense, ahead or behind, what color the other team wore, what cheers would be appropriate to call. But from the stands, in the midst of adults, it was different. The boys running out onto the field were like soldiers rushing into battle in the war movies my father liked to watch. The grownups shouted "Hit! Fight! Kill!" as if they would really be heard and obeyed from the bleachers, happy when they saw their sons slam into the bodies of other children, ecstatic when dreams in the form of pigskin eggs flew over the goal line. Sometimes they looked at the cheerleaders, answering their verses and whistling when somebody flattened her skirt with an especially hard shake, but I suspected that the boys were their real motive for getting out of bed early Saturday morning after a week of what my father called "high-blood-pressure livin'."

Despite the explosive majesty of the teams running out, TJ's game was a boring one. They just pushed back and forth across the field, scoring inch by inch, yard by hard-fought yard, all sweat and blood and grunting, no heroics. My father said it was like that because both defensive lines were on their job, and I nodded as if I understood.

I busied myself with watching the older cheerleaders. The crowd of young and not-so-young men at the gate thickened when the thirteen- to fifteen-year-old girls took the track. These girls were taller, longer, thicker than us. They got their hair done for the games, not in twisted ponytails, but in Shirley Temple curls or cornrows with complex designs or pressed straight down. Breasts pushed against their vests, and real booty and hips, not just force, shook the hard polyester skirts that flew up around full thighs. Their curves seemed unobtrusive and well placed while mine poked out of the fat on my body in strange ways and knocked me off balance. I glanced at my father, who had his camera trained hard on the football field. My mother shifted on the bleachers and sighed loudly, trying to make sure we noticed and appreciated her boredom. I didn't dare move, not even when my stomach felt concave with hunger and the smells drifting from the snack shack—nacho cheese, relish, chili, jalapeños—blended and cooked on a breeze that blew right into my face. By the third quarter, I began to wonder if I'd ever been so miserable in my life. My father even stopped filming and lowered the camera, which my mother took as a cue to pounce.

"Tannah, I don't think anything you catch on that thing today is going on ESPN," she said. When she turned our way, sunlight slipped in from under the picnic umbrella and illuminated the bottom half of her oval face, her slender, mole-spotted neck, her full cleavage, and the coppery skin that shone against the deep cranberry of her blouse. Her eyes, peering out at us from beneath the umbrella's shadow, shone like a cat's. I wondered, with a catch in my breath, why I couldn't be that beautiful. Apparently, it had an effect on my father as well. "Let's see what they do with this quarter," he said grudgingly. "Then we might as well try to beat the crowd out."

My father had barely stopped talking when the ball suddenly sailed into the air, released by a Sheriffs quarterback desperate for a score. "They throwin' it!" my father shouted, standing up and fumbling with the camera. One of the Sheriffs ran towards the ball, wide open in a nearly empty corner of the field. Our team, the Cougars, unprepared for that kind of offense, scattered outwards, but only one player made it out far enough, leapt up so that his feet looked like they were level with the other players' heads, and grabbed the ball down into his belly. The receiving Sheriff was left so suddenly empty-handed that he still clasped onto the air, holding so tight for such a long second he must have imagined that he actually had the ball, that someone hadn't been faster than him, that he hadn't made that fatal mistake, that he wouldn't replay this moment in his championship game in his head for weeks to come. Meanwhile, the Cougar who caught the ball took off with a short, bowlegged skip backwards to gain momentum that would have identified him as TJ to me if I hadn't already seen the number fifteen large and bright on his back. My father always told him it was a bad habit, that skip, but it didn't stop him this time.

TJ shot through clumps of bulky, off-balance players like a buttered beam of light. He ran a straight, smooth path, abandoning his usual showoff tactics of shaking tackles by twisting backwards, of faking and darting side to side. The running backs joined him and swept out from his sides like angel wings, dangerous, heavy wings that knocked aside anybody that came near his path. He picked up speed, dusting even his protectors, and swept over the goal line untouched. The screaming of the crowd and the cheerleaders rose with his every step, and thickened into a delirious roar when he spiked the ball down and broke into the Cabbage Patch dance, pumping his arms and turning in a circle. My father laughed and shook our entire row with his heavy stomping. I jumped up and down, forgetting how mad I was at TJ, and even my mother, though she was the only one in the crowd still sitting, rocked back in her seat and shook her head in amazement. "The boy is good," she allowed.

We won the game 7–0. The football players grouped up, hopping and hollering, falling over each other and spraying apple cider bottles, while the cheerleaders jumped around them like they had something to do with the victory. TJ was at the center of the huddle, taller than most of them, holding the game ball high above the crowd. After a catch and run like that, he would be unbearable for weeks, but he wouldn't be able to annoy me. The end of football season always marked the end of me seeing my brother on a regular basis. The sharp realization of that stabbed at the last handful of anger I'd been holding on to.

The players peeled themselves from the celebration huddle and filed away to do their sportsmanship walk across the field. The drama over, my father seemed to remember I was there and finally turned the camera on me. "My, look at that pretty girl sitting next to me," he crooned from behind the eyepiece, and I managed a smile. My mother followed his lens onto me as if she were looking at me for the first time that day. She wrinkled her nose at what she saw. "Lord, I'm glad this season is over. If I had to wash those shoes one more time..."

A familiar voice called out through the din of laughter, victory chants, and shouting children. We turned and saw Charlotte approaching us, heavy and sweat-streaked, rolling her big hips over one another. "What's up, Tannah? Rebecca?" she called as she got closer. I wondered at her boldness. I could count on my hands the number of times in my life that I'd seen Charlotte and my mother actually speak to one another. My mother raised one perfectly arched eyebrow and looked Charlotte up and down. "Hey," she finally said in a thick, flat voice, drawing me to her side and holding tightly, her fingers stiff.

"And hello, Tanis," Charlotte persisted. I looked at her, torn between the manners my mother had taught me and the loathing for this woman she'd taught me as well. My mother's clenching hand gave no clue as to which way to go.

"Hi," I said as low as I could. "How are you?" Acrylic nails dug into my arm.

"I'm doing okay, sweetheart. Just going to get that boy home so he can get on that homework. 'Cause he got this football thang down, don't he, Tannah?"

"That's for damn sure," my father laughed. "You saw that shit, that interception! I got it right here on tape." He patted the leather bag and laughed again, and my mother stood, her hands on her denim-hugged hips, her body between them. "*We'll* make you a copy," she told Charlotte, finality in her tone.

"*I* appreciate that, Rebecca," Charlotte smiled, not obeying the hint, and looked right past her to my father. "You know they gon' want to take the boys to nationals now, right? I heard it's in Florida this year."

"That far, huh?" my father grunted.

"Yeah, he gon' need plane, hotel fare, all that."

"I hear you. Come on, Tanis," he said to me, though I was already standing up, my bag over my arm.

"And you still gon' come help me move his stuff out to my new place, right?"

Quiet fell over our part of the bleachers, as if the crowd had stopped celebrating just to see what my father would do. Not responding right away, he took his time reaching down for the soda cooler and hoisting it over his big shoulder. "I said I would, didn't I?" he finally answered. I heard my mother's hair swoosh through the air, she turned her head towards him so fast and hard. My father caught it, too. Grabbing the crook of her elbow, he hustled us away. "Tell TJ he had a good game; Ima call him," he said over his shoulder as he steered us down the creaking bleacher steps. My mother let him hold onto her as she navigated the bleachers in her heels, but shook him away as soon as we hit solid ground. "I guess the bitch never heard of a U-Haul," she snapped as we walked to the truck, her stalking several strides ahead.

"Becky, don't be like that."

"Like what? Got me out here today to just humiliate me, I guess. That woman coming all up in your face like I'm not there."

"She spoke to you."

My mother went on as if she hadn't heard him. "And this one," she gestured to me. "Acting like that in front of everybody, getting kicked off the field. What do you have to say to that,

Tannah? I'm always the one who has to say something." My father looked at me and patted his camera case. "I got that shit on tape, too," he said. "That little heffa sure did bounce."

I laughed, and my mother made an exasperated sound and stalked ahead, stomping up dust. My father jogged up behind her, shifting the cooler. He slid his spare arm around her and lifted her easily off the ground. She laughed and kicked until her black clog came off, and held his shoulder to steady herself as he bent down to slide it back onto her foot.

Chapter Four

As usual after a game weekend, I returned to school hoarse on Monday. When Mrs. Ackerson-Smith called my name in the roll, I croaked out a response, knowing as well as everyone else did that I was exaggerating for attention. "Tanis Victoria," she said, riding my full name on a tight sigh. "I'm sure you can speak more audibly than that."

"I had a game," I protested in a whisper. She looked back at me with the eraser of her pencil pressed into her chin. Mrs. Ackerson-Smith didn't like shenanigans in roll call. No funny voices, no requests to be called by a nickname, no hesitation, no pretended losses of hearing to make the other kids in the class laugh. Most of us had come from pink-cheeked, fresh-out-of-college Mr. Marks's fourth-grade class, where we had quickly learned that the longer we could stretch out roll call, the less time we would have for actual work. He had been sweet and eager, young enough to feel invested in his job teaching inner-city kids, and bewildered as to why he never got through his lesson plans on schedule. Mrs. Ackerson-Smith, who had taught at our school for as long as anyone could remember, didn't play that. There was a bit of comfort in the constancy of her meanness. With Mr. Marks or a sub, you never really knew how far was too far to push.

We had heard legends about Mrs. Ackerson-Smith from the bigger kids on the yard since we were in first grade. Supposedly, she had been in the army, had one eye shot out, and replaced it with a glass one that could roll around and see you anywhere in the room. She had gotten married over the summer, which was how the Smith got added to her name, and the general hope was that she would return happier and more mellowed out. This was not the case. Whenever she punished me, I found myself staring at her thick, yellow-gold wedding band and wondering what kind of man her husband was, if they fought, if he made her laugh, if he ever walked up behind her and held her skinny hips when she was cooking.

School had always been easy for me. My teachers got pissed when I did things like letting out the class snake or raising my hand in an assembly to tell Ms. Patterson that she had food on her blouse from lunch. But I was quick to answer questions, I scored high on standardized tests, and I turned in beautiful projects that I never did myself. My father's hands, large and rough-palmed with dirt pressed permanently beneath the finger-nails, could make anything. Whenever I had a project, I worked at the dining room table in the most walked-through part of the house, knowing that he would pass by and see me sitting blank and helpless before piles of Popsicle sticks and papier-mâché. He'd make a few suggestions and glue a few corners, getting more and more into it until I slipped away to watch the *The Cosby Show* on TV. I'd check in with him periodically to nod my approval of the structure coming to life. As if it was never my project, I would admire the little touches he added: real flowers in the yard of my California mission, stones lining its edge, unaware Lego people walking around the base of my volcano who would be killed when tomato-paste lava bubbled down the sides. My mother scolded both of us, but most of the fire died from her voice as she, too, stopped to watch his creations take shape.

However, Mrs. Ackerson-Smith wasn't overly impressed with my volcanoes, dioramas, or log cabins. The way she rose her skinny, drawn-on eyebrows when she looked at the precision of these projects scared me enough to at least sit next to my father as he worked and point out places where he could be more sloppy. She wrote the As she did give me stingy and small at the top of my papers and my lower grades big and red, and she gave six homework assignments a night. Even when I started as soon as I got home, by the time I'd finish it was too dark to take my extension cords outside, tie one end to the gate, and work on my sub-par double-dutch skills.

Internal fifth-grade battles got suspended only when we conspired together against Mrs. Ackerson-Smith. When everyone decided that they were fed up with never making it outside to play on weekday afternoons, we gathered in a clump on the schoolyard to determine a plan of action. To fight her, we decided to draw out the most formidable people we knew: our mothers. Our mothers had knocked us upside our heads, humiliated and cussed us out in public, whipped us until they drew blood, welts, tears, or all three. As surely as we had felt their fury on our ears, hearts, and asses, we knew it would be laid on the outside world in our defense. We each pleaded to them about the craziness of all that homework, how stressed our young minds were, how cruel our teacher was, until we heard the deep-in-the-throat noises and saw the indignant side-cocked hips we loved to see directed towards anyone but us.

The last open house of the semester presented the perfect opportunity for my class to unleash our mothers on Mrs. Ackerson-Smith, just in time to head off the mass of homework she was notorious for giving over Christmas break. I felt connected to my classmates in a way I never had before as we led our parents into the construction-paper-bright room and squeezed beside them at tables too low for their legs. And my mother, beautiful in the coral dress, dark pantyhose, and new pumps she had chosen so carefully for my open house, crossed her ankles, leaned forward, and started the ambush.

"Now, Miss Ackerson," she began.

"Mrs. Ackerson-Smith, please." Our teacher smiled sweetly, and we could see the thin, faded teeth that we hardly ever encountered. My mother opened her wide eyes a little wider and then cut them in half, the way she did whenever she didn't like somebody's tone.

"Mrs. Ackerson-Smith, let me say one thing. I respect you and the job you're doing challenging these kids, but I just think you're going overboard with all this work. Some of these kids have activities in the afternoon, lessons. My baby falls asleep on her books every night. I mean, aren't they supposed to be learning some of this stuff in school with you? Why they have to bring so much of it home?"

A murmur of agreement rippled through the room, and Chantel Becton's mother chimed in. Chantel was what my mother called a ghetto bird. She wore athletic socks with her plastic jelly sandals, talked in husky tones, and cracked her gum as loud and sharp as a jump rope slapping pavement. Her mother's hairstyles were always plastered to her scalp like melted Jujubes and coiled into cone shapes on her head.

"Yeah, I know this class 'sposed to be advanced and everything, but all this going to buy newspapers every day and art supplies every weekend and signing off on every little thang every night is breakin' me. I mean, I got other kids. Why am I getting worked, too?"

We heard a few murmurs and nods, along with a crack of Chantel's gum. Yosi's mother spoke up in her deep, rich voice.

"Academics are very important. We tell our son that every day. But children need to be children, too. They won't have that forever." Women, and one dad, rocked in their small seats and sang "yes" under their breath as if they were in church. We kept our eyes away from Mrs. Ackerson-Smith but swung our legs below our chairs in delight. As quiet fell over the class and Ms. Ass-Lick did not respond, our glee thinned out to a nervous anticipation. In the silence, we could hear the class rabbit rustling around in his cage and small pops of Chantel's gum, until her mother finally shoved her in the shoulder.

Mrs. Ackerson-Smith paced back and forth across the front of the room, lightly slapping her wooden ruler against her hand. She opened her mouth, so heavily painted in red lipstick that it looked as if she had been drinking blood. The lipstick had gotten dry and a little crusty, so that we could see every fold in her thin lips.

"Does anyone have any idea what the job market will be like in ten years, just when your children are moving into the world?" She looked around the room, holding all of us in her greenish gaze. One of her eyes was cloudier and not as focused as the other; word on the yard was that that was the glass one that could look around the room while the other one stayed still. We stared back at her blankly. In ten years, we would be impossibly grown up, twenty and twenty-one years old. Such a future was too unreal to consider.

"Well, I know. Salaries won't increase at the same rate as inflation. Trade jobs will be replaced by new technology and machinery. Unskilled labor will be outsourced to other countries. What only takes a high school diploma now may take a bachelor's degree, what may take a bachelor's will take a master's. The days of finishing high school, finding a job, getting married, and working enough overtime to move into the middle class will end." She spoke slowly but still seemed to say this all in just one breath. Our parents shifted uncomfortably. I knew that for a lot of my friends' parents, most of whom had never gone to college, a city or county job with time-and-a-half was golden, the best they could hope for behind a son making it to the NFL or NBA.

"Education will be the single most important factor dividing those who succeed from those who don't. I am teaching my students to make education their priority. I am equipping them with the skills to handle middle school, high school, and college and beyond. If you want your children to be successful and self-sufficient, I suggest you allow and assist me to do my job. If you are not willing to do that, it is your prerogative to remove your child from my class."

I snapped my head around to my mother, hard barrettes hitting my face. No one talked to my mother like that. But she bit her wine-painted lip and said nothing. The other parents, also chastised, listened attentively for the rest of the night. They raved over our portfolios, clapped for our newscast presentation, and sat alert as Mrs. Ackerson-Smith talked animatedly about what we had been doing in American history and our end-of-the-year trip to Washington DC. Our teacher's excitement about all things American was strange and feverish. You couldn't help but catch a little of it, and most of the parents filed out in a pleasant mood. My mother steered me away with clicking heels and cat-digging nails in my shoulder.

We were about halfway home when our car overheated. My mother climbed out to pour water in the radiator from the plastic jug she kept in the trunk. Just in case the car blew up before she could cool it down, she made me get out and stand several feet away, forcing her to yell her tirade.

"Got me in there, running my mouth to that woman, embarrassing the hell out of me. Having me look like a fool 'cause you don't want to do what you're supposed to do." She swiped at tears from the steam billowing out of our old Duster's hood. "She's right. If me and your daddy did what we were supposed to do, we wouldn't have to go through this kind of shit. We just got our GEDs. Your daddy barely did that. I used to be smart in school." I stayed quiet and waited until she said it was safe to get back into the car. We made it home, the Duster puffing and coughing into the driveway. My mother shook her head at the guys hanging out on the porch next door, who didn't acknowledge her.

"Leave for work, they're sitting out there, get back, they're still sitting out there. Don't ever mess with boys like that, Tanis, ever. Don't throw it away on somebody who's not worth the trouble. You get pregnant by the wrong one, it's over."

I dropped the hand I'd been raising to wave at Butch, one of the guys who always called me Little Mama and got my basketballs out of the street.

"You hook yourself up with somebody who's going somewhere in life, and don't mess it up. You hear me? You promise me that?"

"I promise, Mommy, not to get pregnant by anybody like Mr. Butch."

We entered the house to find my father sitting at the dining room table with his civil service exam books spread out around him. Green laminated with black spiral binding, they said Foreman, Janitor, and Welder in big block letters on the front.

"Got some more tests coming up," he told us. He grabbed my mother's arm as she passed the table and pulled her down to him. "You smell good, baby." She kissed him back, quickly, then stood up straight and broke indignantly into the story about my open house. My father laughed out loud.

"That shit wasn't funny, T."

"If that ain't funny, I don't know what is. A bunch of grown-ass folks riding in like cowboys and getting shut down like that in front of they kids by that little bit of nothing teacher." I considered this. Mrs. Ackerson-Smith was ballerina-skinny and almost as short as some of us, but I had never thought of her that way. She always seemed like a female Goliath looking down on me, and I didn't have a rock.

"I'm glad you're so amused," my mother fumed. "This is Tanis's future we're talking about. Don't you want her to have more choices than this?" She gestured at the exam books on the table, and I saw my father's face tighten.

"Is it bad as all that, Becky?" My mother opened her mouth to respond, and I sprang in to distract them.

"I do want to go on that Washington DC trip. It sounds fun."

"That's going to cost money." My mother snatched up a glass my father had been drinking out of and his full ashtray and stalked into the kitchen.

"No, it's a class trip," I said, turning to my father. "Don't the schools pay for class trips?"

"Since you got so much work, why don't you grab your books, baby, and come study with me."

With our mothers defeated, my class simply surrendered to

Mrs. Ackerson-Smith. We prepared our newscasts, our California missions, our constant book reports, and our charts of the different branches of the US government. We stuffed our complaints behind gritted teeth and hid our sighs in our noses. On one subject only, the Washington DC trip, did her excitement latch onto us like germs from water fountains. When she talked about that, the corners of her eyes lifted and she bared her brittle teeth in smiles that made her almost, almost pretty. As we cried out questions about when it was, the places we would go, what we would see, she allowed us the delicious freedom of talking out of turn.

"This is going to be fun, man!" My desk partner Denise flipped through the packet. "Ooooh, we're staying in a hotel. Me and my parents stayed in a hotel in Disney World. It was phat!"

"Yeah, hotels are so fun," I said, though I couldn't remember ever being in one in my life. "I can't wait!" I liked the new smell of the brochure, the glossy feel of the pages, the glowing faces of kids carefully placed so that there was at least one of color in each crowd. They smiled in front of the Lincoln Memorial, grinned in front of the White House, laughed as if something was incredibly funny at the gate to the Arlington Cemetery. They surrounded a white man who had some look of being important, gazing up at him with attentive, serious eyes and taking diligent notes, as if they were solving one of the world's great problems. They looked as if they had the kind of houses where there was always food in the refrigerator, where classical music played from somewhere you couldn't see, and parents never cussed or screamed. I had never been in one of these houses but knew that they existed, just as I had never been outside of Los Angeles but knew other places existed. The desire came at me, hard and breathless, to get on a plane and to go somewhere, to stay in a hotel, and to be one of these shiny, cardigan-wearing, food-in-the-fridge kids.

"We have some funding from the magnet program," Mrs. Ackerson-Smith told us. "And we will be doing some more fundraisers to help with the cost. Your parents will only have to pay a balance of five hundred dollars."

I had never heard someone say a thing like that before, *"only five hundred dollars."* I set my packet down on my desk, nudging it around until it was completely straight. For once, I was glad when Mrs. Ackerson-Smith called us back to attention and started passing out a worksheet, putting an end to the excited chatter.

I wasn't one of those kids who didn't know the value of money. It was something I learned about very young. There was one Christmas when I was six and decided to buy my own gifts. My mother, the designated shopper in my family, always bought gifts and slapped my name on the tag without consulting me or bothering to take me along. My father would open the present I obviously hadn't wrapped, crooning, "Oooh, what did my baby get me?" I would wonder, too, until he said, "Oooh, some new socks and boxers. Thank you, baby, I sure did need that," and called me over for a kiss and hug that made me feel like a liar and a cheat. My mother picked up small, practical things for me to give, and always shook me off when I tried to tag along, saying, "Girl, how I'm supposed to get anything done in a store with you whining and pulling on me?"

I wanted to buy my own gifts; I wanted to know what they were and wrap them myself and hand them to the person with pride. So that year, I started saving whatever money I could get my hands on in my Hello Kitty caboodle. I would stop in a street to pick up loose change, fish for coins in the couch, and hoard the moist, crumpled dollars my half-blind great-grandmother dug out of her Maidenform bra whenever my mother took me by her house. By mid-December, I had saved $29, which I presented proudly to my mother before launching into a lavish description of all the wonderful things I would buy. "Girl," she said absently. She was directing my father in hanging the Christmas lights, which always had to follow the trends she got out of *Good House-keeping* magazine, and always had to be the best on the block. "Don't you know that little twenty-nine dollars won't do much of nothing? Might as well give me that for gas this month."

I remembered clutching my money to my chest, how sad those dirty coins and few crumpled bills looked after that. I never tried to save again after that year. I knew how little $29 could do. And now I knew how much $500 could do. Surely it would take at least that much to paint the house, get the car fixed, stop bill collectors from calling our home so much and at so many times of the day that we no longer answered the phone. We ignored the ringer, let the answering machine pick up, and listened for the person's voice to come on the line. I couldn't hand my mother that number, $500, especially right before Christmas, and watch her eyes roll upwards in exasperation then slant over to my father, who would take another drag of his cigarette and avoid our gaze.

It surprised me to see my father's pickup outside the gate as I left school that afternoon. Since the time had changed and football season ended, I wasn't used to seeing my father in day-light hours. He was smoking, and when I climbed in, his ashtray was already full. I wrinkled up my nose and rolled down my window as we pulled away from the curb. "Daddy, tobacco increases the chances of heart and lung disease," I said.

"Tanis, I ain't in the mood for that shit today," he growled back.

I felt like I had been hit in the chest. I started wrestling with the car door handle, though we had already started moving.

"What the hell you doin'?"

"I'm going to walk home!" I cried, actually opening the door and sticking my foot out towards traffic.

"Girl, get back!" He reached over me, slammed my door shut, and shoved down the lock. "You lost your mind?" I folded my arms and looked straight ahead.

"I'm sorry, baby," he said a few moments later in a quieter tone. "Daddy shouldna talked to you like that. Your daddy had a bad day."

I stayed firm, sucking back tears.

"We finished the house we was working on, and Mitch tried to screw us on the overtime. Some of them Mexicans, they just take the goddamn check, scared to say shit, I guess, but I wanted what he owed me." I was quiet. My father had never confided in me about work, and I felt both helpless and grown up.

"He probably ain't gon' call me for the next job." He took another long drag. "Fuck him. Don't ever let somebody run over you, baby. Don't take less than what you worth. You gon' be worth a lot more than Daddy, one day. You hear me?"

I nodded.

"You forgive me?" he asked as softly as his heavy voice could manage.

"Yeah, I guess," I said, finally.

"You wasn't really gon' jump out the car, was you?" he chuckled. I shrugged.

"Just like your mama sometimes," he laughed, drawing in smoke he'd just let out, and the laughter turned into a fit of coughing.

"I just don't want you to die," I told him.

"Girl, I ain't goin' nowhere. My cigarettes just help me relax sometimes, when I be stressed out. Don't you ever smoke 'em, though." How like him, and every other grownup, to tell me not to do things while they did the same things themselves. Like my mother cussing as she chastised me for saying a bad word.

"I won't. They make people's lips black and ugly." My father glanced at me.

"I guess that's why you don't kiss your daddy no more," he said. I didn't answer. He was the one who stopped kissing me, turning his lips away when I tilted my mouth up to his, offering me his bristly cheek instead.

"How was school?" my father asked. "Anything happen?"

"Like what?" I asked.

"I don't know. Looked like you was thinking so hard when you walked out. Anything you want to tell me 'bout?" I thought of the Washington DC packet in my backpack, fat and new smelling between my social studies book and my binder. "No," I told him. "Nothing."

My mother arrived home a few hours after us, backing through the doorway with groceries in her arms. My father and I got up, wordlessly, to go get the rest of the groceries out of the car, knowing my mother would not touch another bag once she saw us. She collapsed on the couch and kicked off her heels, wiggling her stocking feet, which she stood on all day as a sales clerk (or customer service representative, as she liked to correct people). My mother refused to wear flats, saying that they ruined your arches. She had small feet with insteps as liquid and bowed as a ballerina's, unlike the Flintstone flat feet I'd inherited from my father. "Lord, I'm glad you could get her today," she called from the living room, pressing her thumbs into her soles. "I finally got some real shopping done." We heard the refrigerator door open and slam close. "Watch him just throw all the stuff in there any kind of way," my mother muttered under her breath. "Get in there and help."

I took a pack of frozen cutlets into the kitchen, the icy film on it dampening my blouse.

"Why'd you get through so early, anyway?" my mother's voice called after me.

"Job ended today. They about to send us somewhere else." My father eyed me as he took the meat from my arms and tossed it into the freezer. I jumped forward and slammed the door before it could fall back out.

Chapter Five

For weeks, my father got up and left at the same time every morning while it was still dark, looking for pickup work. I knew what that meant, standing outside hardware and home-improvement stores on the other side of town with the Mexicans, who people would almost always go for before taking a six-foot, two-hundred-pound black man to their house. I hated to think of him standing there in his flannel jacket holding his tools and hoping someone would wave him over. I'd heard him say once that looking for pickup work felt like hooking outside a motel on Figueroa. He must not have gotten any play because after a few weeks of this, he finally told my mother about his job. "Ima get back on something soon, don't worry about nothin'," he told her.

"Don't worry about nothing, huh?" she repeated in a tired voice, keeping her large eyes on the soot-stained stove top, her back to us, straight and stiff. She turned, leaning against the stove, and wiped her hands on a dingy dishtowel. "Go on and eat. I made rice and beans, some chicken," she said simply. My father fixed his plate, moving carefully around her so that they never touched. I waited until he finished and left for the living room before I approached the stove with my own plate. "Did you wash your hands?" my mother asked sharply.

"Yes," I said, even though I hadn't. She shot a look at me. "And when did you do that?" I turned wordlessly, padded in my socks across the yellowing linoleum to the sink, and squirted dishwashing liquid into my hands.

"Don't use too much of that," she snapped. I screwed the top completely off and let some of the thick, lemon-scented liquid slide off my hand back into the bottle's mouth. My mother just looked at me and rolled her eyes upward. "Girl, you're a mess. Get your food and go on somewhere." I took my plate into the living room, where my father leaned into his recliner with his battered TV tray set up in front of him. A few minutes later, my mother followed and nestled into her favorite spot in the right-hand corner of the couch. Normally, the living room TV was my father's domain, but we all gravitated there since we had cut off the cable in the other rooms. My father still controlled the living room remote control. My mother didn't say a word as he channel-surfed over all her favorite soaps, as if she realized that the living room TV was one thing she should just go ahead and let him have. He finally settled on an old episode of *Family Matters* that we had seen a million times before. We knew exactly what the problem was, when the laugh tracks were coming, and what the chocolate-sweet resolution would be, but we still laughed every time we were supposed to. Despite a load of homework from Mrs. Ackerson-Smith, I stayed in the living room even after I finished eating, not wanting to leave the peacefulness of my parents watching television, of them laughing at the same things at the same times.

We tuned out the phone at first. We always let the answering machine pick up to screen out bill collectors and certain family members from the people we actually wanted to talk to. But it kept ringing insistently, a human impatience pushing through the tones. Still, we didn't move until a voice came on the line that made both my parents stiffen before leaping towards it. My father, though much bigger and further away, moved faster.

"Charlotte? Why you calling here...what's wrong? He did what? Yeah. Yeah, I know. I'll be through there." He hung up. My mother's voice came out trembling and low. "I *know* that bitch didn't just call my house." She snatched the phone to her by pulling the coiled beige cord with her foot and started punching in numbers on the keypad. Apparently, she knew Charlotte's number by heart. My father snatched the cord back. It pulled out of the phone, tumbled over our dark-green carpet like a cut-off Shirley Temple curl, and shimmied up to my knee.

"Give it to me, Tanis." My mother held out her hand.

"Don't you move, Tanis," said my father. I picked up the cord and wavered, beginning to wish I'd done my homework in my room after all. My mother started towards me, and my father snatched her arm. "Becky, calm down, it ain't that serious."

"She's not supposed to call here; you promised me that much."

"Except for emergencies with my son."

"What's wrong with him?" My mother folded her arms.

"He done ran away." My father got up and grabbed his thick flannel jacket from the couch arm where he slung it every day, sending its musky tobacco scent across the room. "Talking about how he ain't movin to no Valley."

"So, I guess you're going over there," my mother said in a defeated voice, watching him tie his clunky work boots. He raised his eyes to hers.

"I'm not gon' to sit up in her house all night, if that's what you think. Ima drive around, look for him. I know some people he kicks it with over 'round there."

"Hmmph. You better not wear your blue coat, you plan on driving slow on that side of town."

"I'll be all right. Glad you care, though." He tried to grin at her, but she turned her face away.

"I'll be back, Toodle Woodle. Don't worry." It hadn't occurred to me to worry until he said that. I suddenly pictured TJ out somewhere in the night, slender and alone, no football padding and helmet between him and the darkness.

My mother got on the phone with Trish after my father left and complained bitterly as she cleaned up the kitchen, slinging and banging pots. She forgot to make me take a bath or comb my hair for the next day, and she went to bed without grilling me about my unfinished homework. I sat in the living room with my social studies book open on my lap until midnight, reading the same lines over and over. I didn't know that I had fallen asleep until the ringing phone made it into my dream. I jerked my head up and snatched the phone on reflex, beating the answer machine to the person's voice.

"Hello?" I asked groggily.

"Hey, Tiny." TJ's voice, usually swaggering, was soft and shaky. "What you doin' up?"

"Homework. Where are you?"

"At a pay phone. I was at my girlfriend's house, but her mama said I had to go home."

"Her mama wouldn't take you home?"

"Well, see, she had caught me in her room. She said I had to get out, go home."

"Oh."

"The bus ain't running no more. My pops there?"

"He's out looking for you."

"No, he ain't."

"Yeah, he is. Your mama called, and he went over to look for you."

"Nah, my pops don't care about me. All he care about is you."

"How you gonna say something like that? You're more stupid than I thought. First you run away with nowhere to go, then you say something stupid like that."

"Don't be calling me stupid," he said so half-hardheartedly I didn't bother to retort. "It's cold out here."

"You better call your mama."

"Nah, I don't wanna talk to her. She talked all this shit when I said I didn't want to move. Talking about how I held her back long enough, I could go to hell, all that. That's the way she feel, I can get out her life. Ain't gon' buy her no house, either, when I blow up." His voice was thick, and I wondered if he was crying. "Hold on, TJ," I told him. He snorted back snot in reply. I went to my mother's room and turned on the light, wondering where I had gotten this courage.

"Girl?" My mother lifted her head from where she'd burrowed completely under the covers. We both slept that way, and my father teased us about it, saying we would mess around one day and suffocate ourselves in bed. "Your daddy call?"

"No, TJ's on the phone. He needs somebody to pick him up."

"Somebody like who?" She bugged her eyes.

"He doesn't want to call his mama."

"Since when does what he want have anything to do with me?"

"He's out there stranded, Mommy, and he won't call his house." She was quiet.

"Mommy," I insisted.

"Shit," she replied, sitting up and throwing the covers off her legs.

We found him shivering on a corner of Normandie and 49th in his letterman jacket, sneakers, and boxers. Apparently, his girlfriend's mama hadn't given him much time to get out. My mother honked as she passed him, made a U-turn, and came back around to the curb. He climbed sheepishly into the backseat, and I twisted around to look at him.

"Where your pants at?" I grinned.

"Shut up," he growled.

"Don't you tell my child to shut up," my mother said, even though she said "shut up" to me all the time.

"I'm sorry, Miss Becky," TJ said right away, more respectfully than I ever thought he could sound.

"And Tanis, it's where are your pants, not where your pants at," my mother told me, reaching to turn on the creaky car heater. "Where are your pants, boy?"

He didn't answer, sinking lower into the torn interior of the backseat.

"I guess you can get a pair of Tannah's at the house. You know I'm not going over to your mother's."

"That's cool. I don't wanna go back there." He stared out of the window as if there was some kind of view besides the uncertain shapes of rickety houses and junky cars parked on their lawns.

"Hmmmph," I said. "You sure aren't too good at running away." He kicked the back of my seat, but my mother didn't see that. "Tanis," she warned. "Leave the boy alone." I stared at her in surprise as she steered into the left lane of the 110 freeway.

We arrived home, and my mother gave TJ sheets and blankets to make a pallet on the couch. "I have a trundle bed," I piped up, but my mother just cut her eyes at me and continued stuffing a sofa cushion into a pillowcase.

"The couch is good," TJ said, stretching his long arms up, grabbing on to the archway that separated our living and dining room. "Good for the back."

"I thought that was the floor," I pointed out. He made a fist at me when my mother turned her back.

"Go on and go to bed," my mother told me.

I undressed and got into bed slowly, conscious of the movements of my mother and TJ in the house, the bathroom, the living room. I could hear TJ lift the toilet seat, the hard rush of his urine against the water, a thinner, crisper stream than my father's. I heard the lid clatter down and the flush, but no sound of water for washing hands, and his footsteps, heavier than my mother's but lighter than my father's, as he made his way back to the living room. I imagined that I could hear his breath, slow and blending with mine as he fell asleep on the couch. I opened my door after I had my pajamas on, and soft gold light from the hall slanted into my room. It brought with it light snores, like my father's massive, rumbling snores would sound if they got bleached in the sun. It was like having a real, full brother to have TJ fold his height into the backseat of my mother's car, to have him sleeping near me, under one roof. I hadn't really known how lonely I was in my parents' house, how small I was all crunched up between them. I wanted to hold on to the moment, to my brother's pee and footsteps and snores. I only drifted in and out of a light sleep that night, so I woke up immediately when the bass from my father's speakers pumped into my dreams. His car door slammed, and my mother's house shoes slapped out of her room.

"Tannah, are you crazy, coming up in here with all that

noise?" I heard her snap even as the front door creaked open. "We have neighbors. We have kids asleep."

"Kids?" My father paused. I supposed he must have seen the hump of TJ's sleeping body on the couch. "He's here? Damn, Becky, why didn't you call somebody?"

"I shouldn't have to call anybody house to look for my husband. I figured you were where you wanted to be. What are you doing?"

"Calling Charlotte to let her know he's all right."

"Hmmph. Must not have been too worried, if she didn't bother to check his girlfriend's house."

"That boy got a different girlfriend every month."

"Wonder where he gets that."

"Char. He's over here...Yeah, he sleep...Guess he took the bus, don't worry about it. Look, I gotta go, he's cool. Ima have him call you tomorrow. Bye." The phone clicked back into the cradle, and it was quiet. The silence was never peace, only my mother's way of preparing for another attack. I was lying tensely on my side by then, the covers pushed off my head, every sound as distinguishable to me as if my parents had been there in my room. My parents' fighting was always like the scene in a scary movie to me: I didn't want to see it, I took no pleasure in it, but it excited me as much as I dreaded it, and I had to know exactly what would happen. The old springs in the couch creaked loudly, and my parents seemed to silently agree to move to their bedroom. I heard no words, just their footsteps, light and heavy, going through the hall.

"How he get here?" I heard the clunk of my father's boots, one by one, on the floor.

"He sure didn't catch a bus."

"You went to get him?"

"You think I'd leave anybody's child out on Normandie in the middle of the night? You think I'm that cold?"

"I thought I looked for that boy everywhere."

"Yeah, I bet you did."

"What the fuck is that supposed to mean?"

"Tannah, don't play with me. How were you really out looking for your son, all this time?"

"So he is my son, now?"

"He sure knows how to fuck himself over for a piece of ass. I'd say he got that from you."

"Becky, you really think Ima go over there and do some shit like that, knowing you know where I was going, knowing my boy's out there in the streets somewhere? You really believe that shit?" A pause. "Becky. Becky!"

"Just take a shower before you get in my bed."

A few minutes later, I heard the water in the bathroom run.

Chapter Six

The next morning was a strange one, with my father home from work and TJ padding barefoot around the house, my father's pajama pants sagging off his behind. He had been uncertain and tentative the night before, the way you are when you sleep over at someone's house for the first time, walking lightly, asking gingerly where the towels were, guiltily placing dishes in the sink. He seemed more confident when he woke up to find my father there. He strode to the bathroom in the morning as if the house was his domain, teased me every time we passed, and straddled the kitchen chair backwards. My mother, who usually drank coffee in the morning and left me to fend for myself with cereal, got up early and made toast and sausage and eggs. I had never woken up to food cooking on a weekday morning, and I kept sneaking curious glances at my mother as she set our plates in front of us along with tall glasses of juice. My father lectured TJ about running away through the whole meal, and I could tell he wasn't listening, though he nodded vigorously between mouthfuls so big that even my father chided him.

"Hold on, boy, we ain't in Somalia. You can slow down."

"Lord have mercy." My mother shook her head after they left for TJ's school, TJ looking ridiculous in some of my father's pants with the belt looped twice around. "Not one, but two heathens at my table." She piled dishes in the sink.

"That breakfast was good, Mommy," I commented.

"Yeah," she agreed. "His mama can't say I didn't feed him well. She can say what she wants about me but can't say I never took care of her child."

I went to school that morning sleepy but strangely happy, belly full of a hot breakfast and excited that my brother had spent the night with us, that he might be there again when I got home. It wasn't until we all took our seats and the homework monitors began coming around that a horrible truth sank in. I had never finished my homework. Out of five assignments, a science worksheet and some definitions of vocabulary words was all that I had completed. I looked up and around at the quiet bustle in the classroom, my peers smugly removing neat sheets of college rule from their notebooks, the snap of three ring binders and the thudding open of heavy, brown-paper-covered books. Mrs. Ackerson-Smith's homework-collecting process moved like a military operation. Different monitors filed around for different subjects and brought the papers to her desk, where she immediately discarded anything too messy to read, obviously incomplete, or not headed correctly. The things she accepted she meticulously marked in her book, and any person whose assignment wasn't present got one card pulled from the Wall.

The Wall was a poster board mounted next to Mrs. Ackerson-Smith's desk holding twenty-four pockets, each one with one of our names above it. Each pocket held five cards: pink, green, yellow, orange, and the last, dreaded one, red. Everyone started the day out on pink, and she pulled a card out every time you did something wrong. Sometimes she'd pull one out for everyone in the class if we didn't quiet down quickly enough when she was trying to get our attention. Whatever color you ended up on every day got recorded on a progress report sent home to your parents every week, on top of whatever punishments Mrs. Acker-son-Smith had doled out. I think she took a lot of pleasure in pulling our cards. Her color would always heighten as she strode to The Wall in steps larger than her body. She'd lick her fingers to get a better grip when she ripped a card from its pocket, making a loud slapping sound. I think the students who didn't give her a reason to pull their cards irritated her. Kristin Tyler, who stayed in the pink zone all week, was a homework monitor who kept her mouth closed and hands folded on her desk (and earned a fair amount of tormenting on the schoolyard for her trouble), but Mrs. Ackerson-Smith couldn't stand her. The one time Mrs. Ackerson-Smith had pulled everyone's cards and Kristin ended up on green, the girl had put her forehead on her desk and cried out loud, right there. Mrs. Ackerson-Smith watched her with what we all later swore was a chilling, delighted smile.

I wavered pretty reliably between green and orange, which was acceptable enough to my mother. I could never stay on pink for more than a day, but I'd never been in yellow, and certainly not red, the regular domain of a few really "bad" kids, like Shemar Harris, who was notorious for schoolyard sexual harassment, or Eric Nichols, with his serious anger-management issues, or even Yosi, who, since we broke up, had started running with a bad crowd at lunchtime.

Anyway, that day I was missing three homework assignments, and I prayed against certainty as the homework monitor left my desk, as Mrs. Ackerson-Smith scrolled down the names in her book. The class, simmering with bustling papers and murmured conversations, quieted as she stood and went to The Wall, as cards began flipping and changing colors. When she got to my name, near the end of the alphabet, my pink disappeared, followed by my green, and my orange. I let out a sigh when the yellow shined from below my name, thinking the worst was over. Then my teacher's long nails fastened on the yellow card, and red glared out at me. I jumped up from my seat.

"Mrs. Ackerson-Smith!" I cried. "I only missed three!" She glared at me, only one gray eye focusing. "Where do your name and date belong, class?" she addressed the whole class, her gaze on me. "In the right-hand corner," they droned. Distracted by the TV and then Charlotte's call, I had headed my vocabulary homework incorrectly.

"But that's not fair!" I cried shrilly, knowing the pointlessness of the protest before it shrieked its way out. "You know that's not fair!" I repeated. I don't know where I had gotten my concept that things in life were supposed to be fair. It certainly wasn't a philosophy most adults in my life ascribed to. Bug-eyed and straight-mouthed at my raised voice, Mrs. Ackerson-Smith fumbled for my card pocket, but there were no more to pull. "Sit down," she said in a voice like broken asphalt. "Or you'll stay in for recess." I stood for a second, glaring at her, but I wasn't that brave. I plopped heavy into my wooden seat, fat hot tears making soggy spots on the notebook paper in front of me, blurring the red and blue lines. A hand brushed my back and I turned in that direction.

"Don't cry," whispered Yosi. "Red's not that bad. I'll be your boyfriend again, if you want." I answered him with a swift punch to the shoulder.

"Tanis!" Mrs. Ackerson-Smith had turned away from me, but I guess the glass eye rolled on around and got me. "That's it. You won't go out this recess, and you'll start out on red tomorrow." I shrugged, not caring. There was something very liberating in being in the red, in knowing you were already "bad." You could do anything you wanted when you knew you couldn't go any lower, that things couldn't get any worse.

For the rest of the morning, I was unable to concentrate on anything and only hoped that someone else would get into trouble so that I wouldn't have to spend recess alone with Mrs. Ackerson-Smith. I thought it was horrible to have to be alone in the room with a teacher or any person of authority, uncomfortably intimate. But after my outburst, the class seemed to communally agree to avoid my eyes, looking instead at their own folded hands. When the recess bell rang, I sat at my desk, watching my class march out in neat double file lines. Mrs. Ackerson-Smith walked them out and returned, smoothing her long skirt. She walked past me to her desk, took out a plastic container with a sandwich inside, and began eating it in small bites, staring down at it the whole time with the same singleness of purpose with which she did everything else. I had never seen a teacher eat before and I didn't want to now. It felt too personal. I lowered my eyes to my desk, not wanting to attract her attention and get some kind of task to do. But the silence in the room with two people there grew so heavy and overbearing I felt like I could bite into it. I could never stay so quiet for too long, and I had to break it.

"What's that you're eating?" I heard myself ask, feeling immediately like a fool. She looked up in surprise and held a paper napkin over her lips while she swallowed.

"Tuna fish. Would you like some?"

"No, thank you," I said quickly. She got up from her desk and made her way over to me, her long brown skirt like something out of *Little House on the Prairie* moving around her bony, stocking-covered ankles. She sat in the desk opposite of me, Kristin Tyler's desk, fitting as perfectly as I did. "Here." She held out the sandwich. "You would usually get a snack at recess, wouldn't you?"

I looked at the sandwich with her red lipstick smeared into a half circle on the last bite she had taken, and my stomach jumped back inside me. Nowhere in my mother's book was eating after someone, even a teacher, okay. "You never know where people put their mouths when nobody's looking," she always said. But Mrs. Ackerson-Smith was insistent. I gingerly broke off a tiny piece from the opposite end of where she had bitten and held it in my hand.

"You have to appreciate the difficulty of the position you put me in, Tanis Victoria, with your open defiance in class." I looked at her blankly.

"This world works when we work together, when we obey the rules, and a classroom is a miniature version of the world. We have to have order here."

I nibbled a small piece of hard-boiled egg from my small chunk of her sandwich. "But it's not fair."

"It is fair," Mrs. Ackerson-Smith insisted. "If you are a good citizen." I looked into her earnest gray eyes, feeling with all my ten-year-old certainty that she was horribly wrong.

"Have I ever told you, Tanis, that you are one of my brightest students?"

"No."

"You are. You are one of the smartest young ladies I have ever taught."

"Smarter than Kristin Tyler?" I dared, and her answer shocked me.

"Yes," she said without hesitation. She winked her good eye.

"But don't tell anyone I said that." A secret. I had a secret with Mrs. Ackerson-Smith. I was still deciding how to feel about that when she leaned towards me, the scent of tuna fish strong on her breath. "I haven't gotten your paperwork on the Washington DC trip. Are you planning on attending?"

"My parents are still, uh, thinking about it."

"You should definitely come. I think it would benefit you so much to see our nation's capital. You can't imagine how much you will get out of it." A glow came into her cheeks, distinguishing itself from the harsh, unblended strokes of too-bright blush. "I will talk to your parents for you, if you like."

The end of recess bell rang then, saving me. Mrs. Ackerson-Smith straightened back erect, placed the top back on her Tupperware, and smoothed her skirt. She smiled at me with her faded teeth before leaving the room to collect the class, and I smiled back weakly. As soon as she was gone, I ran to the trash and scraped the mashed piece of tuna fish sandwich off my hand.

I managed to push the thought of the red card out of my mind for the rest of the day as we rode home from school. My mother would be pissed, I knew, but I wouldn't have to deal with that until the end of the week, when progress reports went out. Besides, I knew something else now, that Mrs. Ackerson-Smith liked me, that she thought that I was one of her smartest students. There was nothing I liked so much as being thought of as better than somebody else, as standing out in a good way. When we got home, I actually made my way to the table and took out my homework without being prompted.

"What?" my mother said in mock amazement as I flipped open my social studies book. "Is she actually doing her homework right away? Without me telling her? I can hardly believe my eyes." I bit my lip as I headed my paper, correctly. My mother had a way of making me feel bad about even the things that I did right, always calling attention to the fact that I didn't always do them.

"I want to get done early tonight," I said defensively.

"Yeah, you better, so you can get to sleep early. I know all that stuff last night messed up your sleep. Lord knows I didn't need it. If they aren't messing with my life in one way, it's another, Jesus help me. I'm glad your daddy took that boy on home."

My pencil paused above my notebook. "TJ went home?"

"You didn't think he was staying here, did you?" She sliced her eyes at me.

"Maybe," I admitted. "He said he didn't want to go home."

"This world isn't about what you want, girl, you should know that by now." I lowered my pencil to my notebook again, biting back disappointment I hadn't known I would feel.

As humiliating as it had been for me to get put on red, the story of how I actually stood up and yelled at Mrs. Ackerson-Smith got out and exaggerated and gave me a sort of notoriety at school that week. I knew how brief the fame would be so I milked it for all it was worth, despite the fact that I now worked harder than ever in Mrs. Ackerson-Smith's class. While part of me would always hate her, another part warmed to her claim that I was one of her smartest students and wanted her brittle smile to land in my direction. Of course, I didn't tell this to the group of tall, self-assured sixth-grade girls that approached me at lunchtime. I often spent lunchtime alone since Yosi didn't come near me anymore, and I was too embarrassed by my limited double-dutch skills to join in with the other girls. It was hard to practice double-dutch when you were an only child and your mother didn't let you play with the other "hoodrats" on the block; somebody had to turn the ropes.

The coolest sixth-grade crew was led by a lanky, fair-skinned girl named Simone Bevens. Simone wore her hair in cornrows in neat, zigzagged patterns with such clear pathways of silky hair and pale scalp, they always looked freshly done. Her and her crew wore the fly latest styles, big flannel button ups over little spaghetti strap shirts showing smooth long torsos and the outline of new apple-sized breasts with baggy jeans or tight stirrup leggings. They wore three, sometimes four pairs of slouch socks over leggings or with their jeans pants pushed up. They painted on chicken grease layers of lip-gloss and had juicy "baby hair" sideburns slicked down with the Pro Styl gel and dirty toothbrushes they all kept in zip-locked bags in their backpacks. A few of them even had long, bright-colored press-on nails. My mother, when she caught sight of them when she picked me up from school, thought they were horrendous. "Look like funky boys mixed with grown-ass women," she said. "Nails. In elementary school? I was barely thinking about nails and lipstick when I was sixteen years old." Sixteen was also the age when my mother first got pregnant by my father, but neither of us decided to mention that.

When those sixth-grade girls came up to me sitting by myself on a bench near the handball courts, I braced myself for torment. There were plenty of things to get on: my J.C. Penney's plaid jumper, my clunky saddle oxford shoes, my thick pink-framed glasses or swollen ponytails trimmed with pastel days-of-the-week barrettes. But Simone sat down next to me, lounging with legs apart, one booted foot up on the bench and one long arm slouched over it, somehow looking feminine in that posture. There was grace she wasn't aware of in her slouch, in the arm draped across her leg, in the fall of her big flannel shirt. "Girl, we heard you put Ms. Ass-Lick in her place!" She snapped her gum. Her friends nodded and murmured assent.

"Yeah," I confirmed, trying to sound hard. "She gets on my nerves, you know?"

"Don't I." She blew another bubble, killed it with her teeth. "I can't stand that bitch." She looked me up and down. "You want to roll with us today?" Her raised eyebrow told me how acutely I was supposed to feel the honor of being invited, and my heart beat quickly. "That's cool," I tried to say in a casual way.

"Rolling" with Simone and her crew consisted of walking from the boy's b-ball game to the tetherball corner and back, talking shit. Every person who walked by they either talked to or talked about, sometimes both. I stayed quiet, focused on trying to keep up with their longer strides.

"Look at Monique, today," said Simone, after waving to a girl with thick, aging "dookie" braids, the back of her sweater snagged from the burnt tips that kept the braids together. "You know it's time to get that hair redone."

"I know that's right," said Simone's head clone, a short, thick girl named Quinesha. The other two, a skinny, athletic girl named Crystal and a curly-headed girl named Nyla, so pretty she probably would have been leader if she had anything to say, laughed.

"But that Dominic sure is looking fine today." We had circled back around to the basketball court, where Dominic, a popular sixth grader nearly as tall as a man, dribbled up and down the asphalt. His eyes were hazel and contrasted (creepily, I thought) with skin such a creamy dark brown it looked like chocolate bars melted and stirred up. He had wavy black hair rippling close to his scalp, and there were rumors of basketball scouts and scholarships to private middle schools. Young athletes were treasured in our world, their futures speculated on from the time they scored their first Pop Warner MVP trophy. The quiet smart boys with the so-so hand-eye coordination were ignored, as if the elusive world of college teams and pro athletics were the most surefire path out of the hood. Yosi stood with his new crew on the edge of the court, watching the game with scornful eyes. Only I knew how Yosi would try to practice so he could join lunch games without embarrassment, shooting baskets every day with an undersized ball into a little hoop mounted above his bedroom door. There was no room to play outside his apartment building, and his parents thought the nearby park was too dangerous.

"That boy over there is black as night!" Crystal pointed out, cocking her head towards Yosi.

"Sure is," agreed Simone. "All you see is teeth." The rest of them burst out in laughter too loud for her comment, sagging against one another. She pushed their weight off when they tried to lean on her and looked expectantly at me. "What you think, girl?" I stared back at her. She was pretty, but there was a substantial gap in her front teeth, and the slight scattering of acne around her forehead and cheeks was tipped in raw pink. La Quinesha's hair, pulled back into a fat bun, was thin and damaged around the edges, and when you looked really close, the black cotton sock used to plump up her bun peeked through. This was how you kept people's eyes off your faults, I realized, by keeping them occupied with their own.

"He tried to get with me," I referred to Yosi.

"For real? That's your man, huh?"

"Puh-leeze." I put one hand on a cocked hip. "If you pushed him in the La Brea tar pits, no one could save him, 'cause homie would blend right in." They laughed loudly, in that way girls laugh when they want everyone to see that they are laughing, that they have something to laugh at that no one else has access to, that they are as special as they want to believe they are.

Chapter Seven

I looked forward to going to school after winter break, knowing I would have a group to hang with. I started waking before my mother had a chance to shove the soapy towel in my face, dressing in the least preppy or childish clothes I could find in my closet. I didn't understand why my mother insisted on me dressing this way, the way her grandmother dressed her, as if it would keep me from doing what she still did despite knee length skirts and "ladylike" leather shoes.

My mother took me to see her grandmother every Sunday, dressing up so that we could pretend we were coming from the chapel we only passed through on Christmas and Easter. Grandmere, as she called her, still lived in a large yellow house on a dry yellow yard in a part of West Adams that had only been middle class some time long before I was born. It was one of those houses that my father admired, a Craftsman with low overhangs on the porch, thick, jutting-out trim, and a limestone porch; but it was old and battered with dull, uncertain paint, a rusty barbed-wire fence, a roof flaking like eczema on someone's scalp. It looked like someone who was not just old, but old and had lived really hard.

Grandmere couldn't live by herself anymore and was taken care of by one of my mother's second cousins, whom both my mother and Trish hated in that intense, swallowed-down way only female family members could hate each other. According to my mother, Cousin Neesie had "moved in on" Grandmere when my mother got pregnant and never unloosened her hooks since.

Neesie had illegitimate children of her own, but my mother explained to me that she, and not Neesie, was kicked out because she was the only one of whom Grandmere expected more. "She invested more in me than the other ones. She knew I could have done better for myself, done big things," my mother said as she kicked at the bottom of the rusty gate and led me up the weed-choked walk. She pulled at my dress and smoothed my hair, even though Grandmere was half-blind. She yanked at her own skirt, pressing out every ripple, and drew her hair neat behind her ears as we waited after she had knocked on the door by reaching through a hole in the screen.

Cousin Neesie answered the door after a full five minutes. She was my mother's height but twice her size, with hips so wide it looked as if a grown man could perch on one and ride comfortably. She carried it all on my mother's family's characteristically tiny ankles. Her wrists were small, too, overwhelmed by clunky bright gold bangles. She also had the family's large, long-lashed eyes, however dull they were, nearly hidden by a mass of hair that had been fried and dyed into rough, brassy curls. She wore blue biker shorts riding up rippling thighs and a faded tee shirt with Martin Luther King, Jr.'s face on the front, the wearing off of the screen-printing causing gaps in his mustache and brown skin. The smells of boiled cabbage, cigarette smoke, stale pear body splash, and stuffed-up disappointment poured out of the doorway behind her. We could see past her into the living room, into dark shapes of furniture that hadn't changed in fifteen years, stained carpet, yellowed doilies, and thick plastic couch covers.

"Hey, Becky." Her voice was dry and monotone.

"Neesie." My mother stood back on one leg with a hand on one round but tight hip, looking her slovenly cousin up and down. "Where is my grandmother?"

"She in her room."

"I'm here to see her."

"I told you she in her room."

"Can you bring her out? It's a nice day. She should be out in the fresh air some every day." Neesie rolled her eyes, but she let the screen door fall closed, almost catching my mother's freshly done nails, and rocked back into the house.

"Damn shame," my mother muttered, running a hand through her hair again. "All that money she gets from the social security people and disability people, can't do no better than this." She turned to the flowerbed, which held more cigarette butts and ice cream paper wrappers than blooms. "Look at these rosebushes. Grandmere used to have the best roses on the block. Best roses anywhere, even the ones outside the church. Some people don't want to be bothered with taking care of roses, but you put something into them, roses always pay you back." She jabbed at the brown, petal-naked twig nearest to us with her car key.

"Don't die easy, either. You see, Tanis?"

"See what?"

"Open your eyes up, look closer." I leaned over the flowerbed, saw the faintly green bud on the side of the dry, thorny branch.

"Bet nobody's touched these bushes in years, but there's still a flower in there, waiting for somebody to come see about it."

There was a clatter at the door, a large groan as the screen squeaked open. Neesie struggled through, Grandmere leaning heavily on her arm and shuffling in fuzzy thick house shoes my mother bought her a pair of every Christmas. My mother rushed to get the other arm and, together, the two helped Grandmere to the flower-cushioned porch swing, which creaked under her massive weight. Grandmere was a big woman. Most old people I knew started completely reversing in height once they hit a certain age. My grandmother on my father's side had barely been taller than me. But Grandmere, though she had lost pretty much everything else, had held on to her nearly six feet of height, her big-bonedness, her long silvery braid. The delicacy of her daughters' children clearly didn't come from her line, though the large eyes did. Her eyes, when she lifted them, were frightening in their huge, cloudy whiteness, and made me think of the X-Men character Storm in comic books Yosi used to show me at lunch.

"How are you doing, Grandmere?" my mother asked, plumping a pillow behind her as Neesie pushed back on a house shoe that had fallen half off her heavy foot.

"Who's that there?"

"It's Rebecca, Grandmere. I brought my little girl, Tanis. You remember, don't you?" She pushed me forward with a hand on my shoulder more tender than usual. I stood, not sure what I was supposed to do at first, but then bent and lightly kissed my great-grandmother's papery cheek. Her cloudy eyes and stuffed-up, mediciney smell made me a little sick to my stomach. She gripped my arm as I bent over her, and her pinching, digging fingers could have been my mother's, only larger and stronger. "You have any babies yet?" she asked me.

"Grandmere!" my mother cut in quickly. "Tanis is going on eleven. She's just a little girl."

"Old enough for blood," Grandmere muttered. "I smell it on her. Be here soon." She let me go, and I stepped away gladly. My mother sat next to Grandmere on the swing. Neesie moved away, sat heavily on the porch steps, and lit a cigarette, staring out at the knotted, litter-choked grass and cracked glass at the curb, the park across the street where no kids ever played.

"So how have you been feeling, Grandmere?" my mother asked again, her hands again smoothing down her skirt, as if her grandmother's vacant eyes could spot a wrinkle. Grandmere didn't answer, pushing at the scarred-up porch boards with her faux-fur-covered feet, the rubber soles sliding over the wood ineffectually. It occurred to me that she was trying to push herself on the swing, so I walked around it and shoved, breathing hard at her weight until the momentum got it going. It seemed like a good great-granddaughter-like thing to do. My hands brushed her long braid as she rocked back and forth; it was surprisingly coarse to the touch.

"Things are good with me," my mother rattled on. "I might make assistant manager at my job." This was news to me. "Next time we come, I'll bring my husband. He would like to see you." This was a flat-out lie. My father would never come near Grandmere; not only could they not stand each other since my mother's teenage days, he was scared of her, said she was a crazy down south lady with voodoo ways and had cursed him, literally, on more than one occasion. My mother just liked saying "my husband" around her female relatives who had never been married; she liked flashing the gold band on her left ring finger in their faces. "Tanis is doing good in school." This was mostly true. Following that horrible red card, I'd brought home solid greens and good scores on my quizzes.

Grandmere continued to rock, grunting in her throat whenever I let the swing go completely still, the only sign since she first spoke that she was aware I was there. My mother, so neat in her pencil skirt and stockings and sweptback hair, stopped trying to talk, just stood up near the swing and lightly patted Grandmere's broad shoulder. I counted the seconds until we could leave. What was an appropriate time to spend with your half-blind, half-crazy grandmother sitting and doing nothing? Ten minutes, twenty? An hour?

Half an hour into our visit, Neesie came out from where she'd gone back inside, her hip shoving open the creaky door. "I gotta go scrub down Uncle Nate." Uncle Nate was Grandmere's baby brother, who had been crazy a lot longer than she had. I had never even seen him; he'd lived in the back room ever since my mother was little. Not only did my mother never talk about him, a disgusted look crossed her face every time his name was uttered. "If she fall asleep out here, ain't gon' be able to get her back inside," Neesie continued.

"All right," my mother said. I think she was relieved. "Just make sure she gets some fresh air every day, Denise."

"Yeah, uh-huh." Neesie put out a cigarette under her foot. My mother bent and awkwardly hugged Grandmere. I had a feeling they hadn't hugged much, even when she was in her right mind. As she bent over her, Grandmere gripped my mother's elbow with her still-strong right hand. "Rebecca was a good and faithful wife in the Bible."

"I know, Grandmere. I know."

"I picked it. Wasn't right. Should have let your mama name her own child. It's not the right name for you."

"It's okay, Grandmere."

"You be careful, Rebecca. I see death around you."

"Grandmere, I gotta get you back to bed," Neesie interrupted. "She talk that crazy Bayou stuff all the time, Becca," she said to my mother, actually seeming as if she wanted to help. "And she don't like taking them pills that calm her down." My mother still looked shaken, but together, they heaved Grandmere off of the porch swing. Grandmere fell quiet, her head drooping.

"Call me if she needs anything, Neesie."

"Yeah, I will."

I knew my mother was as glad as I was to leave Grandmere's house. Still, she fumed all the way home. "Shut up in there with that smoke, filthiness, crazy-ass Uncle Nate. Don't know how Neesie can bear to bathe him." Her knuckles lightened on the steering wheel. "I'd put that bastard in a home in a second. That's what I need to do, take Neesie's ass to court, put him in a place somewhere, take my grandmother home. That's what I need to do." I shuddered, imagining Grandmere living with us, those cloudy eyes following me around the house. "She scares me, Mommy. All those predictions and stuff. Daddy says she has voodoo powers."

"Daddy doesn't know what he's talking about. That's just Alzheimer's and that stroke she had, back when you were little." Her voice was weak, and neither one of us completely believed her. "Why?" she looked me up and down. "Was something she said true? You haven't gotten your period yet, have you?"

"No!" I shifted in my seat uncomfortably. The weather was already warming up but not enough for my mother to use the AC, and the seat of the car was sticky on my thighs.

"And you haven't let nobody touch you anywhere, have you? You would tell Mommy, wouldn't you?" She reached out and took my face in her right hand, her fingertips, with their precise nails, digging into my cheekbones. As she looked at me with that wide-eyed, alarmed stare, the car swerved slightly.

"God, Mommy." I shook my face from her grasp and felt for nail-shaped dents. "Nobody's done anything to me. What about that other stuff she said?"

"Don't you worry about any of that. Don't you pay that stuff any attention." She braked hard for a red light, holding her arm across me as she always did when the car stopped suddenly, as if a single slender limb could stop me from flying through the windshield and crashing into the road beyond.

Chapter Eight

My own birthday that March was eclipsed when invitations went out for Simone Bevens's twelfth birthday, a slumber party for her closest girlfriends. I had been making satisfactory headway into Simone's clique throughout the spring semester. After a lot of begging, I'd finally gotten my mother to buy me a pair of black and white high top Converse All Stars, which I wore almost every day. I'd used my ice cream truck money on dark lip liner from the drugstore that I mixed in with my ChapStick, and rolled up my skirts a few inches at the waist in the bathroom after I got dropped off at school. My biggest triumph had been getting my first perm.

The perm came about after a morning when my parents had fought. Tension had been thick in the house since my father started leaving to "see about TJ" more and more. TJ hated the Valley, was getting into trouble at his new school, though my mother always accused the reports of being exaggerated. And with my father still doing unsteady pickup work and odd jobs, he kept frustrating hours, with no work phone number where my mother could reliably reach him. "He could be anywhere, for all I know," I heard her say more than once on the phone. I knew, though, that if it wasn't about TJ, or TJ's mother, or his job, it would be something else. It always was. That morning's fight had started over my father letting water over-boil, setting off the fire alarm and scorching my mother's favorite pot, which led to the morning scolding about how we could never have anything nice.

After a few minutes of their raised voices, I heard the usual sound of his engine revving up, the bass pumping through his speakers as he skidded backwards down the driveway. My mother came to my doorway, breathless, and told me to get my jacket.

"Where are we going?" I asked, trying to keep up with her trotting steps to the car.

"A goddamn new set of pots," she said through gritted teeth.

We drove way across town to Costco, that magical land of a warehouse where you could buy anything, where servers with trays of samples dwelled in almost every aisle. I loved Costco, the bustle, the oversized boxes and cartons like provisions for other-worldly giants, the servers smiling as they handed you carne asada strips or roasted chicken or chunks of potato salad ske-wered on toothpicks I always sucked clean. My mother grabbed one of the oversized red carts and headed to the kitchen hard-ware aisle, silent with purpose. She skipped the cheaper end of the aisle completely.

"These, these are the good ones," she said, making me pull a box of bright red Cuisinarts out of the bottom shelf so she wouldn't have to bend over in her black jersey dress. She did squat down a little bit, knees carefully together, to help me hoist them onto the bottom tray of the cart. "Three things you never buy off brand, Tanis: your shoes, your tampons, and your kitchen pots. They just won't last you." We heaved the full stainless steel set onto the cart and wheeled away, but my mother didn't stop there. There was something urgent and frightening about the way she shopped, like a fever in clicking heels racing through the aisles. She picked up fleece underwear though winter was almost over because it was on sale, a party-sized box of frozen taquitos, oversized tubs of dill pickles, and Q-tips. I saw her mood and slipped things into the cart I hoped she would let through at the checkout counter: family packs of Double Stuf Oreo cookies, a tank of strawberry ice cream, and, when we passed through the hair supply aisle, the no-lye Just For Me relaxer kit I had seen advertised on TV, with the prettiest, happiest-looking black girls I had ever seen giggling on the box. She paid for everything with a bright-silver American Express I had never seen before, barely looking at the items sliding down the rubber belt.

"Did you put this in here?" she asked later, eyeing the bubble-gum-colored Just For Me box. Even marketers of damaging hair chemicals had learned that you could sell anything to young girls if you packaged it in bright pink.

"Huh?" I decided to just play it dumb as I felt out her reaction. She turned the box over in one hand, tapping it with her nails, and, to my surprise, shrugged. "Shit, why not? You're eleven now. He's not the one who has to comb it."

My new hair fell around my face, softening the features I finally seemed to be growing into, poured thick and shiny over my shoulders, where the thickness my mother had conditioned and oiled and wrestled with for years grew liquid and controlled. I begged to wear my hair down every day, shook it back, admired it in every reflective surface I passed, threaded my fingers through the front like the white girls on TV. This all irritated my father, who had opposed me having any chemicals in my hair and didn't like my new habits. "Leave your head alone," he bristled whenever he caught me preening and styling. "Your little ass still ain't grown." I shook my hair back defiantly, trying not to show how much his rough tone hurt my feelings.

But the hair, new shoes, and lip liner all combined to help me fit in more and more with Simone's group. However, there was one thing they prized in me above all else: my habit for blurting out whatever was on my mind, which they interpreted as a gift for "clowning" others, putting them down. Calling the dozens and trash talking were the keys to supremacy on the yard. Having someone say something to you that sent an impressed groan through the crowd and not having a comeback, or worse yet, coming back with something weak, was the ultimate humiliation, as bad as getting publicly beat down. There were times when a crowd drew around two kids who were going at it or yelling across the lunch table that made me think of the Roman Coliseum we had learned about in Ancient History, gladiators approaching one another with all of our small but sharpened weapons: some-body's musty underarms, bumpy or too dark skin, worn-out shoes that were separating at the soles, alcoholic mama who had picked them up from school with rollers in her hair and tequila on her breath. I became a queen of these battles. The world was every man for himself, every kid for herself, and fairness no longer held great attraction.

So my stats at school went up, but I still wasn't certain of my new position until Simone made a slow walk around the pushed-together benches we would lounge on after school and dropped a square pink invitation on my lap. "You the only fifth grader invited," she made sure to inform me. "Fly Chick number five." I felt the honor as acutely as I was supposed to. Fly Chicks was the name Simone's clique had come up with for themselves, which I used to think was really stupid when Simone explained it. "See, it's like we fly and we chicks, but it's also bomb because chicks are birds and they fly." I wanted to tell her that chicks didn't fly but forgot that as soon as I got my own designation. Simone looked at me expectantly, smacking on a Blow Pop that had stained her teeth a faint blue. "I'll be there," I told her.

My father had a different idea when I got home and showed my parents the invitation. I had waited until they were together because I thought my father could act as a mediator, a champion for me against my mother, as he had done so many times before. I didn't like to see them fight but I wasn't completely above dividing them to get closer to what I wanted. But they both looked at each other skeptically, passing the invitation between them. "This is that grown-looking girl?" my mother asked.

"She's tall," I answered, playing dumb, as if I didn't know what my mother meant by grown.

"Don't see the point in people sleeping over people's houses," my father grumbled, "when they got beds of they own at home."

"'Cause it's a slumber party," I pleaded. "A time-honored tradition for young female bonding." My father guffawed at that, but he still shook his head and handed the invitation back to me. "Y'all can bond at recess. You ain't going to spend the night over nobody's house." I stared at him in disbelief. I knew that if I wasn't at that party, it was over. The comfort of finally having a slot in a group, the safety and specialness of being a Fly Chick, would be done. People always talked about and isolated that person who wasn't there, so the key was to be there, wherever there was, all the time.

"But I've never been invited to anything before," I said in a small voice not put on for show. "Nobody ever liked me." I saw a crumple pass through my mother's forehead and knew she was thinking of her own time growing up. She had always been too pretty, and Grandmere had imbued her with such a certainty of being better than other people that other girls hated her. She didn't have any friends until Aunt Trish moved up from Louisiana. Girls used to try to jump her every day after school, corner her in the bathrooms. The day my father pulled alongside her in his apple green low-rider as she tried to lose a group of bullies on her tail must have looked like escape in more ways than one.

"If they like you enough to invite you this time, they will next time, too," my father said, sensibly and stupidly. "When you older."

"You act like I'm a baby," I protested, my voice rising. My father's eyebrows came rough and thick together. "You're my baby. And I done said all Ima say on it."

Disappointment and desperation seized me, and I jumped up. "I hate you!" I shrieked, and then ran out of the living room, knowing I better get as far away as I could. I sprinted to my room and slammed my door. I heard my father yelling after me and my mother's surprisingly calm voice. "Leave her alone. It's those hormones coming down."

"You heard what she said to me?" I could hear hurt deep in his voice.

"Well, what you expect? Telling her no after you spoiled the hell out of her all these years." My mother seemed a little gleeful, that for once it wasn't my father and I allied against her.

"What that got to do with anything? You want her to go?"

"Well, it's not like she's ever been anywhere before," my mother said, a little weakly. I didn't think she wanted me to sleep over Simone Bevens's house any more than my father did, but agreeing with him too easily was always something difficult for her to do.

Meanwhile, my fifth-grade class buzzed more and more over

the Washington DC trip. Mrs. Ackerson-Smith had us memorize all the branches of government, the Supreme Court judges' names, and had us pick Congress people to do reports on. I chose Maxine Waters, only because I knew she was black and often heard her name on the radio when my mother listened to stations like KJLH. Mrs. Ackerson-Smith also paired us up with pen pals from some Northern California school that would be going on the trip at the same time. I hated to get my pen pal letters, from a redheaded white girl named Sara (she sent me a school picture), and we talked about superficial things. Carefully written lines in fat cursive passed back and forth, with a laundry list of enough facts and favorites to reach three quarters of a page. It was as if I had somehow decided, even at eleven years old, how different that white girl's life must be from my own, and she quietly complied with my refusal to genuinely get to know her.

I still hadn't gotten the courage to ask my parents to pay for the trip. For all my dislike of the pen pal project and continued unease around Mrs. Ackerson-Smith, I desperately, inexplicably, wanted to go. I had never been on a plane or even a long car ride, never gathered up my stuff and spent time in another place, never slept on the crisp (I imagined) fresh sheets of a hotel. And more urgently than that, I didn't want to be left behind. To be one of the kids in class who wouldn't be able to chime in when everyone came back buzzing with news, bubbling over with stories they wouldn't bother to translate to everyone else, pretending they had more fun than they actually had. To be lumped in with the other kids who obviously couldn't afford it, like Anisha Dennis, who wore the same purple nylon sweat suit to school almost twice a week. Even ghetto bird Chantel bragged that she had already paid her deposit. "My mama said if we meet that

George Bush, I'm supposed to tell him to kiss her ass," she proclaimed proudly, out of Mrs. Ackerson-Smith's hearing.

I did my work diligently but looked forward more and more to getting out to lunch, hanging with my Fly Chicks. Their laughter at my jokes and putdowns, their embracing of my worst impulses, their occasional fierce kindness and protectiveness only extended to one of their crew gave me a sense of safety, kept me in the warmth of the spotlight I had always craved. It felt almost like real friendship, something close to unconditional love. We'd taken to hanging out on a group of benches pushed together right in the path of the lunch tables and the basketball courts, where the boys passed through every day. Several of them passed by one Wednesday after playing a rowdy, no-rules game. They were led by Dominic, who somehow seemed less dirty and shabby than the rest, even with his sweat-streaked face and a tee shirt stretched out around the neck. They all carried their school shirts flung over their shoulders. Dominic had his basketball tucked under his arm.

"What y'all doin' here?" he plopped down on the benches with us. "Nothing," he answered his own question, smugly. "Girls don't do nothing but sit around."

"As a matter of fact, we were having an important discussion," Simone said.

"About what?" He sat up, close to me. I could feel the moist heat coming off his skin and smell his scent, a not-unpleasant mix of puppy dog must, teenage boy corn chip funk, and chewy grape candy.

"Wouldn't you like to know?" she said slyly. Dominic grinned, and even the gap in the side of his mouth was cute.

"I heard you having a party."

110

"Well, I heard you ain't invited. Just the girls."

"Didn't nobody say they wanted to come to your funky party no way." Dominic took my legs from where they lay, cross-legged on the bench, and put them onto his lap on the pretense of moving closer into our group. He did this and kept talking like normal, like nothing was strange. I had never had my legs in a boy's lap before and it seemed like an incredibly wrong—and also a kind of right—place for them to be. I tried to join in the conversation as if nothing had happened, thinking about my legs: the rolled-up-at-the-waist skirt that suddenly made me feel naked, the two or three band-aids on them from trying to sneak and shave, all the patches of fine new hair I had missed. I thought about how many ways my mother would kick my ass if she could see me and how much I hoped everyone else would notice. I wanted him to push them off; I wanted him to keep them there. I saw the other Fly Chicks talk more loudly, cutting their eyes at my legs, at me, and at one another. I tried to breathe normally and shook back my hair, somehow realizing, without seeing, that Dominic had watched me do that.

The "freeze" bell rang, the one that meant everyone was supposed to stop what they were doing before the bell signaling it was time to walk to our class lines. When I was little, we'd all make a game of the freeze bell while taking it very seriously, freezing our bodies in exaggerated positions, in mid throw at the softball cage, on one leg on the hopscotch court. Those of us who thought of ourselves as grown pushed the envelope, continuing our conversations and love taps, dragging to our lines at the last second. I couldn't yet tune the freeze bell out, and as it sounded, while the Fly Chicks and the boys talked on, I instinctively turned my attention to my class's area, wondering how I would pull away to line up on time without looking like a nerd. When I looked over towards the building, my legs still across Dominic's lap, my eyes locked onto the cold gaze of Mrs. Ackerson-Smith.

Mrs. Ackerson-Smith said almost nothing to me for the rest of the work afternoon, though it seemed to me that she watched me closely. She had been far away from the Fly Chicks and the boys and me, but somehow I still felt sure that she had seen me with my legs in Dominic's lap. Mrs. Ackerson-Smith was very strict about that kind of thing, very insistent on us always being gentlemen and ladies. She'd gone against her usual rules and permitted all of the girls to hit Shemar Harris, repeatedly if need be, if he grabbed at our budding breasts, snapped our bra straps, or smacked our butts. Anyone caught playing Hide and Go Get It or anything similar would be sent to the office with a recommendation to be suspended, and any boyfriend/girlfriend talk was strictly forbidden. If any of that kind of thing got back to her, your parents would be called. Knowing all this, I sat in fear for the rest of the day, watching her face for a clue as to what she had seen, what and when she would tell. When school ended without it coming up at all, I was both relieved and more anxious than before.

My father's truck, unmistakable with his loud music, sat at the curb when I got out of the front gate. We had barely talked since my blowup over Simone's party, and I dragged my feet over. I stood outside the truck door for a second, staring at the door, and yanked it open. I climbed up, settled my overstuffed backpack between my feet, and focused straight ahead.

"Your mama had an extra shift," was all he said, a little helplessly, as he started the truck up and pulled into the street.

We started on our long winding path home. My father didn't

like the freeway, said it gave him a feeling of being trapped; you couldn't go as slow as you wanted, couldn't really roll your windows down without getting too much air blowing in your face, couldn't turn around if you wanted, and had to wait miles between exits to get off, knowing you were going even further and further out of your way. He liked to roll, especially if we were in our neighborhood; he liked to bang his music and hit corners and lift his hand to everyone he knew that we passed. It was one of the points where he and my mother were different. She'd hop on the freeway to go three streets and save five minutes; he only used it if he had to. Usually, I liked the long rides with my father, the putting off of the moment we drove into the driveway, delaying the inevitability of my mother's mouth, of chores, of a pile of homework. That day I sat stiff and uncomfortable.

My father was playing his favorite mixed tape of Prince hits. He loved Prince, and I heard him say on several occasions, "That sugary little dude got some of the best music ever made in the world." He turned up "Betcha by Golly, Wow" to as high as the speakers would let him and started wailing along. A smile pulled at the corners of my mouth, but I resisted. He sang through "Purple Rain" and then "Kiss." When "The Most Beautiful Girl in the World" came on, he turned it down a little so that his voice, softer now, blanketed itself over Prince's, out of key but low and earnest and soothing. He began looking and gesturing towards me as he sang, until I couldn't help but giggle. I felt my chin shake, tears gather on my lashes. I was almost broken by the time he pulled into the parking lot of a liquor store around the corner from our house. The liquor store was a ratty brown building with a trash-filled parking lot, handwritten sign to replace the one that had been broken and never fixed, old advertisements for movies and cigarettes and perm kits plastered across the door and windows. No point in making things pretty for people who would always come regardless. The same crowd of bleary-eyed men surrounded the door, leaned against the front wall.

"Gotta pick up a little somethin'," my father said, turning off the ignition. "You comin' in with me?"

"No," I said quickly.

"Make sure you keep these doors locked, then." He got out and moved across the parking lot with his rocking gait, giving a head nod to the guys he passed. There was urgency in his movement.

I hated going into the liquor store. Whether it was the Korean man who owned it staring at my hands and pockets as I browsed through the Blow Pops and Snapples or the funky-looking grown men who openly eyed the rise of my skirt in the back, I always came out feeling oily, like I'd been rubbed down in chicken grease by those eyes. And I didn't like to see my father go to the back case full of gold cans and brown-filled bottles, to see him gulp out of a brown paper bag. I waited, and changed the radio to FM, flipped to a popular hip-hop station. I loved Prince, but since I was hanging with the Fly Chicks, I needed to be up on the latest songs.

My father came back quickly, two brown paper bags in his fists, and handed one to me. I opened it curiously to find a Moon-Pie, one of those s'more-like marshmallow cakes I used to love when I was little, that took forever to chew and get down and made the whole world sweet and muffled for the whole time. My mother would never buy them for me, saying baby fat eventually turned to the real thing.

"Won't tell your mama 'bout yours if you don't tell her 'bout mine," my father said, putting his own bag under his seat.

"I won't," I told him. We were allied again. "Thank you, Daddy."

"You're welcome, baby."

"I have a project due soon," I told him. "On the Revolution and the Boston Tea Party. I want to build the tea party ship. Mommy already bought the stuff."

"Well then. We better get on home, get started."

With Mrs. Ackerson-Smith's class, it was difficult to bullshit somewhere in between doing well and doing badly, and I had finally resolved to do well. Doing too badly meant being moved to a Regular class, and not even the bad kids wanted to be Regular after being in the Highly Gifted Program. We had been trained to think we were chosen, special, better, the Oreo frosting middles of the school. Being considered smart was one thing I had. Since our recess spent together in the classroom, Mrs. Ackerson-Smith seemed to have finally realized my genius, stamping upturned faces on my papers and showing my work as examples to the class.

I finished my MoonPie before my father pulled into the driveway, and he stuck the remainder of his beer way back in the refrigerator. We spread newspapers out on the floor, and I brought out the Popsicle sticks, clay, and glue that my mother and I had bought at Michael's with the light bill money, as she had reminded me several times.

"So what is this tea party thing all about and what a ship got to do with it?" my father asked as he looked from the book illustration to the piles of thin wood in front of him, flexing his fingers.

"Daddy, you know what the Boston Tea Party is," I said in a voice more exasperated than I had meant for it to sound. My father crunched down one eyebrow.

"'Fraid I don't, baby. Daddy ain't as smart as you."

I lowered my face. "It was one of the events that led to the start of our great nation. The Whigs—those are the good guys, the patriots—they got on a ship from England in the Boston Harbor in the middle of the night and threw all the crates of tea overboard."

"Why they do something like that?" The rib shape was already beginning to take form under my father's hands while I sat there stupidly holding a glue gun. It amazed me how, when it came to building things, he always knew what to do.

"Because England was taxing them too much. It was taxation without representation, and that was wrong."

"I guess so. Maybe I need to go find me a ship to throw something off of. Did a construction job for this dude who made the checks and the W9s out all legit 'stead of just sliding it under the table like everybody else do, taxes musta ate that shit up. So who's out there representin' me?" I started rattling off the names of our representatives in state legislature and Congress that I had had to memorize, but my father just chuckled.

My mother came in about an hour after we had started, a May Company shopping bag over her arm. She slid down onto the couch and pushed each of her shoes off with the toes of the other foot, letting out a huge groan.

"Don't know why you wear them things," my father muttered.

"Can't I look nice if I want to?" She sat up, stretching out her toes. "And this is just a little top I got on clearance. With my discount it was hardly anything."

"I didn't say nothing about your bag. You gon' try it on for us?" He grinned at her, and her face relaxed a little. She settled back into the sagging couch cushions, watching the progress of my ship. "That's looking like a real boat," she conceded. "Make sure you all don't get anything on my carpet, now." We nodded, and she got up and headed for her room. After my father reached and took the glue gun from me completely, I slipped away to the couch and peeked into my mother's bag. The blouse was a violet color and as silky as baby oil, way too nice to get stuffed on a clearance rack. It already smelled like my mother, her Elizabeth Arden perfume, her olive hair oil, the musky hollow between her breasts. I wondered how long she had had it on, how long she had turned in the dressing room, debating.

"Tanis, get me some empty toilet paper rolls," my father ordered from the floor. He looked like a big contented child, so focused, his legs spread out on the floor. "I think Ima use those to make this mast."

When the phone rang a couple of hours later, we all tuned it out, as usual. When Mrs. Ackerson-Smith's voice came crackling onto the line, I stiffened, my stomach heating up and plummeting inside me. I knew she had seen me that day with my legs in Dominic's lap, but I hadn't thought she would go so far as to call my house. I could already picture how my father would look away from me, could hear my mother's rant on what fast-tailed little girls grew up to be. Too focused on draping sails to notice my teacher's voice, my father stayed hunched over the stick structure on the floor. My mother, however, ran out of the kitchen with dish suds on her hands and snatched up the receiver.

"Hello? Mrs. Ackerson-Smith? Sorry, we just walked in the door. How are you doing? Tanis, she didn't do anything wrong, did she?" My mother cut her eyes at me the way she had when Mr. Foster called about the class snake. "Oh, that's good... Oh, that's wonderful!" My mother's narrowed eyes widened into surprised approval. "No, I didn't know... No, you mentioned it at that open house, but Tanis hasn't brought anything home and I didn't think...I see..." Her look towards me grew threatening again, and I shifted my feet. "How much?" I saw my mother's eyes roll up in the way I'd foreseen, and I sat down and picked at the old, stained green carpet. "Well, thank you for calling, but I'll have to discuss that with my husband and get back to you... Oh, really? Is that so? That's generous, but I don't think... No, well, I really need to discuss this with her father, we might have family plans around that time, so...Yes, yes, no, thank you, thank you so much for calling. Goodbye."

"What was that all about?" my father asked, scooting back from his—my—work to appraise it.

"Apparently, Tanis's class is going to Washington DC in a couple of weeks," my mother answered, wiping her soapy hands on her bleached leggings.

"I thought they wasn't doing that anymore."

"That's what I thought, too, since Tanis never brought any information home." She glanced at me, but I kept my eyes down at the floor.

"Well, I know that cost some money, right?"

"Three hundred dollars, due next week."

My father whistled low, wiped his glue-covered hand across his forehead. "You might not be meeting the president this time around, baby," he said to me.

"I thought it was more than that," I said to my mother.

"Well, she was talking about how they have some fundraiser

money they can use to help sponsor one student." She peered at me. "You didn't tell them we didn't have the money, did you?"

"Shit, we don't," my father broke in, looking from my book to the clay he was spreading on top of the ship's stick skeleton. "Not before it was just five hundred and not now." My mother only stared at him until he looked up at her, as if he could feel her gaze boring into the top of his head.

"What?" he demanded gruffly.

"Her teacher was saying how it's a big opportunity, and she's one of her smartest students, and she would get a lot out of it. How it could inspire her to be a politician or something like that, one day."

"She don't have to go on this trip, this time, to be somebody. We ain't got it."

"You had it to give that bitch to send that boy to his championships in Florida. Oh?" She smirked when he started, snatching his head up. "You thought I didn't know about that, huh? I know more than you think."

"You don't know shit, Becky." My father jumped up and towards her, tripping over my ship in the process and crunching a dent into the side of it. She hopped back, snatching a vase from the nearby curio shelf and sloshing water across the wall. "What, you gon' run up on me now?" she cried, her breathing heavy. My father stood still, his arms and shoulders dropping. He moved his eyes from my mother brandishing a vase, to me frozen near the couch, to the half-ruined ship on the floor. "Fuck it," he said, and none of us knew whom, or what, he was talking to. He turned and headed towards the door, snatching his keys, wallet, and cigarette pack from the side table on the way.

The house was quiet for the rest of the evening, the air heavy.

I heard my father's truck rumble up a few hours later but he never did finish the ship, and he was up and gone again early in the morning. I wrestled with the ship for a few minutes before I decided I just didn't care anymore. I would take it to school just like it was.

Chapter Nine

After the disappointment over the DC trip, which I guess I had still been hoping would somehow magically happen, my parents had agreed to let me go to Simone's birthday party. "Keep your head on straight," my father had told me as he looked at the address, printed in metallic cursive on the thin, rose-colored invitation. "And remember ain't no one better than you, no matter what they got." He must have been familiar with the area to say that. The directions took us further west than even Baldwin Hills, beyond Ladera Heights, and I could see my mother's mind working as we passed landscaped yards complete with fountains and statues, bougainvillea trees and terra cotta courtyards, as houses grew second stories and Mexican nannies pushing pale babies in strollers sprouted from hilly, smooth-paved sidewalks. "It sure is nice around here," she murmured more than once.

We finally pulled up to a Spanish-style house with lights in the flowerbed washing the big banana plants and white stucco walls in a soft tropical glow. "You be careful about touching things in here," my mother warned as we made our way up the walk. "Say please and thank you. Don't act like you've never seen anything before." I thought, as my mother gingerly rang the bell and made hissed observations about everything from the Lexus in the driveway to the trellis vines on the porch, that she was the one acting like she'd never seen anything before.

The rooms inside of Simone's house looked like the ones all set up in my mother's catalogs, everything quiet and color coded and untouched. No worn spots in the carpet, no junk that didn't fit anywhere else pushed into corners, no open magazines lying about. I wondered why Simone would come east of the 405 freeway to go to school, until Nyla clued me in that this was just her dad's house, where she only spent vacations and weekends. Her father appeared briefly when our parents first dropped us off, lifted a hand without smiling, and ducked back into his home office. It was her white stepmother who shook our wary parents' hands, showed us where to put our bags, and led us to the kitchen for a snack. She was all dried-out blond hair and veneered teeth, aging Disney princess voice and feverish trying too hard as she lined us up at the kitchen island and asked us bright-eyed questions about school. "Dang, Katie, you trying to get their life stories?" Simone snapped after five minutes of us muttering noncommittal answers over the smoothies Katie had made us. "They only here for one night."

Katie turned eyes too dark for her hair and eyebrow color on Simone with a look in them like the edge of a broken bottle, but clearly she didn't know how or didn't have the energy to fight her. "I'm sorry," she finally said. "You girls go on. You probably shouldn't drink those on the new carpet, though." Simone picked up her big soda-shop-style goblet as if she hadn't heard the last part, so we tentatively followed her lead and slipped off the island stools on to the cool ceramic floor.

"Dang, you mean, Simone," Crystal murmured in that observant way that was more admiring than critical as we tumbled down the hall. "I think she was trying to hang out."

"'Cause she don't have no life," Simone responded. "Bitch." I snapped my head around, wondering if she had said that loud enough for Katie to hear.

"She seems nice," I ventured, surprising myself. Simone narrowed her eyes at me. Fly Chicks, especially brand-new fifth-grade Fly Chicks, did not disagree with Queen Chick. "You don't know her," she said. "She messed up everything." I looked at the hard line of Simone's full mouth and decided not to ask any questions.

We piled into Simone's room. It was pretty, with cherry wood furniture and a full bed dressed in lavender ruffles, but it seemed bare, and it didn't look like her. "I'm still working on it," she told us, flipping the TV to a music channel. We watched music videos, dancing and singing along to SWV and Boyz II Men. With no cable at home, I hadn't seen most of the videos but I tried to act like I knew what was up. We watched for hours, talking and laughing, grabbing additional snacks from the kitchen, gossiping about people at school. I was the only one in the gifted program, and they teased me lightly. "You one of the eggheads, aren't you, T?" asked Crystal. "I hate all y'all."

"Yeah, you know, the *gifted* kids," La Quinesha put quotation marks in the air with her fingers, "get better books, more field trips, everything."

"It's okay, Tanis still know how to get down," Simone said.

"Yeah, like she been getting down with Dominic at lunchtime," slipped in Crystal.

"It's not even like that," I said weakly. Since the day Dominic had put my legs on his lap, he'd been paying me more and more attention, calling me cutie, sitting next to me whenever the boys came by the benches we had claimed, playing with my hair.

"Maybe he likes you," chimed in Nyla.

"Dominic doesn't know what he likes," Simone cut her off. "You know how he be flirting with everybody all the time. You know who's really fine, that one white boy in Color Me Badd." We agreed in a chorus and broke out into the lyrics for "I Wanna Sex You Up," rolling our torsos and hips in hard, snapping circles. I mouthed the words, glad, for once, that the attention had moved off of me, imagining how quickly my mother would snatch me if she heard me singing that song at home. This was what I had always wanted, to be part of a group, comfortable in my pajamas on the plush carpet of the most popular girl in school, but I felt like I was locked in a yard of sleeping pit bulls who could wake up, sniff, and realize I wasn't supposed to be there. Watching my mouth and acting grown and trying not to say the wrong thing at lunchtime was one thing, doing it for a whole night was quite another.

Pronouncing herself bored with music videos, Simone picked up the remote and started channel cruising. She reminded me of my father, how he'd flip through channels, stopping on one thing just long enough for you to get attached, then moving on. She finally stopped when she got to the regular channels, where the ten o' clock news was playing on most stations.

"What's going on?" said Quin in the smallest voice I had ever heard her use.

"The police are kicking somebody's ass, that's what's going on," Simone snapped with only some of her usual sass. We watched as a dark-skinned man crawled around in the grainy video, police officers in a circle around him. I was in awe of how their faces glowed in the dark, like his light pants and white car. It was blurry, but you could see him trying to pull himself up, slipping, scrambling around on his hands and knees as batons and boots cracked against his back, his head, his cocked legs. One officer standing off to the side held a cord attached to the man like a skinny leash. The other police stood casually around, some with their hands on their hips. They looked like they were just chilling, watching a show, the way kids did at school when someone was in the middle of the crowd getting clowned. Sometimes one of them stepped forward a little, like they felt sorry for him, like I would sometimes feel sorry for kids getting clowned but stay quiet because it was better them than me. A dark car drove by, slowed down, then drove on. The man kept pushing himself to his hands and knees, collapsing again as leather and metal drummed on his flesh. His pants were hitched up and his socks showed above his shoes, which made it all seem more pathetic, more real.

"Dang, dude, just stay down," La Quinesha murmured, as if the man would hear and listen to her through the screen. The video seemed to go on forever, but less than two minutes had gone by when the camera flashed back to an anchorman, who started talking in a nasally voice about how the man had been arrested for speeding. Simone lost interest and flicked off the TV. "Damn, they got that fool," she said.

"When y'all get your licenses, don't drive too fast!" quipped Crystal. She was obviously proud of her joke, but the timing was off and our laughter weak.

"I hate the police," said Nyla in her soft voice, twisting one of her curls around her finger. "They stopped my brother and my cousin before for no reason. They were just going to their friend's house. The police made them lay on the ground with their faces down and everything and searched all through my mama's car. I mean, why they had to put their faces on the dirty ground where people walk and spit and stuff?" I had hardly heard Nyla say so much at once. Even as she talked about that, I watched the movement of her hair with envy.

It turned out that we all had a story about someone we knew getting pulled over, shaken down, beaten up, even shot by the police. We traded them until Simone became frustrated, the attention too far drawn from her. "This getting too heavy for my birthday, now," she broke in. "Let's do something else." Though we wouldn't have fought her anyway, we were happy to agree. We raided the kitchen for second helpings of cake and pulled out some board games, but the party mood was killed by then. I was relieved and exhausted when we finally gave up and started settling down to go to sleep. I began unrolling my Beauty and the Beast sleeping bag, wishing I had thought to get my mother to buy me another one. Crystal and La Quinesha had claimed the spots on either side of Simone on her bed.

"Uh-uh, Quin. Your feet stink, get off my bed," Simone laughed as La Quinesha settled back into her mound of lace-edged pillows.

"That's not me!" La Quinesha cried, almost stuttering with anger. "How you know that's me?"

"Please, girl, you was wearing Birkenstocks with no socks. Who had on sandals today? Tanis...Tanis, you want to sleep on my bed?"

"I'm okay." I moved my body to cover the smiling, blue-eyed face on my Disney sleeping bag.

"No, come up here and sleep on my bed." La Quinesha gave me a withering look as we changed places. Not wanting to be the first one to fall asleep, I held myself tense until I heard everyone's breath slow and steady. I was finally beginning to get that fuzzy, heavy-falling motion when I felt Simone stir and move closer to me. Her breath was on my neck, her press-on nails in my shoulder.

"I want to ask you something, Tanis."

"What is it?" I asked groggily.

"Do you like Dominic?"

I knew better than to tell the truth.

"No."

"Are you lying?" Her breath smelled like steam and strawberry sheet cake.

"Nah, I don't even look at him like that. That's like, my big play brother. For real."

"Hmmph." She quieted, but her breath didn't slow into sleep. "Your daddy live with you?" she asked.

"Yeah," I whispered with a faint note of pride. Most of the kids I knew didn't have their real fathers actually living in their house with the same last name as their mothers.

"Yeah, my dad used to live with us, too, when I was real little." Her voice lowered, and she didn't seem to be talking to me anymore. "I had to beg to do my party over here. Beg. I haven't even hardly been over here in months."

I didn't know what to say to that, so I just didn't say anything, holding my own breath until hers deepened into long, soft snores.

I slept hard and deep without dreaming. Only the sun slanting through the periwinkle blinds in a hot, sliced-up glow pawed at my eyes in the morning. I reached for a pillow to throw over my head and pushed my face into the sheets, but they smelled different, too crisp, too new. Other smells seeped into my consciousness: the Pro Styl gel all the other girls wore, French toast from the direction of the kitchen, the sleep skin and morning breath of Crystal and Simone still snoring in the bed with me. I sat up slowly, feeling more than a little nauseated. La Quinesha and Nyla, who were chattering groggily in their sleeping bags, only rolled their eyes at me and turned back to each other. I slipped out of bed and went to the bathroom that was attached, right there in her room, something I had never seen before. I could still smell the paint, and there were crystal knobs on the faucet. At home, we shared one little bathroom with yellowed linoleum that was coming up off the floor.

I squatted above the seat, remembering what my mother always told me: "I don't care how clean you think people are, don't put your ass on anybody's toilet." I pulled my eyelet lace-edged panties down and blinked in confusion when I saw the thick, wet, rusty stain. I stood and yanked them back up, as if that would make it not be there anymore, gazing at the small window high in the bathroom wall that led out into the yard. I could feel the moistness against me but I still prayed that I had somehow seen wrong as I inched them back down. Not only was the stain still there, I could see that it had soaked through the thin shorts of the pale pink pajamas my mother had bought specifically for the party. She had wanted me to look cute and feminine when I changed to go to sleep, but I probably would have been better off in the thick fleece sweats that I preferred.

"Ew, who the fuck got this on my sheets?" Simone's voice pierced my ears from the other side of the door, and a chorus of squeals followed.

"Uuuuugh, it must have been her!" said La Quinesha gleefully. "I told you not to invite no fifth graders." Someone beat on the bathroom door. There was no escape; the only way out of the bathroom was through her room. I considered the tiny window above the pink-tiled shower.

"Girls, I have breakfast," I heard Katie say. "What's going on in here?"

"Katie, she messed up my new bedset!"

"What?" I heard a pause. "Oh, I see. Where is she...in there? Sweetheart?" she called softly. "Are you okay?"

"Yeah," I lied.

"Is this your first period?" I heard laughter outside the door again, and Katie's hissed shushing. I didn't bother answering.

"Do you have pads?"

"No."

"I only have tampons. Do any of you girls have pads?" I heard twittering outside the door as no one, out of four almost-teenage girls, could produce a single pad.

"Sweetie, I'll bring you your things to wash up and then I'm going to go to the store, okay?"

"No, that's okay. Just let me call my mom."

"Are you sure?"

"Yeah. Just let me call my mom. I want to go home." I no longer cared about trying to hang or looking like a baby. My top priority at that moment was to get away. By the time I had showered, stuffed some tissue into the crotch of my underwear, and called my mother, Katie had herded the other girls into the den. I made no attempt to say goodbye to them before I left, but Katie hugged me as if we had known each other for years.

"I'm sorry about the sheets," I mumbled into the warm, freckled skin of her cleavage.

"Oh, don't worry about that. I just wish you were staying." She looked up at my mother with a hand on my shoulder. "She's such a good kid." I thought about all the people I had made fun of over the past few months as part of the Fly Chicks, and knew that that wasn't true.

"I guess Grandmere was right, after all," my mother murmured as we buckled our seat belts. "Mine was early, too. Your stomach hurt?"

"No."

"It will. We better pick up something." She glanced back at Simone's father's house as we drove down the street. "That sure was a nice big beautiful house. Does her stepmother work?"

"I don't think so. Simone's always saying she doesn't have a life, she doesn't do anything. Her dad has some kind of business. All he does is work."

"Hmmmph. Left a black woman to take care of a white one. Oh well, if that's what he wants to do. Some men have it like that, where they can just take care of you."

"Didn't you say you should never let somebody take care of you?"

"There's nothing wrong with letting a man take care of you as long as you know in your head that he doesn't really have to. Shit, that woman probably has a housekeeper and everything. All she has to do is watch the kids and lay on her back."

I didn't get that at first, but it dawned on me. "Mommy!"

"Well, you're getting old enough to know some of these things now. You got your period, that means you're a woman now. You can make a baby. I wasn't that much older than you when I made one. Shit, I wish somebody had told me some of this stuff. Men will give what they think they need to give to get what they want back. It's just a matter of how much you think what you got to give is worth." I looked at her blankly, wondering if she ever really saw me at all. Why she couldn't see how miserable I was, why she could never reach out and draw me to her and touch my hair, the way TV mothers did, and lie that everything would be all right.

We walked in the door to find my father watching TV in his chair. The video we had seen on the news the night before of the man getting beaten was playing.

"God, they're playing that again?" asked my mother, closing the door behind us.

"I taped it," my father answered.

"You and that recorder." My mother shook her head. "You didn't get enough of this shit last night?"

"I figured it's one of those things I should catch. Might be history, one day."

"I don't see how. Just another black man getting beat down."

"But on tape, and all out in the open like this. People ain't gonna forget this one, mark my words. Fucking bastards."

"They did get him something terrible." My mother sat on the couch. "But he was probably doing something he didn't have any business doing."

"So what, he deserved it?" My father turned towards us and seemed to notice me for the first time. "Hey, baby, you home early. You had a good time?" I managed a nod, glad my father was too caught up in the video to ask any more questions. I watched the man in the white pants crawl around the circle of police with tears in my eyes, conceding that his day was a little worse than mine.

My mother let me stay home on Monday, but she couldn't be talked into letting me transfer schools.

"Girl, have you lost your mind? After all I went through to get you in a halfway decent school? Everybody gets a period, including those heffas you're acting so afraid of. They'll get theirs soon, if they haven't yet."

I knew everybody went through it, but I was sure everybody didn't go through it on the white windowpane sheets of the most popular girl in school. In elementary school, menstruation was still a big deal, a gross and mysterious novelty. As I predicted, the news of my "accident" had trickled through every fifth- and sixth-grade class. People snickered at me, ducked their heads and whispered when I walked into a room. A boy sitting next to me in the computer lab for gifted students kept lifting his nose, sniffing the air and saying, "I smell fish. Don't y'all smell that? Where could that be coming from? Is somebody on the rag?" I spent recess in the library but had to go outside for lunch. I stood in the line for the school lunch, trying to take up as much time as possible, then sat on the edge of my class table alone. No one talked to me. I had pissed many of them off during my rise with the Fly Chicks, and they were gleeful at my fall. So it shocked me when Simone and Crystal walked by and stopped near me like nothing had ever happened.

"Fly Chick number five, why you ain't eating with us?" Simone said. I looked up at her in surprise.

"I thought..." I began stammering. I stopped, looked around at my curious classmates, and lowered my voice. "Y'all told everybody," I hissed.

"Nah, that musta been Quin. You know how she is." Simone waved a hand.

"It's not that big a deal," Crystal added.

"For real?" I asked, warily.

"Yeah, and just to show you so, we got you something," Simone said. I barely had time to shoot her a suspicious look before Crystal raised a bag, and thick, pink-wrapped maxi pads spilled over my lunch tray and lap.

The cafeteria seemed to fall silent even as a dull roar filled my ears, followed by gasps and shrieks. I thought nothing, felt nothing but the scratchy texture of synthetic braids in my hands, the smoothness and moistness of skin beneath my nails, soft flesh connecting with my knuckles and knees and the hard shell toes of my new Adidas, of strong adult arms coming around my waist from behind. Somewhere through the din and lights before my eyes my classmates' chorus reached me, screaming, "Get her! Get her!" I had no idea who they were talking to, me or Simone or Crystal or all of us, and it really didn't seem to matter. Someone yelled, "Beat her like Rodney King!" And loud laughter sounded as I was finally wrenched, flailing, out of the crowd.

More than a week after my fight, my mother was still barely speaking to me. I had tried to remind her of how she always told me to stand up for myself, to fight back. But she was embarrassed, and there were few things my mother hated as much as getting embarrassed. Not only had we had to have a meeting at school with the principal, I got suspended for three days. Not long after, Mrs. Ackerson-Smith sent home a progress report that said I was "defiant" and that I had problems with "impulse control," whatever that meant. Mrs. Ackerson-Smith had seemed to stop favoring me after I didn't go on her precious DC trip; I was just another kid in her class who no longer tried to cover up the fact that I didn't like her. I was staying out of my mother's way at home as much as possible. She seemed to prefer it that way, until one day, when she called me out into the living room.

"Tanis, I want you to see this," she told me, turning up the TV.

The news was playing a fuzzy tape from a liquor store not unlike the one by our house. A black girl not that much older than me struggled with an Asian lady. The lady grabbed her book bag and her sweater, she pulled away and hit the woman in the face. She left a bottle on the counter and turned around; the lady threw a stool at her and reached under the counter. I turned away, not wanting to see the rest, sick of videos of things I couldn't do anything about.

"Why do I have to look at this?"

"Because that woman killed that little girl, that's why. Shot her in the back of the head over some goddamn orange juice she had put in her backpack. The girl had her money in her hand." I looked back at the screen. It had gone back to the anchorwoman, who identified the girl as Latasha Harlins, pronouncing her first name as if she was having trouble getting her mouth around the sound. The girl's black and white picture, with her thick kitchen-bumped bangs, smiled from the top corner of the screen.

"I don't want to look at this, Mommy. What does this have to do with me?"

"You're black aren't you? You're hardheaded, aren't you? That girl was black and hardheaded. She shouldn't have tried to do things her way. She should have kept the damn juice in her hand in plain sight until she paid her money and got out the store. She shouldn't have tried to fight that woman."

"But that lady was wrong."

"She was wrong, and she's alive. That little girl's not."

"You saying it's her fault she got killed?"

"I'm saying this world doesn't care about you, that's what I'm saying, it doesn't give a damn about you and it doesn't care about being fair, and the sooner you calm down and understand that, the better off you'll be."

Chapter Ten

Thankfully, my mother was soon distracted from me by better news. After many exams, interviews, and months of waiting, my father had finally gotten hired as a maintenance worker by the City of Los Angeles. My parents were acting like we won the lotto, and their excitement was contagious. I didn't know much about my father's hourly wage or benefits or retirement package. But the few men I knew who had city jobs in our neighborhood, where a lot of guys didn't have steady jobs at all, drove shiny trucks and put the best lights up at Christmas, and wore their cotton hats with the city seal on them with pride.

"Don't have to come all out the pocket no more for doctor's appointments and medicine and glasses and braces now, Becky," my father told my mother proudly as she ironed his new blue city work shirts.

"Shit, the braces'll be ready to come off next year," she responded, but she couldn't help smiling when he came closer to her. They kissed wetly over the ironing board, and I groaned out loud but smiled, too. There was a part of me that didn't get what all the fuss was about. We still had the same beaten-up cars, and there hadn't been any talk about my father's new job getting us one of the ice cream-colored houses on the west side of town. But we had three kinds of juice in the house and enough stuff in the fridge for me to avoid the ticket line at lunchtime. My mother told me I could get my room painted, and I chose a deep purple, which she said was much too dark for a young girl. I loved it; going in there at the end of the day was like crawling into a cocoon where I couldn't hear the taunts at school. The color muffled the sounds of my parents fighting and making love. There was more of the latter since my father started bringing home the checks from his new job, but the former hadn't disappeared. Our house was just as small, our walls just as thin, and nothing they said to one another was a secret.

"Becky," my father's voice revved through the soft din of my mother's recorded soap operas and dogs barking outside. I jumped at my new dresser where I had been practicing hairstyles and dropped my looping ponytail before I could get my hair band around it. His voice, already heavy, had the loudness of someone who has been preparing to say something for a long time.

"I need to talk to you 'bout somethin'."

"What?" my mother said. "Did something happen with your job? Please don't tell me something's wrong."

"Why it gotta be like that all the time, Becky? That somethin's wrong?"

"Well, something usually is. But go ahead and tell me."

"TJ is moving in with us. My man Mitch over at Dorsey got him signed up for tenth grade, and he's gonna move here in time to start summer practice with the football team."

"Is that so?" my mother's voice said on a steely laugh.

"That's so." My father's voice was firm.

"Where's he supposed to sleep?"

"We clean out the den, put a sofa bed in there." The "den" was a tiny, cold room in the back of the house that used to be part of the back porch. It was kind of a catchall, packed with old appliances, my father's sports memorabilia my mother wouldn't allow anywhere else, her old clothes that she wouldn't get rid of, my discarded toys and handed-back school projects.

"There's no insulation in that room."

"We get a fan and a space heater. He can sleep on an air mattress in Tanis's room if it gets that bad."

"A grown-ass boy? No, I don't think so."

"Becky, that's her brother."

"You think that's stopping something? I don't want him in her room or in this house with her alone."

"That's some sick thinking, Rebecca."

"And you're naïve as all hell. He's a young man, she's a young lady now, and I haven't seen any proof of blood linking them. How are you going to come and tell me who's going to live in my house?"

"Just like I'm doing now. That's my son, and this is my house, too. I ain't gon' keep letting you just run everything how you want, and you ain't gon' run me."

"Oh, I get it. You got a little touch of money now, so now you're big and bad? Now you think you want to run things, huh?"

"I think I'm gonna do what I shoulda did a long time ago, as a father."

"Do what you're supposed to do here! You have a child here!"

"You think I don't know that? I'm thinking about her, too. She ain't got no friends. You got her thinking she too good to kick it with the kids around here, the same way your granny did you. She could use her big brother being around her more, but you always blockin' him out."

"She would have a brother around if it wasn't for—"

"What?" He raised his voice. "What? Go ahead, Becky, I want

to hear you say it; tell me again how that was my fault."

"You didn't even want to name him!" Her voice traveled to a hoarse, desperate shriek like an animal sound. My father was quiet for a long time.

"Becky, what's the point in bringing that up?" he finally said, his voice tight.

"You lied to me! Talking about how it would hurt me to name him. 'Cause you were too busy naming that bitch's baby the name I was going to give him."

"I ain't getting into this shit with you."

I heard the bedroom door crash against the wall. My father's heavy footsteps poured a rumbling path from their room to the front door, and my mother's lighter, but still pounding ones, followed behind them.

"Look at it this way, Becky. After TJ moves in, if I drive out to Charlotte's, you'll know it's 'cause I'm going to get fucked." He slammed the door, just in time to catch something crashing against it. I jumped, letting my hair, which I'd forgotten I was still holding, fall around my shoulders. I tiptoed into the hallway and looked to see what had gotten broken this time. It was the small, frosted-glass nativity set that had been sitting on the coffee table since Christmas; my mother had never put it away. She dropped down on her knees and started picking up the small lambs and robed bodies that lay dismembered in silvery shards. I went to help her.

"No, leave that alone, you might cut yourself," she said thickly, snatching Baby Jesus's tiny head before I could. "Go on." Her voice was rough, and I backed away. She started to cry in deep, jagged gasps. I had never seen or heard my mother cry before. I'd heard her fuss and cuss and scream and I had even heard her make cat sounds at night but I had never heard her cry. She had always seemed solid even in her delicacy, but now, bent over the way she was, her shoulder blades slicing out from her back, making slight boomerang shapes above her tank top, she looked fragile. I wanted to put something over them, cover them up. I wondered if I should do something, pat her back or hug her. But I was scared, scared she would hit me or push me away or hold me back so tight I wouldn't be able to breathe — or do nothing at all. I felt completely helpless and still, like the time when I watched the stray puppy I once brought home run into the street just as a low-riding Chevy sprinted down our block. And suddenly I hated her, hated her for being on her knees, hated her for crying like this, hated her for making me feel so powerless. Something had scabbed over the part of me that used to run to the door so excitedly when I heard my father's truck in the driveway, reach so trustingly for my mother's hand. Now my arms felt completely heavy. I found that the only direction I was able to move in was away from her. I went back to my room and kept trying hairstyles with shaking hands.

My father's truck was in the driveway when I got home from school the next day. When my mother's shifts got changed and my father started picking up overtime, I had started learning to take the bus. The school bus only took me as far as where I was supposed to live, according to the paperwork that my mother signed me up with. From there, I took the city bus, got off at the Vermont stop, and walked the rest of the way home. I was scared the first time, especially when grown men honked and leaned out of the window, but I walked fast and kept my heavy backpack ready to swing. I tried to stay on guard, like my mother had told me the first time I had to ride the bus alone. "You can't be in your own daydream world, Tanis. You better stay alert and watch people because you better believe somebody watching you." I saw so many things happening as I walked home: sour-smelling people in rags and cracked-up feet standing protectively over their shopping carts full of junk, women juggling car seats and grocery bags at the bus stop, police cars cruising slow with hairy forearms hanging casually out of the windows. By the time I got home, I was always exhausted, less by the walk than by the vigilance and constant watching.

As I got closer to the house that day, I saw my dad sitting on the front porch, on the raggedy green couch that my mother wanted to get rid of so badly. "It just looks so ghetto," she would say, shaking her head whenever he went out on the porch and sat on it. He was staring into space and smoking.

"What you doing here?" He looked at his watch. "Damn, it's later than I thought. I would have come to get you."

"What are you doing here?" I couldn't help asking before wondering if that sounded too smart-mouthed. He just shrugged and took a long drag. "Got off early today. How was school?"

"All right," I said, keeping it simple. If I said how much I had hated school, he would want to know why, and that was something I didn't want to get into. Or he would say that everything would be all right, and I didn't really feel like hearing that, either.

I didn't hear any more about TJ moving in, but, as summer drew closer, my mother told me to start looking through the stuff I had on the back porch and separating out what I still wanted. I didn't want to get excited in case he ended up not really coming, and I didn't want to act too happy since my mother was so unhappy about it. I wasn't completely sure of how I felt about the whole thing. I had always wanted another sibling, a real one who lived in the house with me like a regular brother or sister. But as the hope of that had died over the last couple of years, so had some of the desire for it. I was used to having my house and my parents, as crazy as they were, to myself. I was used to hearing only my bare feet padding the linoleum in the quiet of weekend mornings when my parents slept in and murmured behind their door.

It was hot outside by the middle of April, and I was excited. My mother was taking me shopping for summer clothes, and the school year was more than halfway over. No one had messed with me since I fought Simone and Crystal, but no one had been friendly with me, either. I planned to renew my campaign to get my mother to let me change schools. The last thing on my mind was "Take Your Daughters to Work Day." I saw the ads and commercials and knew the teachers were excusing absences from school, but I didn't get what the big deal was. The only reason I could see to get excited was if your parents had some kind of big, important job, which wasn't the case for most kids I knew. When I was little, Take Your Daughters to Work Day happened every time I had to go with my mother to the store when she couldn't find a babysitter, helping her fold the tables in her department and hiding behind the sales counter when her supervisor came by.

So I was surprised when my father said before dinner, as he was getting his TV tray out, "You got anything going at school you can't miss tomorrow?"

"Not really," I said, even though I had an essay due.

"Good, 'cause they having this thing at my job for Take Your Daughters to Work, and I wanted you to go."

"Oh," I said, surprised. "Okay. They had a slip we were supposed to fill out for that; I didn't take it in." Why I brought that up I didn't know; it wasn't as if I wanted to go to school.

"I can write you a note, can't I?"

"Yeah, I guess." My mother turned from the stove where she was scrubbing grease spots from the chicken she had fried and looked at me.

"I mean 'yes.'" I refrained from rolling my eyes.

"Good then," my father said, brushing against my mother as he fixed his plate. "Go to bed early, we gotta get up at five." He went into the living room, and we heard the TV come on.

"Five o'clock?" I repeated to my mother with wide eyes.

"Yes, five. His ass breaks my sleep every day when he gets up, too, opening and slamming every drawer and turning on every damn light he can. You better take your bath tonight. And I don't know any of these people he's taking you around or how safe that place is, so you stay close to your father and listen to what he says." It occurred to me that as contagious as the joy had been about my father getting a city job, I had no idea what he did.

My father woke me gently, when it was still dark outside. I heard his deep, murmuring voice and felt his large, warm hand on my shoulder long before I actually woke up. It blended into my dream and made me feel safe and content. He shook me a little harder, and I gasped sharply, the way you do whenever you get snatched out of a deep and comfortable sleep. I sat up and looked around in confusion. My father was already wearing his crisp blue work shirt. He smelled like Old Spice Body Wash and cigarette smoke and black shoe polish.

"I let you sleep long as I could. Get dressed. I made you breakfast."

My father had made his special dark eggs. He fried them in old cooking grease so that they were brown and oily and carried the faint flavor of chicken and ground beef. My mother fussed at him whenever he did this and refused to eat them, but I liked them that way. We ate quietly, my father's smacking the loudest thing in the room. The sky faded into a thick, violet-tinged gray as we finished up and got ready, and the birds began to sing. It wasn't like preparing for the day with my mother, with the TV going, hot comb sizzling on the stove, heels clicking back and forth on the floor, her fussing that she was going to be late and asking why I didn't do something better with my hair.

The first thing I noticed when we pulled up to my father's big, gray building that took up an entire block was the smell. It was awful, like chitterlings that hadn't been cleaned yet. My father drove his truck into the underground parking and held out his security badge to an electronic scanner.

"This is real important," he told me. "If somebody got in here and messed with the wrong thing, it could be a big environmental hazard. You got to know what you doing in here." I nodded.

My father took me to the lounge first to meet some of his co-workers. All of them were black and Latino and ranged from early twenties to late middle age.

"This is my little girl, Tanis Victoria," he said over and over again as new guys came in, his hand clasped on my shoulder. "Ain't she pretty?"

"She sure is," they all answered him. I didn't know if they were humoring him or really thought so but I enjoyed the attention. I gave them a small smile and wave as they clapped my father on the back and said things like "she must have got it from her mama 'cause she sure didn't get it from your ugly ass!" in the way only men could talk to one another. I felt an urge to reach for my father's hand and stand closer to him but I knew I was much too old for that.

Next, he took me to another room in the same building where the lounge was. There was a TV set up and several kids sitting at a conference table. I wouldn't be following him around throughout the day as I had pictured and didn't mind if he was going to where that funky smell was. Left alone with the other kids, though, I was quiet and wary. We spoke briefly and left it at that, and I played with my hair until a sandy-haired man in a lab coat came in. He showed us a video that explained in cheery, bell tones how all the city's waste from sewers and storm drains flowed into this plant, where it was cleaned out and chemically treated before it was sent to the ocean. He turned the video off and opened himself to questions as if it were the most thrilling topic in the world. I was surprised that most of the kids were excited and curious, asking what would happen to someone who fell in one of the tanks and how excrement for manure was shipped to farmlands, and squealing with disgusted delight at his answers.

Next, the guy gave us all earplugs to protect our ears from the machinery sounds when we toured the plant. I turned mine down at first, having no intention of going on the tour, but, on second thought, took them and tucked them into my little backpack purse. I could use them at home, though all the nudging in the world would not convince me to use them at the plant. The man supervising turned red as I sat firm in my seat; all the kids were supposed to be kept together and do as they were told. I stared at him with that blank look that so perplexed my mother and teachers and ended up staying in the conference room for an hour by myself. I pictured my father lowering himself into one of those tanks to clean the walls, as the video had said all the maintenance workers had to do whenever one of the tanks was drained.

I didn't see my father again until lunchtime. By then, my appetite was gone. He took me for lunch at a Jamaican place nearby that piled every section of your Styrofoam carton so high that it couldn't even be closed good. Usually, I would have been thrilled and digging in, especially with my mother not around to correct my dinner table posture. Now, I only picked at my plantains and jerked chicken.

"You cool?" my father asked gruffly. "Never seen you waste food before."

"I'm fine."

"You sure, baby?"

"I'm not a baby," I blurted out, suddenly irritated. "Not anymore."

His bushy eyebrows met, and he looked away to gulp his soda. "Well, what do you want to be called Missy Miss?"

"I don't know," I mumbled. We were quiet for a few minutes, except for his smacking.

"Things are going to be good for us. I got this better job; you'll have your brother around. How you feel about all that?"

"Good, I guess." I couldn't get the sound of my mother's sobs out of my head.

"Yeah, we gon' be all right." He took another gulp of soda.

"Daddy," I said. "You know they use some of the same ingredients that are in soda to clean freeways?"

My father smiled. "Naw, I didn't know that." He looked at his watch. "It's almost 'bout time to go back."

A grimace crossed my face that I hoped he didn't see.

"You really like this job, Daddy?"

"Yeah, girl, you know how long I been tryin' to get in with the city. City's best place to work for; city won't shut down they factories or close down or move away like everyone been doing, and they pay decent. A good job is real hard to come by these days."

"I know, but do you really like the job?"

He reached across the table and poured all of our leftovers into one carton and closed the top. "One day, Tanis, you and TJ are gon' go to college, and y'all may get the kind of jobs where you work 'cause you want to and make good money for doing things you like, and I hope to God that happens. That being said, though, yeah, I like my job. It ain't the prettiest thing in the world, but without this place there'd be all kinds of bacteria, diseases, nasty stuff all over the place making people sick. I'm helping keep the city healthy and safe, and I'm proud of that. I could be like them boys on the porch next door, doing nothing."

I listened and nodded but felt my mind drifting to the next day of school, when the girls who went on Take Your Daughters to Work Day would be talking about their parents' jobs. I knew, with all the strikes already against me, that I wasn't going to open my mouth. I understood that what my father did was important. But I wasn't going to get up and tell everyone that my father cleaned toilet water for a living.

Chapter Eleven

TJ came to stay late that summer, and Trish came over that day to help my mother get ready. I think my mother felt like she needed backup, someone to hold her up in the presence of my father's son and his obvious joy. Why she had finally agreed to it, I didn't know. Maybe because my father making more money gave him more say-so, maybe because having TJ there would keep Daddy from needing to go out to Charlotte's, maybe she just got tired of fighting it. But she still wasn't very happy.

"What's so bad about it?" Trish said, helping my mother tuck in a quilted blue bedspread over the single bed we'd put in the "den." "I don't know nobody whose man don't have a child somewhere else, whether he claim it or not."

"That's the thing, though. I didn't want to be like everybody else." My mother checked that a corner was sharp and stood up straight. "I got pregnant young and all, but we got married, we got a house. We were supposed to try to do things the right way."

"What's the right way, Rebecca? There ain't no way but one way, the way things happen, and that's what you gotta deal with. It could be worse; the boy could be a gangster. He wants to come over here, so he should act right."

"Yeah, I'm not really worried about all that. He's not a hoodlum, and anyway, Tannah's the one who's going to deal with him. It's just looking at him every day and remembering all that. How I left my school, my Grandmere, everything, and T was out there messing around. How they were born the same damn week."

"Well, be glad one made it to this world safe. Be thankful for the child you got here." She gestured to me playing with the old Barbie dolls I had found when I was cleaning my toys out of what was now TJ's room. My mother's eyes focused on me.

"You were supposed to get rid of stuff, not collect more stuff. Aren't you too old for those things?"

I defensively gripped my Christie doll with her swirling green eyes in a chocolate-brown face and pink miniskirt-kissing hair.

"Oh, let her play," said Trish, smiling at me. She had beige skin and thick lips and wore so many gold earrings in her much-pierced ears that I could always hear her on the porch before she knocked. The sound always made me happy. "Mine are too busy being grown to play with dolls."

"Oh, don't think she's not grown, too. She's steady talking back, and she thinks I don't know how she rolls up that skirt almost until her panties show. Tanis, get that stuff out of here. He'll be here soon, and I don't want you hanging out in this room with him, you hear me? You all can be in the living room or the kitchen and the yard, but I don't want him in your room and I don't want you back here. You understand?" Her voice rose, and I bit my tongue and nodded, gathering up the Barbies and their tiny, hot-colored clothes. It had been my instinct to ask why I couldn't hang out with my brother anywhere I wanted to but I didn't really want to hear the explanation.

"And change those shorts. Those shorts are too short and too tight. You're getting older, and you can't walk around any kind of way with your daddy and a grown boy in the house."

I rolled my eyes with my back facing her. I loved my old faded pink shorts that said Cheer on the butt. But I went to my room, dumped the dolls on my new canopy bed, and dug the PE shorts that we had accidentally bought too big out of my dresser. I put them on and sagged them down around my hips, like the boys tried to get away with doing at school. I pulled my big tee shirt over the waistband and walked back out, Fresh Prince-limping hard.

"Lord," my mother breathed when she saw me, rolling her eyes up in her head.

"What does it matter?" Trish chuckled, more amused than my mother, as she always was by me. "You need help with anything else?"

"No, I think I'm good in here," my mother said, dusting off her hands and looking around. "Why, you're not leaving, are you?"

"Well, I was gon' stop at the store, you don't need anything else."

"The store will be open later. I want you to stay 'til they get here."

"I ain't moving no boxes."

"You don't have to do any of that. Tannah brought the big stuff already. I want you to stay 'til they come." There was an unsure softness in my mother's voice I wasn't used to hearing, a trembling around her large eyes that made them young and beautiful.

"You can help me cook," my mother continued, leaving TJ's room and heading towards the kitchen. "I want to have a good meal waiting. I don't want him going home telling his fat-ass mama that I don't feed him well, 'cause Lord knows they're eating good over there." She and Trish both laughed.

"Girl, I barely cook at my house."

"I'm making a really big pot of spaghetti. You can take half of it home. Last you half the week."

"Is that so?" Trish rolled up her sleeves. "Let me get in here, then. Tanis, are you coming to help?" Trish turned to look at me where I'd followed them into the kitchen.

"No, Tanis is going to study," my mother snapped, turning on the faucet. "Tanis's last quarter grades were terrible. I think she was trying to scam me into putting her in another school but all she did was get herself sent to summer school. So, Tanis is going to go to her room right now and get in those books, and I better not come in there to check on her and find her messing with those dolls. And if I see any eyes rolling, I'll slap them out of her face." I stopped the instinctual roll before it could complete itself and dragged my feet out of the kitchen.

"And pick up your feet when you walk!" my mother called after me. I picked them up and stomped back to my room. I heard Trish's laughter and my mother's angry voice, but I knew she was too wrapped up with getting ready to spend much more time on me. I sat cross-legged on my bed, pulled out my social studies book, and looked at it for an hour. The words blurred together, and I was happy to toss it aside when I heard my father's music booming from the driveway, the voices of the guys next door calling out to him. I got up and made the short walk to the living room. My mother walked to the doorjamb of the kitchen, bringing the smell of onions and tomato sauce and simmering hamburger meat with her. We locked eyes for a second, and she turned back towards the door. Trish came up behind her and put her hand on her shoulder.

I heard the heavy footsteps on the porch, my father's deep voice, and saw the doorknob turn. Then TJ burst in like music from a block party. He hit me with his crooked smile, and I was in his arms before I felt my feet carry me over, inhaling the cool red leather of his letterman jacket and feeling his hands in my hair.

"Hey, Tiny. What happened to the Afro puffs?"

"I haven't had those for a long time, you dummy," I said, snorting back tears and snot.

"Oh yeah, I forgot." He pushed me in the head and walked over to Trish, who had walked out to meet him.

"I don't think I've seen you since you was little. You remember me, Trish."

"Yeah, I remember you, Miss Trisha. How you doin'?"

"Good, good as can be. You done turned into a really nice looking young man."

"Thanks." He looked past her at my mother, who hadn't moved from the doorframe. I held my breath.

"How you doin', Miss Rebecca?"

"I'm fine, TJ, how are you?" she said stiffly.

"I'm good." Then he walked over to her and bent to hug her. He was almost a foot taller than she was, and his red-wrapped body enveloped hers completely. He hugged her full, and I saw one of the hands that had been hanging by her sides reach up to pat his back before she stepped away.

"You may as well call me Becky now since you're staying here. Go put your stuff down in the back. I made some spaghetti." He nodded and walked towards the back, and my father smiled a relieved smile at me from the front door.

At dinner that night, after Trisha packed up extra spaghetti in Tupperware and left, we all actually sat around the table and ate. My father's smacking was as loud as ever, but either my mother wasn't as quick to criticize him in front of TJ or she didn't know what to do if he left the kitchen. Daddy and TJ dominated the conversation, talking about football, and I enjoyed it the way I used to when we rode to practice, though I felt a touch of jealousy, too. I never knew what to talk to my father about anymore, but for them, it was so easy.

"Yeah, their stats are good. I know the scouts from all the schools out here be at those big games. You get on varsity and make it past first playoff, they'll see you. You young now, but it won't hurt you to get on they radar early."

"Man, as long as that USC coach comes out," TJ said, shoveling in spaghetti. "I look good in red." He posed in his jacket, and I giggled.

"It's burgundy," I said. "My school took a field trip there, and their colors are gold and burgundy."

"Man, ain't no difference," TJ said, batting me in the head, and I felt like a real little sister.

"A big difference around here though, son," my father said, suddenly serious. "I know you like your jacket, but you not in the Valley no more, you can't be wearing all that red around here."

"Man, this jacket got my all-star letters, Pops."

"You can take 'em off, put them on the new one you gon' get at Dorsey."

"It's bad luck to move letters." He leaned back on the back legs of his chair, mock threw the football that seemed permanently fused in his hand or under his arm. "And I need my luck for USC!" He did a little bark. I glanced at my mother. I had never been allowed to play around at the table, let alone that kind of rowdiness. I could see her lips pursing as she tried to hold in something, but they lost.

"TJ, put your chair down right, put the ball down, and eat your food," she said firmly. TJ looked at her and paused, and my father and I both stopped with forks halfway to our mouths. After a few seconds, TJ let his chair down with a boom and set the ball on the linoleum underneath it. "I'm sorry, Miss Becky," he said. He made goofy doe eyes at her with his thick, girly eyelashes. "You still love me, right?" She didn't answer, but she swatted him lightly with the dishtowel and laughed a little, and we all relaxed. For the rest of the night I pretended that it had always been this way—father, mother, boy, girl—and that he was my mother's baby who lived and Charlotte was never in the picture and that he looked more like us.

I ducked my head in his room that night as he talked on the phone and hung up shirts in the armoire we'd gotten from IKEA.

"Yeah, I'm with my Pops, now, girl...Yeah, right off Vermont...'Cause the Valley was mad wack, and I'm trying to get recruited...Yeah, Pops is cool, I got a stepmom, though...Nah, you probably can't slide through no time soon, you know how it is...Girl, don't trip." He dropped his voice an octave and pulled a pair of jeans out of his suitcase with a bored look on his face. I imagined some stupid girl on the other end sitting still, hanging on his every word. "You know I really came out here to be closer to you. You know how I feel about you." He saw me in the doorway and winked at me. "Yeah, yeah, you too. I gotta go now, though, I'll call you later." He hung up, and I was happy he had interrupted his phone call for me.

"Hey, Tiny. So how you been, what you been up to?"

"Nothing." I smiled and shrugged.

"What about school, how you like your school?"

"I hate it."

"For real?" he sat on his bed, long legs splayed. "I need to come kick somebody's ass?"

"Do you fight girls?"

"Nah, but I got some females on my jock that I can get to do it."

"Do you lie to girls, TJ?"

"Nah, I just tell 'em what they want to hear. That's how you game it."

"Is that what I should do? With boys?"

"Nah, dudes are different. You gotta have a little attitude with them, make 'em think they can't get you."

"Oh."

"Why, you like somebody?" I thought about Dominic, who never even made eye contact with me anymore if we passed each other. I had fallen below even play sister status. "No," I answered. "Just curious."

"Don't lie, you do. Come tell me about it and help me put up these clothes." I became conscious of the bulge in his pajama pants and the thinness of my nightgown, thought about all my mother's warnings. "You not gon' game me into putting up your stuff," I said sassily to cover up my nervousness.

"Come on, Tiny, help a brother out." He got up, kicked his suitcase back open. I shifted my feet, not knowing how to tell my brother I wasn't supposed to come in his room. "No," I finally said, checking behind me for my mother. "I have to go to bed."

He shrugged and picked up the phone. "Good night, then."

"Good night," I mumbled. I scurried back to my room, feeling jittery and confused.

Chapter Twelve

TJ had lived with us for a few months before he spotted Kiana Jacobs, the girl who lived across the street from us and represented everything my mother wanted me to be. She lived with both her parents, but we hardly ever saw her mother, who didn't even have her own car. Kiana's father had worked for the city for a very long time; their house was the nicest on the block, and security placards in the yard and on the high iron gate screamed for everyone to stay away. My mother pointed Kiana out to me constantly, how neat she was, how polite, how well she "carried herself," how she was the only girl in our neighborhood worth my time.

I would never burst my mother's bubble by telling her that she thought more of Kiana than Kiana's parents thought of me. We had played together when we were younger, when our age difference of three years didn't seem like much, and I was practically the only kid on the block they let her play with. But I still remembered how they never invited me in, how I had to stay out on the porch when her unsmiling father went back inside to get her, how the curtain would move several times an hour until she was roughly called in. She still smiled and waved when she saw me on her path between her father's car and her front yard, the only time I ever saw her outside. She never walked to the candy house or the corner store; she never took the bus. She had grown tall, long legged, a deep-chocolate brown, and she wore her crinkly black hair in a single thick French braid with a ribbon tied on the bottom. Her arms were always full of books, a heavy book bag always hung off her slender back.

One day, TJ and I sat on the front porch eating pollaseeds, making a pile of sharp, wet shells in the grass. We watched Kiana Jacobs as she slid inch by inch out of the passenger seat of her father's car. The fold-down socks appeared first, the ones that made her seem younger than she was, followed by long, smooth legs in a plaid uniform skirt and a woman's body on top of them. She waved and smiled at me, and I waved back. Her father glanced towards us with his usual grouchy look as he held open the gate for her to walk through first and locked it behind them. Kiana's skirt swayed slightly above the back of her knees as she went up the brick steps, and her back was straight in her white blouse. I found myself sitting up a little straighter on the porch. I glanced over at TJ, who looked like a baby seeing colors for the first time.

"Who is that?" he asked.

"Why you wanna know?" I asked slyly.

"Don't play, Tiny. Why I ain't never seen that girl before? She just move here?"

"She's been here forever, knucklehead. Before you were here."

"Nah, I would have noticed something that fine."

"Not if you were too busy with your football and your basketball and your own big head," I said, more bitterly than I intended. But in the months since TJ moved in, if we weren't fighting over the cable TV or how he inhaled the last of everything good to eat or drink in the house, he was gone to practices, camps, tryouts, clinics, games, or out with friends, even when he was supposed to be on punishment for bad grades. I picked a lot of our fights just to get him to look at me for ten seconds at a time. It was mostly times like that day, when my mother expelled us both from the house for making a mess, that we sat quietly together.

"What's her name?" he asked with a reverent softness in his voice that I usually didn't hear when he talked about girls. Jealousy nipped at me. I had started my sixth-grade year at a new magnet K–8 school I got bussed to on the West side, away from anyone I knew at King Elementary, which was what I had wanted. Save for a few shallow lunchtime acquaintances, no one, female or male, paid me much mind. I wondered if a boy would ever ask who I was in that tone of voice.

"Kiana Jacobs," I answered stiffly, not wanting her name to sound so perfect, to roll too sweetly off my tongue.

"Kiana," he repeated. "You know her, right, Tiny? You gotta hook me up!"

I started to tell him I hadn't talked directly to that girl in years, that I was sure she didn't have time for anything I had to say. But as I watched his eager face, I found I liked the idea of having access to something he wanted.

"Kiana's not the type of girl you hook up with like that. She's a smart girl. Not like those stupid girls who be calling here." My mother had told off more than one girl who called the house for TJ late at night. "Does your mama know you're on the phone this late? Go get her. No, I didn't think so. Don't you call my house after eight. Should be letting the damn boy run after you, not the other way around." I no longer answered the phone when the high-pitched voices came over the machine's tape.

"She smart, huh?" TJ spit a shell out through a slim gap in his front teeth. It made a neat arc before pitching into the lawn. I tried to do the same and ended up choking.

"Yeah," I answered, leaning forward to spray half-cracked sunflower seed shells off my lips. "She's classy. You can't do all that baby baby baby stuff with her."

The smooth harmonizing of the O'Jays sang into the air, and we both turned to watch my father's truck come around the corner. He was home late. There was a carefulness in his movement as he hopped out of the truck, kissed my hair, and knocked TJ affectionately in the head, and I knew he had been to the liquor store and to hang out in the old neighborhood, as he had been doing more often. My mother came to the door and leaned against it, looking very tall as she stood above us. "Overtime?" she asked, eyebrows uplifted.

"Come on, Becky. Don't start nothing."

"Hmmph." She stepped aside. "It's getting dark out here, you all better come in and eat." I'd noticed that my mother was less likely to go off on my father whenever TJ was around. Maybe it was because he sometimes still felt like a guest, and my mother was always one to keep it cool in front of outsiders. Maybe it was because she didn't want him telling Charlotte on his visits home that her and her husband didn't get along. Whatever it was, I wasn't used to her calm voice, her anger stitched tight into the lines around her mouth. The quiet put both me and my father on guard, made the air in the house electric and hard to breathe. And TJ, the cause of it all, seemed oblivious, hard-bobbing his head to rappers with big medallions and funny little names.

"This is good, Becky," TJ said, wiping his mouth after inhaling a pork chop and rice only moments after we had fixed our plates. "Can I have some more?"

"TJ, don't get greedy, now," my father warned lowly, and I

thought about how my mother had been on the phone that day, fussing to Trish about how TJ was eating and drinking us out of house and home.

"I made plenty, T," my mother said, surprising us. "But you're getting it yourself, TJ, there aren't any maids around here."

"Will be when I go pro and get them dollars!" TJ cried as he got up and scooped another chop and some more gravy onto his plate. "Ima buy my mama a big house and Ima get y'all one, too." I saw my mother bristle at the mention of his mother and swallow her food down hard.

"In Baldwin Hills!" I piped up, trying to be a distraction. "I want a house in Baldwin Hills! With my own bathroom in my room."

"Then that's what you gon' get, Tiny. What kind of car you want?"

"A nineteen sixty-eight cotton-candy pink convertible Volkswagen Beetle," I said promptly. "With chrome wheels and cream leather interior." Everyone looked at me and laughed.

"She know what she want, don't she?" my father chuckled, wiping his mouth with a balled-up napkin. I didn't know why they were so amused. I knew cars. I always played Contact when I rode with my parents, memorizing every feature of the cars I saw that I liked. But it was nice to look around the table and see everyone smiling at the same time.

"Yeah, Ima get you that. But Ima get that new Benz." TJ sat back down with his plate. "What car you want, Becky?"

My mother considered, patting her mouth with a paper towel. "I want a convertible, too. Your daddy used to have a convertible low-rider, apple green. I used to love riding around in that car with that air on my face."

"I didn't know that," my father said, grinning at her. "You always said it was too loud. You made me get rid of it."

"I did not."

"Did too. Said we was getting married, I couldn't have no flashy picking-up-women kind of car, and since there wasn't no seatbelts in the back, we couldn't put a car-seat in it—" He stopped abruptly as my mother's face flushed. The baby that we never talked about suddenly squirmed, carelessly conjured in the air over our warped kitchen table. TJ looked from one of my parents to the other one, confusion frowning up his face. It occurred to me that maybe he didn't even know about him, the kid who would have been here if my mother had gotten her long-ago wish that things had happened the other way around. No one had ever told me; I knew about the baby in the way I knew a lot of things because grownups talk on the phone and over the heads of little kids as if they can't hear. My mother got up with a huge clatter and started clearing the table. She snatched my plate right from under the forkful of rice I was still eating, but I didn't protest.

"Miss Becky, I'm still eating that," TJ said when she grabbed his plate away. She shoved it back towards him and some rice flew onto his jersey. He opened his mouth towards her back, and I pleaded with him with my eyes. He quietly ate a few more bites then looked up again.

"Miss Becky," he started, ignoring the warning of my father's thick, tight-knit eyebrows. "You coming to my game, right?"

"What game?" she said shortly, running the dishwater.

"Homecoming. It's a big one. Coach say there's gon' be a USC scout there."

"The coach says, TJ."

"Yeah, that's right, that what he said."

"I don't know." She turned around, wiping her hands on her jeans and leaning against the sink. She sighed deeply, as if she was pushing something away with her breath. "I guess. I guess so." I looked at her with surprise. She had missed most of TJ's games that year, always finding some excuse.

"Stop bugging those eyes, Tanis, and come start these dishes."

The sky grew dark earlier and the weather grew chillier as homecoming approached. TJ's practices were long, but whenever he could, he watched from the porch or the front window as Kiana Jacobs got out of her parents' car. On the days she came home late, she carried a big black cello case. Sometimes we could hear strains of the cello, long and smooth, moaning through the open windows. Occasionally, and only when her father's old Lincoln Town Car wasn't in the driveway, she came out, dragging the instrument that was almost my size, and practiced on the porch. Her smooth knees shined against the high white socks she had started wearing as it got colder, and she moved her head and neck gracefully with the strokes of her bow, closing her eyes in such a passionate way it was embarrassing to watch, like seeing your parents kiss with their tongues. The music mixed strangely with the other sounds of our street: babies crying, basketballs bouncing off the asphalt, heavy-jawed dogs barking, guys bull-shitting on the porches, NWA lyrics pouring out of the speakers of parked cars, sirens echoing nearby.

"I don't like the sound of that thing," my father complained when she played. "Makes me think of funerals, stuff they play when people die."

"I think it's beautiful," my mother replied, wistfully. "I want

Tanis to take up an instrument like that. Won't you sign up for orchestra or something like that at school?" I rolled my eyes, ducking my head so she couldn't see. I had signed up for pretty much everything at school just to get her off my back, though I rarely went to meetings after the first day.

"TJ really likes that music," I said slyly. My parents both turned towards him leaning against the wall by the window, his headphones around his neck. He looked at us then back out of the window, shrugging. "It's cool."

Kiana had never played her cello on the porch before TJ moved in. I never saw her look his way but I felt like she knew that he was watching. She was one of the first women to teach me to do that, to know without seeing, and to move your legs and neck and hair accordingly.

Our midterm report cards arrived in the mail at almost the same time that month. None of my new school teachers were as hard as Mrs. Ackerson-Smith, and I suppose I had her to thank that I easily got As and Bs. My mother taped my report card to the fridge, and my father congratulated me with a hug and a ten-dollar bill, but TJ's report card took the bulk of his attention. He had gotten an A in PE and geometry, a C in chemistry, and Ds in Spanish, social studies, and English, barely squeaking over the 2.0 he needed to play in the homecoming game.

"Boy, I don't see why you can't do no better than this," my father said, holding out the card as TJ slumped in his recliner. I watched from the kitchen doorway with curiosity. My father had never chastised me, not even when I brought home bad behavior marks from King, not when I got benched at games or suspended. He always left any kind of discipline to my mother. TJ looked up at him sullenly with his big, heavy-lidded eyes. "Look, I'm playing Friday, right?"

"Is that all you worried about? You a helluva player and all, son, but football ain't everything. What if you bust your ass, your knee, your head, what then? You mean to tell me you can do all those things you do out on that field with a D brain? This teacher here said you might have a reading problem you might have to get checked out. You don't get your shit together, you gon' get left back again or they gon' start sending you to school on the short bus, and I didn't raise no dummy."

"Right," TJ answered. "You didn't." He stared at my father with marble eyes. My father stood up straighter, the arm holding the report card falling to his side. Even when my mother cussed at him, I had never seen him look so wounded.

"Well, you here now," he continued, his voice lacking the conviction it had before. "And I'm trying. You gotta give me more, too."

"Can I go now?"

My father nodded, tiredly, and TJ hopped up, untangling his long legs. I darted away before I could be caught spying and acted like I was looking for something in the fridge, but TJ wasn't fooled.

"Hey, Tiny, why you all in my business?" I closed the refrigerator door and crossed my arms.

"You didn't have to say that to Daddy."

"Why not? It's true. He wasn't even around all that much, now he wanna regulate on everything I do. Calling me a dummy and stuff."

"He didn't call you a dummy."

"Might as well have," he said, stubbornly, going into the back porch off of the kitchen that now served as his room. I followed him and sat gingerly on the foot of his messed-up bed, glancing behind me for my mother.

"You're acting like a baby with your lip all poked out like that." He didn't respond to the insult, scooping clothes and papers from certain areas of his room and flinging them into others. TJ had his own sense of order unintelligible to anyone else. I shivered, rubbing my arms. It was getting too cold for anyone to sleep in there.

"That girl Kiana, you say she real smart, huh?" he spoke suddenly, bending to turn up his space heater. "I want to take that girl to my homecoming dance."

I laughed out loud. "That girl's not going to any dance with you." His forehead folded tight together and his eyelashes dipped in a way that made me feel bad about laughing.

"I mean, even if her parents would let her, which they won't, she doesn't know you from Adam," I said.

"Maybe not homecoming, then. Anyway, I got my freak lined up for homecoming. But some kinda way, Ima get her."

"Yeah, whatever you say."

The colors for TJ's new school were green and white. I dressed carefully for his game, putting on four slouch socks, two green, two white, alternating so that the same colors didn't touch each other when I stood with my feet together. So you could see my socks, I put on a knee-length denim skirt and a green tee shirt tucked in, and pulled my hair back in a ponytail with a wide green ribbon. My father had gone ahead to get TJ there early and was coming back for us in a few minutes, so I walked down the hall to my mother's room to see if she was getting dressed. I found her laying on her bed, staring at the wall, a cup of milk on the night table, an *Essence* magazine open and face down on her stomach. She had changed from her work clothes to one of my father's blue city tee shirts and her faded, around-the-house leggings.

"Mommy," I said. She didn't budge. "Mommy. Mommy!"

She jumped and looked at me, her eyes slowly focusing as if she was trying to remember who I was. "Oh. Hey, baby. You look cute."

"It's the school colors. For TJ's school, remember?" She waved her hand as if she were lazily batting a fly and turned back to the wall. I heard my dad's music and motor in the driveway. He honked for us.

"Mommy, Daddy's here," I said helplessly.

"I hear him." She didn't look my way. I went out to the driveway as my father got out of his truck.

"Hey, baby. You look like a green honey chocolate drop."

I dimpled in reply. These days, it wasn't often that my father noticed me enough to say things like that.

"Where's your mama?"

I stopped smiling and shrugged. He knit his eyebrows and headed purposefully into the house. I followed him into the house and went to my room. I filled my Hello Kitty backpack purse with a small comb, a maxi pad, and ChapStick, and looked for a jacket that would match my green ensemble, listening to my parents' voices rise and fall.

"Damn, Becky. You told the boy you would go."

"He has you, Tanis, his real mama there. He's not thinking about me."

"He didn't care, he wouldna asked you."

"I just can't."

"You do everything else you want to do when you want to do it."

"Is that bitch going to be there?"

"You don't think you should stop calling her that, with him livin' here? What if you slip, say that in front of him?"

"Is that bitch going to be there?"

"We ain't gotta sit with her if you don't want to."

"I don't care. I'm not coming. Tell TJ I'm sorry."

"Yeah, you sorry all right. You sorry as all hell."

"Yeah, I learned from the best, didn't I?"

I heard the bedroom door slam, my father's footsteps stomping through the house. "Come on, Tanis!" he roared. I jumped, grabbed my purse and sweater, and followed him out. The drive to TJ's school was quiet. I didn't even say anything when my father started smoking, though I rolled the window down all the way and stuck my head out like a dog.

We got to TJ's school, and I tried to put the image of my mother sitting in the house alone, staring at the wall, out of my head. It became easier when we walked through the gate, pressed in on all sides by loud, raucous high school kids. I loved watching the older guys in their baggy jeans and flat-top haircuts, the girls in their crayon-colored outfits and red lipstick. They flirted and gossiped and talked shit to one another at the snack-stand and bleachers. They yelled for no good reason and throbbed hard to the brass band blaring popular radio tunes. A few of them actually watched the game, and I realized that, in high school, going to the games was less about the game itself than about being seen there. No one was more seen than the cheerleaders, and I watched them hard, marveling at how their pressed hair stayed straight and in place as they jiggled their hips to the drum line. I had stopped cheering for the Cougars since TJ left to play in high school and my dad got too busy with TJ and overtime to take me. I looked around at the faces of girls in the stands, from the cute girl in her head-to-toe Cross Colours outfit to the big, dumpy one playing the trombone in the band, and it seemed like all of them would rather be kicking their legs up with their names and flashing green bloomers to the crowd. I promised myself that when I was in high school that would be me down on that track.

As the night went on, the sky went from redbone to blue-black, and a frothy mist rose and mixed with the hot, white glow of the field lights. The cheerleaders' hair wasn't straight any more, and my bare legs started to shiver. It was a close game, with each side scoring and making good plays and constant upsets. Washington's defense was tough, their offense quick, and the Dorsey coaches were on guard. By the third quarter, they still hadn't played much of the second string. I knew that if TJ didn't get to play, he was going to be in a funky mood after the game. Eventually, my father turned off his video camera to save the battery. "You be nice to your brother, now," he warned me. "None of them cracks about his jersey still being so clean." I bit back a smile.

By the fourth quarter, Dorsey had pulled into the lead, but Washington had the ball and was trying to break through Dorsey's tough defense. The tops of their helmets made it look like a bunch of colored beetles down on the field, pushing back and forth. TJ's coach finally put two of his second stringers in, and my father cheered as TJ trotted onto the field as if he had already done something. We watched the players set up, everybody squatting down, and the handoff to the Washington quarterback, tense and bent over in his bright red and blue. Suddenly, instead of running forward and getting caught up in the fist of green bodies waiting for him, he doubled back and swung back the arm clasping the ball.

"They throwin' it!" my father called as if they could hear him on the field. "Look out, they throwin' it!" The brown ball left the blue quarterback's tape-wrapped hand and swung a neat, whistling arc high into the air, straight towards the hands of another Washington guy waiting near the end zone. I cried out and restrained myself from covering my eyes. TJ's mood if he didn't get to shine would have been bad enough, but it would be infinitely worse if his team lost their homecoming game.

Just as the ball was almost touching the fingertips of the Washington player, a green blur jumped up so high he looked like something out of a martial arts movie and clasped the ball to his belly. I didn't need the long legs, the brief leg pop back before he took off, or the blurred number fifty-three to know who it was.

"Interception!" I shrieked. "TJ made the interception!" I hit my father in the shoulder over and over again, jumping up and down as he struggled to focus the video camera. TJ shot through the field in nylon zigzags, ducking every attack. He had gotten halfway across when huge blue-and-red-covered mounds of boy flesh leapt onto him, one by one, completely covering his body as they all rolled out of bounds. Still, our crowd roared, mini pompoms flew into the air, and the band broke into the fight song, which girls used as a cue to jump up and start shaking spandex-covered butts. TJ hadn't made a touchdown but he had overturned possession, and Washington wouldn't have time to get the ball back before time was up. TJ didn't do anything remarkable in the last ten minutes, but Dorsey did end up winning 21–14. When the players crowded up to do their chants afterwards, TJ wasn't in the center, like he always had been with our Pop Warner team, but I could still pick him out easily, jumping up and down, knocking helmets with the varsity players. My brother was one of those people who seemed to both fit in and stand out everywhere, and it was a gift I envied with all my heart.

We had to wait a long time for TJ after the game. First, the football players spent twenty minutes on their celebration ritual, barking and hugging and roughly pushing each other as their coaches fountained them with bottles of apple cider. The cheerleaders danced and chanted in a tight circle around them, laughing as they jumped away from the cider spray. We climbed down out of the stands, and my father moved closer to get the festivities on film. My chest felt tight as I watched him maneuver around the crowd, laughing. He would always tell me he was proud of me, but he never watched my cheer performances the way he would watch TJ's game films, or rewind to see a particular rhyme or jump the way he would do that beautiful run. I hooked the tip of my tennis shoe in one of the chain links and looked at the sneaker-stamped sand, waiting. TJ left his teammates to hug and kiss Charlotte, who looked like a green blimp in all her game gear. I watched her and my father together, narrowed my eyes at their easy laughter, their simultaneous claps on TJ's back, their brief hug, TJ's smile as he looked from one to the other. Finally, she left, and TJ and my father made it over to the gate. With his jersey and half of his padding stripped off, TJ looked like a dismantled foosball man.

"Hey, Tiny," TJ pushed at my head, messing up my careful ponytail. "Did you see that run?" He hunched his back, tucked a football in his elbow, and lifted his knee in a pose ready for the cover of *Sports Illustrated*.

"It was all right." I rolled my eyes, retying the ribbon he had loosened.

"Did Becky see it?" he asked, craning his neck to look behind us as he tossed the football between his hands. The ball was like spider web, the way it seemed to stick to each hand without being gripped then shoot over to the other.

"Ima show it to her on the tape, son," my father said, clapping his foam-covered shoulder. TJ shrugged him off.

"Figures. I shoulda walked my mama to her car. I'll be back."

Chapter Thirteen

By the end of the football season, TJ had scored more turnovers and yards than any other sophomore. He had been mentioned in the school newspaper, his starting spot on varsity was assured for the following year, and he was too full of himself to bear, "smelling himself," as my father liked to say. He got bold one day as we sat outside eating pollaseeds and watching Kiana Jacobs play the cello on her porch. The whole thing was getting ridiculous. It was cold outside, and she would sometimes mess up and squeak, causing some of the dogs on the block to howl. Of course, TJ didn't notice.

"Ima go talk to her." He stood up suddenly.

"Are you crazy?" I asked, yanking at his baggy pants leg. "Her daddy'll get home and he'll kill you. And anyway, getting all up in her face like you like to do, that won't work."

"Well," he sat back down, looking nervous. He had a pollaseed shell stuck to one lip. "What I'm supposed to do, then?"

"I don't know. Maybe you should write her a letter or something."

"A letter," he repeated. He ran his hands over his high-top fade. "You gon' give it to her for me?"

"I guess, if you want. Just don't go running over there."

"Okay, okay," TJ nodded, shooting another pollaseed shell out of his mouth.

A few days later, TJ gave me his letter. It was on a piece of notebook paper pulled out of his spiral notebook. He had taken the trouble to pull off every rough edge along the side where he'd ripped it out and folded it in about a million little squares. He had even drawn some intertwined hearts and butterflies and music notes on the outside. I wanted to laugh, but when I looked at him, his face was so sincere that I decided not to.

"Can I read it?" I asked.

"Yeah. Tell me if it's good." He shifted his feet. I hadn't seen much of that TJ, nervous and unsure of himself. "Sometimes I kinda mess up words."

I unfolded it and read slowly to myself, stumbling over every other word. TJ's writing was tiny and shaky, the ink barely peeking above the thin college rule lines. He had spelled things like "pretty" and "music" wrong in ways that made no sense, and half the letters, especially his ds and bs, were backwards. I gave up halfway through and looked up at him, not sure what to say. I was wondering how he had gotten the grades he got, even how he had made it to the tenth grade.

"Is it good?" he asked in a low voice, and I felt as if I was the older one.

"Yeah, it's good," I lied. "I'll give it to her tomorrow."

I checked myself carefully after school the next day, ensuring that my hair was pulled back neatly by a headband, unrolling my skirt at the waist so that it hit my knees, making sure my blouse was straight. Though my mother would have been thrilled that I was going to hang out with Kiana Jacobs, she also might have been suspicious. So I waited for her to go out to the store before I put on my coat, pulled out my math book, and walked across the street.

I had to pause at their gate until I saw that the heavy padlock wasn't actually locked, just fastened onto the gate in a way to make it look like it was. I moved it carefully and fixed it back after I walked through. A loud bell attached to the gate rang out as I moved it, and my steps felt loud on the brick path. By the time I got to the porch, the hulking shadow of Mr. Jacobs already filled the doorway. He opened the screen and peered at me, his brown face unsmiling and eyes sharp, as if I was an IRS agent or cop or gangbanger in disguise. TJ owed me big.

"Hello, Mr. Jacobs," I said in my sweetest voice, which felt strange in my throat. "Is Kiana home?"

"Yeah." He looked past me, as if suspecting there was a posse hiding in the bushes. "Studying. What is it you need? She don't have a lot of time to socialize."

"Oh, no, I don't want to socialize. It's just, I know Kiana's in high school, and I just started pre-algebra, and I know she's smart, so I thought maybe she could help me with this problem I can't get. It's just one problem."

"Don't you got a brother, cousin, somebody staying there now can help you?"

"My half-brother is at track practice. Sir, I'm supposed to get my homework done before dark."

He grunted, sounding kind of like my father. But where my father's grunts were pretty nondescript, just sounds he made that could mean any number of things, Mr. Jacobs's grunts were decidedly mean. But he stepped aside and held the door open wider. "Come on in."

I stepped inside, warily, conscious of being alone in a room with a grownup man not related to me. The living room was so dark I could barely make out the flower shapes on the overstuffed couch. A pre-season basketball game played low on TV, and no

175

food smells came from the kitchen. I was glad when he called Kiana's name. She appeared promptly rather than yelling back "what?!" as TJ or I would have done.

"Daddy?" she said as she walked in, moving like liquid. Her eyes were wide and almond shaped, and her skin was darker up close, or maybe it was the dim light in the room. "Hi, Tanis," she said, nicely enough, though there was a patient question mark in her face. I was surprised she remembered my name. "You haven't been over here in forever." We all stood quietly for a long moment. I had forgotten my cover story. Mr. Jacobs slammed the door behind me and I jumped, almost dropping the math book in my hands.

"Math," I burst out. "I need help with my math homework. Pre-algebra. You took that already, right?"

"Oh, sure. Math isn't my best subject, but let's look at it. Can we go in my room, Daddy?"

"Yeah, but remember, you got your own work, too."

"I know." She beckoned me, and I followed her out of the living room and into the hallway. Her house had almost the same floor plan as mine, even if it was a little bigger. It was strange to be inside a house so much like my own but so different. I found myself wondering about everything, was her dad really like that all the time, what her mother was like, how her parents talked to each other, did they still kiss each other, did they ever fight. Kiana's room was clean with fully dressed, unmarked dolls nestled into the mound of pillows on her ruffly comforter. The only clutter I saw was a pair of knee socks on the rug and an open book face down on the bed. Even so, she seemed self-conscious, scooping up and rolling the socks and putting them in a drawer, straightening a few papers on the desk as I looked around.

"Excuse my room. I don't have a lot of company." I just shrugged. My room would have required a flurry of cleaning up to look half as good.

"It's a really nice room," I told her, feeling a pang of resentment for how I had never seen it before, had never been invited inside to play.

"Thank you. So," she sat on the floor and Indian-crossed her long legs in her skirt. I was shocked until I saw that, like me, she wore shorts underneath. "What's the problem?"

I plopped down next to her and showed her the problem I knew perfectly well how to do. I had tried to pick something hard enough that it might seem like I actually needed help, easy enough so that we both wouldn't be embarrassed if this girl, touted to me as brilliant much of my life, couldn't get it.

"Oh, okay," she said, reading the word problem. "It's a proportion problem. So you have to set up the proportion and cross multiply and divide." She talked me patiently through the steps I already knew. I worked slowly, listening to her gentle voice, and purposely made a mistake on my long division.

"No, you just have to make sure your decimal is in the right spot. Let me show you how I would do it, and then you can try yourself, okay?" She took the book from me, as she had probably been craving to do all along, and started reworking the problem. I let my gaze wander around the room. Her cello case lay open on the floor. The glossy wood gleamed so hard its surface seemed to move, pulse, like syrup flowing slowly out of a pitcher. It perfectly matched Kiana's rich, satiny skin that appeared to have skipped puberty bumps altogether.

"You play that really pretty." I gestured towards the cello.

"Oh, thank you, that's so sweet. You can hear me?" I glanced at her. Her face looked genuine, but I didn't buy the surprise. Of course she knew everyone could hear her.

"Yeah. You like practicing outside?" She lowered her head back to the book, biting her bottom lip.

"My dad doesn't like for me to do that. And it's getting too cold for it. The mist is bad for the wood." She paused, then asked the question I had known she would. "That boy living with you guys, he didn't always stay there, did he?"

"No. That's my half-brother. He just came this past summer."

"Oh. Do you like having your brother live with you?"

"It's all right," I shrugged. "He thinks your music is pretty, too." She looked up, the eraser of her pencil pressed into her cheek, and looked back down at the book. "I'm not allowed to have boyfriends," she murmured, as if somebody had already asked her. That was the moment to give her the note. But as I looked around at the certificates and ribbons on the buttercup-yellow walls, the complicated-looking music on the stand, the books lining white shelves, I couldn't help but picture her squinting over that scrawled letter a six-year-old could have written. TJ wasn't always my best friend, but I couldn't stand the thought of what might go through her mind.

"Okay." I peered over her shoulder at the solution she had worked out in neat, light pencil strokes. "I see what you did. I get it."

"Are you sure? I can show you again. Is that the only one?" I looked into her face. She wanted me to stay. Though I suspected she thought she was better than me, I was still someone new in this dark house. Maybe she practiced on the porch not just to show off, but to feel closer to the people she only caught quick looks at between her father's car and her front door. I knew how she felt, but I also knew my mother would be home soon, and I didn't want to get grilled about what I'd been up to. "Yeah," I said again. "I get it. Thanks."

"You're welcome," she answered in her soft voice. She got to her feet, smoothed down her skirt, and walked me to the door.

I dreaded talking to TJ in the weeks after going to see Kiana, sure he would ask me what happened. Luckily, he was easy to avoid. He had begun his training for track season and stayed at the field for hours every day after school, never satisfied with his times, which were all he could talk about when he got home. The habit of eating around the table together, renewed when TJ first moved in, dissipated as the newness of him being there wore off. My father had gotten us each our own cable boxes to stop the bickering, so we usually grabbed our plates and retreated to our rooms. One day I went into the kitchen to find TJ in front of the open fridge, pouring the orange juice I had wanted down his throat directly from the carton. I slapped his arm.

"That's so nasty, TJ. Mommy'll kill you if she catches you doing that again."

"So," he said, gulping, wiping his mouth with the back of his hand. "I don't care."

"You don't care?"

"She don't care about me."

"Don't say stuff like that." He rolled his eyes at me and put the carton back in the fridge. I took it back out and handed it to him. "You might as well finish it now since you started it. I don't want your germs. I don't know where you put your mouth when no one's looking."

"Damn, you just like Becky, always messing with somebody.

Ain't nobody even messing with you." He took another gulp. "Eh, did you ever go across the street?"

"Oh, so now you want something from me." I stood in front of the fridge, hoping in vain that there was something else to drink, but there wasn't. I slammed it in frustration.

"Just to know if you took my letter over there. I put the number at the bottom. But she never called."

"She's not the type of girl who calls over boys' houses."

"Well, if she ain't the type of girl I can go up to and she ain't the type to come outside and she ain't the type to get on the phone, how the hell I'm supposed to get at her?"

"Maybe you're not meant to. Maybe she's just too good for you," I snapped, banging cubes out of the tray to make ice water. The sound of my banging echoed through the kitchen.

"Man, forget you," he said, and his voice was low and husky. "You didn't even go over there." He started to leave the kitchen, and I turned and called after him.

"I did, TJ. For real, I did. I think she likes you, too. It's just that she said she can't have boyfriends or talk to boys. She'll get in a lot of trouble."

"Word?" He pitched the empty juice carton into the trash and raised his hands to grasp the molding on the top of the doorway, which he could reach easily.

"Yeah." I ran water from the purification filter my mother had bought into my glass, facing away from him. "I'm sorry."

"Nah, that's all right, Tiny. Good lookin' out, though."

I just nodded into my glass of water. My mother came into the kitchen, ducking under TJ's arm to get through the doorway and wrinkling her nose.

"Boy, don't you think you better get in the shower and stop

hanging around in doorways like a monkey?"

"You ain't gotta call names, Becky!" His raised voice made my mother snap her head around. "I didn't call you a name, TJ, I was just saying—"

"Calling people monkeys and stuff. Y'all always getting on me about something."

"You better be glad somebody's willing to get on your ass. That somebody gives a damn what you do."

"What's that supposed to mean?" He dropped his arms to his sides, took a step out of the doorway, his whole body tensed. "You talking about my mama?"

"Nobody said anything about your mother, TJ, and I know damn well you're not raising your voice at me. You can go back to your mama, you wanna do that." She turned her back on him, bending to get a pot out of the bottom cabinet. He stared after her with a stormy face for a few seconds, then turned and stomped out.

"I don't know what's wrong with him," my mother muttered, banging a skillet and pot on the stove, opening and shutting cabinets. "In here getting ready to feed his ass, he wants to talk to me like that."

I didn't want to say to her what I knew, that TJ had been upset with her, that the uneasy peace in our house had shifted for the worse ever since she didn't show up at his homecoming. "Do you want help, Mommy?" I asked, knowing that she would say no. My mother had been fretting lately about how it was time for me to learn to cook but never wanted me in her way. "That's okay," she said absently, feeding the faulty gas burner a scrap of a receipt until the fire flared up. "You just get on that homework. He's your daddy's business, but you ain't bringing no Ds in this house."

Chapter Fourteen

Grandmere died in her sleep on my twelfth birthday. I felt some guilt that we had missed a few Sundays of going to see her, but I was mostly annoyed at her timing. We had nothing much planned, just ice cream and cake once my father and TJ came back from his track meet, a trip to the one-hour photo and the movies later, but I had been looking forward to it. I was hanging around the dining room, eyeing the round pink cake box from Kream Krop Bakery I'd been forbidden to touch when my mother came in, swaying slightly.

"Neesie just called. Your Grandmere passed away, Tanis," she said in a thick voice, her eyes red. She spoke slowly, as if that was hard for her to tell me, as if she expected some painful reaction. No tears jumped to my eyes, though; nothing happened inside of me. "When?" I asked.

"Early this morning. And she's just getting around to calling me. Like I'm just nobody. A fucking distant relative. She's the fucking distant relative." She raised the cordless phone that had been clenched in her hand and started to dial, but her hand shook. She leaned against the wall and sank to the floor, lowering her face into her palms. Her hair, freshly pressed and tinted for my annual birthday pictures, fell silky over her slender wrists and forearms. I lowered the purple paper plates I had been setting around the table, wanting to be anywhere else. Seeing my mother cry was no easier then than it had ever been.

"You want me to call Auntie Trish?" I offered. Trish was coming over later with my cousins for my birthday, anyway. My mother nodded, her head and shoulders shaking. Glad to have something to do, I grabbed the phone.

Trish came quickly, but it still felt like I had been waiting forever, watching my mother sit in that same spot against the wall. I was surprised that I heard Trish's knock before I heard the clink of her earrings, and I ran to throw open the door. I was clasped into her hug, her low, soft breasts. She held me back by the shoulders to look at me.

"Look at you, Miss Twelve Year Old. You know, we were worried about you for a while, but you're starting to shape out to be a real pretty girl." I knew Trish didn't lie, and I beamed to hear her say that before remembering Grandmere and forcibly removing the broad smile from my face. "Mommy's real upset," I told her.

"Where is she?" Trish followed me into the house, around the wall separating the living room and dining room area, where my mother still sat slumped on the floor by the wall heater.

"Oh, Bey Bey," Trish said, calling my mother by the nickname I hardly ever heard. She dropped to her knees and wrapped my mother in her arms. I watched, wondering how she did that so easily. How she knew when to hold somebody and how to wrap your arms around a body so that its head fell just right into the warm swing-seat between your neck and shoulder. Trish hadn't taken the time to put in her earrings before she came over. Her earlobes looked tired and bruised, her pierce holes stretched into droopy black slits, some with scabs, some with small, fat keloids in the back.

"I'm all alone now," my mother moaned.

"What you talking about, Bey Bey? You got me, you got your

own family."

"My mama's gone, Daddy's gone, my grandmamma's gone. I don't have anybody to look in the face and see what I'm supposed to be."

"What do you need something like that for? You're whatever you supposed to be already."

"I should have been there, holding her hand, something. They weren't taking good care of her. Big and healthy, last time we saw her."

"And crazy."

"Trish!"

"Well, it's true, ain't it? And when your mind is gone, you need to follow it as soon as you can. You know she glad to be in Heaven where she can pull herself all back together. You know that once you get to Heaven, everything that was wrong with you goes back right." My mother only cried harder, and I couldn't take it anymore. I went to my room and buried my head under my pillow, not caring that I was messing up my freshly touched-up hair. I knew there would be no visit to the one-hour photo that day.

Trish came into my room a few minutes later.

"We gotta go over to Grandmere's to see about some things."

"Oh, God, do I have to?" I wailed.

Trish raised her over-plucked eyebrows.

"That's your great-grandmother, Tanis. I know it's your birthday, but—"

"It's not about my birthday. I don't like going over there. And that old lady scared me."

"Well, she's gone and there ain't nothing left to be scared of now. Anyway, your mama needs you."

"No, she doesn't. She never does." Trish looked at me, touched the side of my face. I wasn't used to being touched and I flinched away. "You just come on," she told me, her voice firm.

We got into Trish's car and headed to Grandmere's, my mother and I still in the matching button-up denim dresses and high boots we'd gotten for my birthday pictures. Trish drove a rattling old Volkswagen Rabbit, and the pictures of her kids tucked into the dashboard were curled with age, freezing them at snaggle-toothed grins. She had said once that that was how she liked to think of them. Jerome Jr., a little older than TJ, had already been to Juvie and was on house arrest; his twin, Jamila, was pregnant. It puzzled me because Trish seemed like a good mother. I had often, when I was little, wished she was mine.

When we pulled up to Grandmere's, cars already filled the driveway. My mother was further insulted that she wasn't even the first one there. "Vultures," she spat every time we got out of earshot of relatives we'd just hugged. "Who here even halfway came to see her? Probably just want to see what they can get." I stayed quiet, submitted myself to tight hugs and wet kisses, to squeezes and comments on my growing body from relatives I barely knew. We were not close to our extended family. My mother had been the only child of a mother who died young and there had been some anger, Trish had told me, over how much Grandmere favored and prized her when she was younger. She'd been raised feeling she was above her cousins and raised me the same way. My mother thought most of my cousins (Trish's kids, too, though she would never tell her so) were a bad influence. Everyone was varying shades of peach, toast, and banana, and I felt dark and out of place.

It was strange to enter Grandmere's dark house after years of going no further than the porch. Neesie sat on the old plastic-covered couch, looking glassy-eyed and accepting hugs, but otherwise seeming disturbingly not disturbed. She was finally free. My mother touched her shoulder but obviously couldn't bring herself to hug her. "We need to talk about the wake and all that. Grandmere was Catholic, she'd want everything done out the right way."

"Mommy, can I go outside?" I asked. She nodded distractedly. I walked out onto the porch and sat on one of the steps, staring at the dismal street, stretching my legs out in front of me. My boots had a heel on them, my first real heel, and my curls tumbled over my shoulders. The curls would be out by the time we made it to the one-hour photo, if we made it at all. Why did the old lady have to pick that day to die? I fumed over that so I wouldn't have to think about Grandmere herself, about what death was like. Did it hurt, did you know when you were about to take your last breath that it would be your last? With her voodoo powers, Grandmere probably knew. She probably knew and thought about things first.

I sat for what felt like hours. More people arrived and left, and I spoke as little as I could get away with. The hairs on my skin rose in that way that lets you know someone is watching you. I glanced out into the yard where a crowd of my teenaged cousins I'd been too scared to try to join hung out. One boy, lanky and caramel colored, kept looking in my direction. I met his eyes and then ducked my head.

"Caleb, you better stop that, you know that's your cousin!" one girl shrieked, and they all burst out into laughter that seemed too raucous for a dead woman's yard.

"Keep looking at her like that, we gon' have some deformed, funny-looking babies show up in the family," added another cousin who I did know, Charisse. There were a lot of girls in my family. Caleb was probably looking at me because I was the only one he hadn't met and didn't know was blood, but still, I felt proud. Trish had called me pretty and my boy cousin had checked me out, all in one day. I had a goofy smile on my face that I shook off as soon as I saw my mother come out of Grandmere's house, her face like a dishtowel that had been wrung dry. She looked at me as if she didn't recognize me, then past me at the dry old bush next to the step where I sat. "Trying to shut me out," she muttered. "Talking about they're taking care of things. Probably just want the damn insurance money to themselves." She bent, I thought towards me, but she reached past me to the old rosebush next to the step where I sat. She fingered one dry leaf. "Look at this shit. Couldn't even take care of her roses." She stood straight suddenly and stalked to the garage. I jumped up. The structure was so slanted and old, it looked like the roof might cave in any second as my mother disappeared inside. She came out a few minutes later, sneezing, dragging a shovel. She looked strange lugging the heavy shovel in her fitted dress and high-heeled boots, and everyone outside the house stopped their conversations to stare. She brought the shovel over to the flowerbed, started digging into the dry soil. Stepping away so that dirt wouldn't get on my dress, I heard a few snickers coming from the yard where my cousins had gathered and felt my ears heat up from the inside out. I ran inside the house and called for Trish, who got up from the couch and followed me outside.

"Bey," she called when she saw what my mother was doing. "Bey!" My mother went on, grunting and coughing, stepping onto the shovel, giving it all her weight, then wrenching down the handle. The branches shook; my mother was stronger than I thought. Trisha shrugged.

"Well, Rebecca, I hope you got a plan for getting that thing home. I'm not trying to have dirt all over the back of my car."

When my father finally pulled up in the driveway, I was sitting at the dining room table, eating a slice of my birthday cake. My mother had picked out exactly what I wanted, a strawberry-filled white cake with lavender buttercream frosting, but she had been locked in her room when I finally decided to go ahead and open it. She'd gone in there as soon as we got home from Grandmere's and untied the rosebush from the top of Trish's car. Trish had waited with me for a while for her to come out and my father to get home, determined to still sing "Happy Birthday," until she finally said she had to go. "Happy birthday, sweetie," she said, pushing a small purple-wrapped package into my hands. She stroked my hair, the curls of which had already started falling. "You are a year older. Try not to care about every single thing so much."

My father and TJ came in later with a lot of noise and a bunch of jewel-toned, heart-shaped balloons. I could see them stopping by the grocery store or some gift shop on the way home, rushing, knowing they were in the doghouse for missing my party. I sat calmly, starting my second piece of cake.

"Hey, birthday girl!" My father barreled into the dining room, TJ close behind him, struggling with his gear. They looked at my open cake box, the plate in front of me.

"Y'all cut it already?"

"I cut it," I replied, not looking at him, taking another bite. He and TJ glanced at each other, and my father sat down at the table.

"I'm sorry we late, baby. It was a bunch of extra teams in that thing; it ran way over. I would have left, but no one could give your brother a ride from way out there to back over this way."

"Yeah, Tiny, I'm sorry," said TJ, sincerely. I glanced at the medal around his neck and back at my plate, picking up my fork to lick it clean.

"Well, here." My father put a pink envelope down in front of me. "You can at least open your card."

I opened it, scanned the message, and took out the money. I knew my mother was the gift buyer in the family, that my father didn't know what to buy me, especially now that I was too old for toys and dolls. Still, I liked the thought of him taking the time to pick something out for me, even if it turned out to be something I didn't like. I put the ten-dollar bill in the front pocket of my denim dress.

"Thank you, Daddy."

"You're welcome, baby. Where's your mama?"

"In there. Grandmere died today." I stood up. "I'm going to my room, now."

TJ came into my room a few minutes later, which he hardly ever did. I don't know if he had picked up on the fact that my mother didn't like him to be in there or if it just didn't hold much interest for him. It was just a girl's room, housing a gingham plaid comforter set that was always sliding off the bed, Bell Biv DeVoe and SWV posters on purple walls, a bunch of other junk, and me. But he came in wearing his green track sweats and knocked my feet aside so he could lounge on the edge of the bed. I tried to kick him off, but he caught my socked feet in his hands and started tickling them on the bottom.

"Stop!" I squealed, thrashing my legs. I wanted so badly not to laugh that I felt an actual sense of panic. I managed to pull away, my socks coming off in his hands.

"Ew," TJ said. "Your feet stink."

"They do not. You're the funky one. Getting your must all over my bed."

He stretched out on the bed, moving his arms and legs like he was making a snow angel in my tousled sheets. "Ah, I'm giving your bed all my aroma."

"Stop!" I pushed at him, a giggle escaping me.

"Wait, hold up!" He grabbed at the air in front of my face, closed his fist in front of my mouth, and stuck his hand in the front pocket of his sweatshirt as if he was putting something away. "I got yo' smile."

"You did not."

"Yeah, I did, and Ima keep it." He patted his front pocket. "Sorry I made Pops miss your party, Tiny."

"It's okay."

"Nah, it's not. You know you pissed. He missed a bunch of my parties when I was little. I used to be real mad at you." He tossed my socks at me, which he had rolled together into a ball, and I pitched them back.

"I didn't know that."

"Yeah. He was with my mama first, you know."

"No, he wasn't."

"He was. For a long time. He married Miss Becky because she was so young and your great granny was gonna have him put in jail and his brother had died in jail. I heard my mama talking about it a bunch of times."

"How do you know that's true?"

"How do you know what your mama say is true?" I laid back into my pillows, my head beginning to ache.

"I didn't see him that much 'til I started playing football. You were real little." He looked past me at a spot on the wall. "Anyway," he reached up and took the medal from around his neck. "This is for you."

"Why would I want your old funky medal?" I said, but my voice was weak. There was nothing TJ prized like his sports trophies, medals, and plaques. He loved them more than girls, more than food, more than Ice Cube and leather sneakers.

"This ain't no old funky nothing. This is history right here, girl. First place for sprinting. My best time ever." He dropped the medal, strung on a wide blue ribbon, in my lap.

"You should keep it, then, if it's that big a deal," I told him.

"Look, my money's funny, right now, but when I get a job this summer, Ima get you something real good, then you can give it back. I just want you to hold it for me 'til then."

I fingered the grooved edges of the medal, the number and block letters carved into it. "Okay. Thanks."

Just then, my mother appeared in the doorway. Her face looked soft and swollen, but her eyes were sharp as she took in TJ sprawled on my messed-up bed, my bare feet in his lap, my denim dress hitched up by our light wrestling.

"TJ," she said in a low, hoarse voice. "Come help your daddy with this bush out here."

TJ rolled onto his back, tossed my sock ball up high, catching it with one hand.

"TJ, you hear me talking to you?" She raised her voice.

"Right now?"

"Yes, now. My grandmother died today, boy. I'm not in the mood for your shit." Groaning, TJ dragged himself up and slow-limped out of the room. My mother leaned flat against the door-jamb as he passed, as if she didn't want his body to touch hers. She crossed her arms and peered at me.

"What, Mommy?"

She said nothing.

"What?"

"You need to get up and clean up this room. It's a mess." She reached in and pulled my door closed.

Chapter Fifteen

That was when things really started to go wrong in our house. Sometimes, I would think it started when my mother missed homecoming. Or when TJ moved in. Or years before I was born, years before TJ existed, years before my parents ever met. All I know is that after Grandmere—who had never even been to our house—died, something seemed to weigh heavy over us, like something weighed over the entire city during those months. My father and I went with my mother to Grandmere's wake, but TJ flat out refused, and once we explained to him what a wake was, no power on earth could change his mind.

"I don't like dead people," he protested.

"There ain't nothing not to like about them," said my father. "They're dead, gone. It's just a shell." That didn't seem to make TJ feel any better.

"That shit is weird. Sitting around, eating, talking with somebody's body just chillin' right there in the room."

"Son, I don't want to go, either, but that's the oldest member of Rebecca's family, and we gotta pay respects."

"Why? You said that old lady didn't like you, and she ain't no family of mine."

"TJ—" my father began.

"That's all right." The front door opened, and my mother came in, carrying two bulging shopping bags from her store. She had started to come home with something almost every day, always claiming it was on clearance, barely anything after her discount. I was surprised we hadn't heard her heels clicking on the porch until I saw she wore sensible, plain flats. This fact scared me more than the thought that she had heard what TJ said.

"That's okay," she said calmly. Her roots were growing in, dark and crinkly, and her hair was tossed up lazily in a red scrunchy. "He doesn't have to go. He can just stay home." We all just stared back at her. She made her way to the hallway and never went near the kitchen the whole night. I hadn't realized how accustomed I had become to my mother cooking for me until she stopped doing it, and I had no clue how to fend for myself. It was TJ who took me in the kitchen and made us grilled cheese sandwiches after my father, who had stared at my mother's closed door for several minutes, said he had some business to take care of and left.

"What's wrong with your moms?" TJ asked, pressing the spatula into the butter-soaked bread in the skillet.

"I don't know," I murmured, standing near him. I had grown much taller without anyone noticing and marveled at the fact that I was almost at his shoulder.

"I'm sorry," he said, flipping the half-blackened sandwich onto my plate. "But I ain't going to nobody's wake. Looking at people's bodies. When I die, I want to be cremated."

"So we can sit you on the mantle and look at you?"

"Nah, spread me on the football field. At Jefferson High. That's the first field where I ever played a real game."

"I want to be cremated, too. I saw this thing on TV where they can take the carbon in your ashes and make a diamond. If they make me a diamond, will you keep me?"

"Yeah, I got you."

"You won't give me to a girl, will you?"

"Nah, Tiny, I won't give you to no girl. I'll put you in a fly-ass medallion, wear you right here." He thumped hard on his chest.

The wake was at Grandmere's, and it disturbed me, going to that house twice in one week. It was becoming too familiar; I was used to it only in the context of our Sunday visits. One of my mother's aunts, who lived in Louisiana, had flown up and taken over things. The yard was cleared out, the house cleaned up, windows washed and opened. Air had blown through that stale odor and the carpet had been vacuumed, though it was still dark inside. Walls were already marked that were going to be knocked out; the house was going to be remodeled and put on the market as soon as possible.

Grandmere's surviving kids and siblings were getting everything, and I knew how much that stung my mother. Maybe she had thought that Grandmere would come to her senses in her last days, that her role as little princess and replacement daughter would be restored. I couldn't tell. She didn't talk to me. She didn't look at me. She didn't even meticulously supervise my wardrobe as I got dressed. I wore a black sweater, tights, my boots with heels, and a plaid skirt I had outgrown that stopped several inches above my knees. My father raised his bushy eyebrows when he saw it, but as my clothes were my mother's domain and she didn't say anything, he didn't say anything, either. He was uncomfortable in his own suit jacket and button-up shirt, pulling at his collar constantly as he planted himself on a chair in the corner.

I walked with my mother to Grandmere's coffin. It was big and white, and she filled the whole thing, no smaller than she had been in life, her silvery hair spread out over the broad shoulders of her rose-colored suit. "This isn't right for her," my mother muttered. "I don't see what they were thinking. It's just tacky. She was classy; she would have wanted classic, classy mahogany. A nice navy suit. She used to say pink was for young girls, for virgins." She touched Grandmere's arm, her forehead, which was still folded in a frown, as if she had been trying to remember something when she died. Other than that, she looked okay, peaceful. I had had nightmares that her toothless mouth would be grinning at me, her filmy eyes open and staring, asking why I didn't cry. I felt nothing as I stood beside that coffin. True, I didn't know Grandmere really well, but I had seen her often enough and heard enough about her to feel *something*. Maybe I wasn't normal. Maybe I had an emotional problem. I reached up to pat my mother's arm, surprised at how hard that was for me to do, to just reach out to touch my mother, how heavy my arm felt. She patted my hand back and held it there. I noticed that her nails were chipped and needed a fill.

"She said she saw death around me, she was seeing her own," my mother murmured.

"I thought you didn't believe in that stuff, Mommy." My mother dropped her hand from mine and didn't answer. I turned towards the chair where my father had parked himself, but he was gone. I went out to the porch, where I found him smoking, leaning against the porch rail. I wanted to warn him not to do that, that the raggedy rail might collapse under his weight, but I changed my mind when I got closer. He smoked in quick, nervous puffs, his whole body shook, and he had undone the top three buttons of his shirt.

"Daddy? Are you okay?" He shook his head, starting another

cigarette. There was moisture on his forehead, though it was chilly outside.

"I don't know what it is. I ain't never liked this house. And that woman." He took another long drag. "I ain't never forgot how her face looked when she cursed me, and I ain't never felt right around her. She was a hard woman, man. She dead, but I still feel them eyes looking at me like I ain't no good, like I don't do the best I can. I can't stay around here. Tell your mama—"

"No." I crossed my arms. "If you want to leave, you have to tell her yourself." He looked at me in surprise, but I didn't move. The standoff was soon broken when my mother came onto the porch.

"Tannah, people are asking where my husband is. There's some family I want you to see."

"Becky, you know damn well none of those people care about me; don't matter one way or the other if I'm here."

"It matters to me."

"Why? So you can show off that you got a husband? Or 'cause you really need me?"

Say you need him, I found myself pleading in my head. *Tell him you need him.*

My mother crossed her arms below her chest. "Fine, Tannah. You want to stay out here, pouting, being unsociable, that's fine with me." I looked at her arms, realizing that mine were folded in the exact same way. I dropped them.

"Actually," my father ran his hand across his close-shaven head. "I'm not feeling that good. I think Ima go on home, lay down."

"We just got here!"

"I don't like this house, Becky, and that woman lying in there couldn't stand me. There's a funny spirit running through here. I don't feel right."

"My grandmother's spirit is in Heaven, Tannah. You surprise me; out of all the things you've been, this is the first time you've acted like a punk."

My father seemed to swell up looking at me and back at my mother. "I done about had it with you talking to me like I'm shit, 'specially in front of her. But we can talk about that later, I'm 'bout to go."

"So you're leaving?"

"Yeah, I'm such a punk, watch me punk out." He stomped down the steps. "I'll be back to pick y'all up."

"Don't bother. Trish'll drive us home." My mother went back inside, banging the ratty screen door, which immediately bounced back open. I sank onto the porch swing, looking after her, listening to the music from my father's speaker fade as his truck moved away.

I was sitting on the porch swing, slouching and scraping up the toe of my boot as I pushed myself back and forth, when I heard the porch creak a footstep rhythm behind me. I sat up straighter, yanking at the skirt that kept gathering around my thighs. When I looked up, Caleb, the lanky, peach-colored cousin who had checked me out before, stood there with a small plate of chicken wings and strawberries. He sat down next to me on the porch swing, which whined in protest. "Hey," he said.

"Hey."

He held out his plate.

"You want some?" I took a small drumstick, its fried skin soggy from the strawberry juice.

"Man, is this boring or what?" he commented.

"Yeah, it is." I took a bite near the top of the wing, where there was the least juice and the most meat. "Did you love Grandmere?" I asked him.

"Uh, I guess. I mean, there's a way you love people 'cause you really love them, 'cause of who they are and what they do and being around you and all, and there's a way you love them just 'cause they kinda belong to you, you know?"

"Yeah, I know."

"You don't hafta love me, though." He grinned and scooted closer to me. "I found out we only second cousins by marriage." I couldn't help but smile.

When Caleb asked me to go around the back of the house so he could show me something, I did. When he asked if he could kiss me, I did that, too. I think that I wanted to feel something, though I don't see why I thought I could get that from another person's slobber, from eyes too wide open in faces closer than faces should ever be. I went home from my great-grandmother's wake with the taste of chicken and strawberries and Carmex on my tongue, glancing at my mother to see if she would notice something different about me. But she never did.

When we got home, my father's truck wasn't in the driveway.

"Go home and lay down, my ass," my mother muttered as we climbed out of Trish's car at the curb.

"Just be cool, Bey. At least he came. I can't get Jerry to go no-where with me."

"You wanna come in, get some coffee?"

"Nah, girl." Trish looked tired. "I gotta get home, see what's going on in my own house."

"All right, then." My mother's hand, with her undone nails, brushed the rusted top of Trish's car as she pulled off. We wobbled up the driveway and porch in our heels, loaded down with foil-covered plates. This was another sign that my mother was not quite right; she usually didn't trust other people's cooking and thought it was unseemly to pack up food to take home from people's houses. She let us into the house, which was dark and quiet, though we could hear music from TJ's room. "He needs to turn on a light in here, anybody could try to break in, walk up in here on him..." she muttered, walking to the back. "TJ! TJ! Why's the house all dark? And there's some food in here—"

I heard a sharp gasp as my mother flung open TJ's door, and I ran behind her and peeked under her arm. All I saw was TJ's sneakered feet on the floor in front of his bed, his heavy jeans around his ankles, his ashy knees, a girl's big behind and slender, naked back before my mother pushed me roughly back. The girl had a splotchy birthmark on the left side of her butt.

"Get out of my house!" my mother screamed. Veins stood out from her slender neck, and her voice sounded hoarse, dragged out of her. "Get out of my house!" The plates dropped from her hands, cold jambalaya, cornbread, rice and beans hit her black skirt and tumbled across the floor. She stood there wringing her hands, screaming, "Get Out of My House!" like a cheerleader until I realized that she was talking to both the girl and TJ. They both, clothes disheveled, flew past me and out of the front door. I saw long black hair and, for a second, imagined it was Kiana Jacobs, but it was a thicker, lighter girl I had never seen before. The whole thing would have been funny if it wasn't for the touch of hysteria in my mother's screams and the hollow, final sound of her slamming her bedroom door.

The next day my father came home with TJ ahead of him, TJ's neck in the grip of his large hand, as my mother flipped through a catalog on the couch. I had told my father what happened when he got home, and he'd called around until he found out TJ was at one of his friend's houses in his old neighborhood. He'd let him stay the night to give my mother time to cool off and gone back to get him that afternoon. TJ looked as if he wanted to be anywhere else, and there was a slight bruise under his eye. My father closed the door behind them, looked at my brother expectantly. TJ stared at the wall with stony eyes. My father shook him.

"I'm sorry, Miss Becky, for disrespecting your house," TJ said quickly. My mother just stared. My father let TJ go, and he rushed back towards his room.

"What's he doing back here?" my mother said softly once we heard the door slam. "I told him to get out."

"Now you got him thinking he ain't wanted."

"He was fucking that girl under my roof. Somebody's daughter. We have a daughter here. What kind of example is that for her?"

"He's a teenage boy, Becky."

"And boys will be boys, huh? What if we caught Tanis in the house with some boy on top of her?" I closed my eyes where I sat studying on the floor, wishing I had had the foresight to not be in the room.

"We might kick her ass. But we wouldn't just kick her out on the street. Or would you, Becky?" My mother calmly dog-eared a page in her catalog.

"Look, I chastised him, he ain't gon' try to pull that shit again."

"But what's next?" my mother murmured.

I got up quietly, slipped to the back, and opened TJ's door.

"Damn, don't nobody in this house know how to knock?" he snapped, shooting rolled-up tee shirts at the basketball hoop mounted on his wall.

"Yeah, that would be better for you, wouldn't it?" I smirked. "Was that the freak you took to homecoming?" He didn't smile.

"Why he make me come back?"

"You live here."

"I don't want to live here no more."

"You don't want to live here, you don't want to live with your mother, where are you going to live?"

"Mark's mama said I could have stayed with them as long as I want."

"'Til they got sick of you, too." I grinned. A heavy Jordan high top came flying at me, and I ducked. It thumped against the wall, just missing my head.

"You almost hit me!"

"Get out of my room, Tanis!"

"TJ, I'm just play—"

"No, just leave me alone!" After a few seconds of stunned, hurt silence, I obeyed.

Chapter Sixteen

As summer came closer, Rodney King seemed to become the most famous person in my world. Except at school, where most of my classmates were completely oblivious and where social studies was strictly limited to memorizing presidents and the dates of wars, his name was constantly in the air. Everywhere black adults came together, I heard them fuss about it, complain about the trial venue change to Simi Valley, recount stories of people they knew who had been beaten up or shot by the police, speculate on how the trial would play out.

"I don't see how they can't convict them," insisted Trish. "I mean, it's right there on tape."

"So was that Korean lady shooting that little girl a while back," my mother reminded her. "She didn't go to jail at all."

"And these people are white," my father said, agreeing with my mother for once. "Police first of all, and white, just like that jury. Ain't nothing much gon' happen to them, mark my words."

That school year, I had transferred to a new magnet school on the west side of town that I had to be bussed to. I hadn't been able to convince my mother to change my school after my Fly Girls humiliation on my own, but she relented quickly when a spot opened up at a K–8 magnet west of the 405. She was very impressed when we visited and saw white kids everywhere. My mother had told me that white people always got better service at the store where she worked because they were never afraid to go over your head and complain, and she was sure they were the same way about their kids' schools. The few black kids there were not from my part of LA, and they acted like some version of black they had gotten from hip-hop videos and *The Fresh Prince of Bel-Air*. I quickly went from being the "white girl" who couldn't stay in a double-dutch turn for more than thirty seconds, pop her gum, or go to the 7-7 skating nights at World on Wheels to having actual street credibility. My white friends, along with not being able to get the leg movement of the butterfly dance, had no clue about the way smog and anger grew hands and choked the air as my bus moved closer to Hyde Park. And that was how I liked things. I wanted to remain the best in double-dutch, and I wanted to think about the spring dance, not juries and dead girls and police brutality.

Under my mother's urging, I had finally joined a club, the drama club. I hadn't gotten any parts yet or attempted to audition. But I went faithfully to the meetings and my name was reflected next to last on the club roster. The drama club met on Wednesdays, and my mother knew that on those days I would stay after school until four-thirty and then take the late bus home. So it shocked me when I saw her walk into the auditorium at four o'clock. I had been sitting as far back in the auditorium as I could get away with, not participating, and completely alone, doodling in my notebook. I wished for the first time that I had actually signed up to try to get a part, that my mother had walked in to find me on the stage. She still wore her Robinsons-May nametag, and her natural, dark-brown hair color now extended halfway through the length of her hair, still not touched up since Grandmere was buried. She beckoned to me impatiently, and my drama club mates watched curiously as I threw my things together and followed my mother out without a word. Though I was almost my mother's height and had longer legs, I had to scamper a bit to keep up with her strides. We hurried to the parking lot and the new little Honda Civic she had gotten after my father's first pay raise on his job.

"Mommy, what's going on?" I finally asked, tired of the anticipation. If I was in trouble, I wanted to get the fallout over with. "Why are you picking me up?"

"They acquitted those officers who beat that man. And I don't know, I just have this bad feeling about it. People been talking crazy. I left work. We're calling your daddy's job and TJ's school as soon as we get to the phone."

"What do you think is going to happen?"

"I don't know." She bit her full bottom lip. "My grandmother used to know things, Tanis. Have dreams and see things that would come true."

"You said that was Alzheimer's."

"I know what I said," she snapped. Then she lowered her sun visor and softened her voice. "I can't sleep lately, the kind of dreams I've been having since she died." I didn't see what this had to do with the police getting acquitted or Rodney King or picking me up from school or anything else, but I saw how agitated my mother was and kept my mouth shut until we got home. She turned on the news as soon as we got into the house. Mayor Bradley was speaking on one channel, saying he was shocked at the verdict, warning Los Angelenos not to "strike out blindly."

"It's a shame." My mother shook her head. "Finally get a black man in office, a good black man, and something like this has to happen on his watch."

"Something like what? What do you think is going to happen,

Mommy?" She never answered me.

My father and TJ got home soon after us, TJ pouting hard. He had hurt his knee in a tournament earlier in the month and was going through physical therapy. He was worried that it wouldn't be healed in time for summer football practice and had stalked around like a human storm cloud for weeks.

"Why I gotta come straight home?" he protested. "Since I can't practice, me and my homies was gon' roll to the mall."

"You don't need to be rolling anywhere, today," my mother snapped, gesturing at the TV with her remote. "Look at all these crowds of people out and about, looking to get into something."

"Who asked you?" The vehemence of his response snapped all our heads around.

"Excuse me?" my mother took a step in his direction, but my father interrupted her.

"Boy, I don't want to hear you talk to Becky like that. You go on back to your room and chill out."

"You always take her side."

"Go on, I said, now." My father raised his voice. TJ swung his jacket around him and stalked to his room, his hurt knee and anger exaggerating his already heavy limp. My father shook his head.

"Don't know what's gotten into him, lately," he tried to say lightly.

"No home training," my mother muttered, turning up the TV.

Throughout the afternoon, my parents stayed in front of the TV, flipping between various news channels. "They all over Normandie," my father murmured. "My brother's store is right over there." Ronnie, my uncle and godfather, had a little electronics store at one of those countless corner plazas that mostly held nail salons, wig shops, and fried fish places. My father used to take me by there a lot when I was little, before TJ came, before my role as his passenger-side "road dawg," as he used to call me, was dramatically reduced. As if on cue, the phone rang. My father, distracted by the news, reached for it without waiting for my mother's okay or for the answering machine to come on.

"Yeah, what's up Ronnie? Yeah, we watching it now... Bro, you better calm down, don't do nothing stupid... Look, Ronnie, Ima be over there. Ima be over there, okay?...Yeah, yeah, see you." By the time he hung up, my mother's eyes were wide and hard.

"I know you're not about to drive in that direction."

"I gotta see about my little brother, Becky. You know how crazy Ronnie is. All those people over by his store making him nervous."

"Making him nervous? What about me? Who's going to come see about you after you drive into that mess?"

"Becky, dammit!" My father clenched his hands at his sides. "Can't I think about nobody but you? That's all you think about: what you want, what you need."

"Is that so?" She combed her fingers through her hair as she watched him. "You don't think I might give a damn what happens to you out there, trying to be a hero?"

My father's face softened. "Look, it ain't gon' get that bad. Let me go see about my brother, calm his ass down. I'll be back."

She shook her head. "I hope you just remember that your ass may be thick, but it's not bulletproof. And you just stay on that freeway as long as you can. Don't be winding all up and down those back side streets like you like to do."

"All right, baby," my father said mildly, shrugging on his jacket and heading out the door. I followed him out onto the porch.

"Daddy." I pulled on his jacket sleeve, remembering a time when I had to cock my head way up to do that. "Be careful." He smiled at me, pulled my head in with his large hand, and kissed my forehead, his mustache bristly, lips wet. "Be careful," I said again, not sure why I felt so sure that he needed to be careful unless my mother's nervousness, like so many of her moods, was contagious.

"Don't worry about me, Toodle Woodle. Tell TJ I'll be back, and tell him to do his homework, and to be cool."

"He won't listen." My father chuckled and headed out into the still-bright afternoon sky. I closed the door behind him.

"Make sure you lock both those locks," said my mother from the couch, her eyes fastened back to the TV.

Later that evening, unable to focus on my homework, I finally pushed it aside and went to TJ's doorway.

"Hey," I said. He didn't answer, bouncing a mini rubber ball against the wall above his bed. *Talk to me*, I pleaded in my head, but I didn't know any way to engage his attention other than attack. "Why you have to be so grouchy all the time?"

"Why you have to be so annoying?"

"What are you talking about? I don't even mess with you."

"You do. You like a little mosquito, buzzing around my head all the time."

"You know, you're the one who tripped on that hurdle; you don't have to take it out on everybody else." He sat straight up. "I didn't trip!"

"Yeah, you did," I laughed, glad to get a reaction. "You bounced on that track, like this." I imitated TJ's fall with sound effects. He stood up, throwing down his ball.

"Get outta here, Tiny! You not supposed to be in here, anyway."

"Who told you that?"

"Y'all think I'm stupid, huh? I'm deaf, I can't hear people talking shit about me?" He lay back on his bed. "That's why Ima go to summer school, try to graduate early, get recruited. I can't wait to get the hell outta here, to get away from y'all." His words and tone stung; I felt wetness in my eyes and hated myself for it.

"Hmmmph. It's gon' take more than one summer of summer school to help you graduate early," I muttered.

"What?" TJ sat up. "What did you say?"

"I said, you gon' need more than summer school to graduate early. I could have wrote that letter you wrote to Kiana Jacobs when I was five years old." His face looked stricken, but I felt my mouth still moving, heard myself going on as if the schoolyard taunts were filling my ears, the crowds pushing me forward. "I bet she thought so, too. How you gon' call a girl pretty and spell it wrong? That's probably why the girl didn't want to call you!" The words were barely out of my mouth before TJ had shot across the room, quicker than I thought his hurt knee would let him. It all moved so fast I didn't feel him grab me, just felt myself being shaken back and forth all of a sudden, fingers digging into my arms, my hair flying across my face, the world looking like it did when I was little and spun around in circles until I collapsed, sick to my stomach, on the lawn.

"You calling me stupid! You calling me stupid! Don't you ever call me stupid!" My brother's repeated, hoarse yells soon blended in with my own shrieks.

"What the hell is going on in here?" I heard my mother cry.

"You take your hands off my child!" I felt myself being wrenched from TJ's grip. I was still dizzy, and my hair still covered my eyes, so I didn't see the slap, but I heard it, sharp as my click-clackers. The sound pierced everything and seemed to immediately stop everything else in the house: the yelling, the TV, my own heartbeat. When I opened my eyes, all I could hear was all of our heavy breathing. I didn't know who had slapped who until I looked at TJ's face and saw the redness on the left golden cheek.

"You don't ever touch my child," my mother said, her breasts heaving with her breath. "That is my child, and you don't ever touch her." TJ took a step back, touched his face, which was already welting, and looked at his hand. "Right," he said. "That's *your* child. And I ain't." They stared at each other for a few seconds before my mother pulled me out of the room.

"What did he do to you?" my mother asked repeatedly, shaking me almost as hard as TJ had been as I sat crying on the couch. "What else did he do to you?"

"Nothing," I sobbed.

"Well, what did you do? Why was he grabbing you like that? Did he hurt you?"

"Nothing, I didn't do anything." I sucked up snot and tears. "Maybe you didn't have to hit him like that, Mommy."

"Shit, he put his hands on you first. I have to have him in my house like he's mine, wash his clothes like he's mine, feed him like he's mine, I should be able to hit him like he's mine, too." She said this saucily enough, but her voice shook. "I can't take this shit anymore. He can go back to his mama, he can go wherever, but I just know—"

Suddenly, she stopped cold, putting her hand to her throat.

"Mommy?" Her eyes focused on a spot on the wall above my head, her pupils large, the color of her irises lighter, her whole face trembling.

"Mommy, what's wrong?"

"I saw this," she murmured and ran back through the kitchen towards TJ's room. I followed and got to the doorway in time to see several drawers of his dresser and the doors of his IKEA wardrobe wide open. The gym bag he usually left sitting by the door was missing, and his favorite football, a game ball signed by his old Crenshaw District teammates, was gone from the holder on his desk. By the time I had taken all these things in, my moth er had run out. I tracked her flash of red blouse into the kitchen and followed the line of her eyes to the wide-open side door.

"Get your jacket," she told me. I obeyed, not asking any questions. She grabbed her keys, and we headed out to the Honda. We drove around the neighborhood for what seemed like hours.

"Lay down in the backseat," my mother instructed me. "People might get nervous seeing someone driving slow like this and shoot at the car."

I climbed into the back and did as she asked. Somehow, lying in the back in case of gunshots heightened the uneasiness I was already feeling into a real, immobilizing fear. I breathed shallowly as my mother circled our block, then all around it. She went to the bus stop on Vermont, but it was empty; the six o'clock bus had already been by. We made another circle, and I started to feel disoriented, carsick. I thought I was imagining the smell of smoke in the air until I heard a gasp in my mother's throat and sat up straight. The liquor store around the corner of my house, that the Korean man owned, was completely lit up in flames and people filled the parking lot, shouting. I wondered where the Korean man was, and his wife. I used to like the days she worked the counter because she didn't watch me as hard as her husband, and always slipped extra green Jolly Ranchers in my bag.

"Get back down," my mother ordered, and I obeyed, my heart knuckle-rapping inside me. Her brakes squealed as she swung us towards home.

Chapter Seventeen

My mother and I did not leave the house for three days. We didn't need the schools being closed or the mayor calling a curfew to tell us to stay put. We huddled in my bedroom, the furthest back except for TJ's, as if being away from the front of the house would keep us safe. No one touched or went near TJ's room; it was frozen at the moment he left it. My mother and I gripped each other as we sat on top of my unmade bed, both quiet and unwashed..When my father wasn't at the hospital, he sat on the porch with his shotgun and water hose ready. We could hear shouting and smell smoke, but people never came onto our block. The liquor store was the closest thing to us that had been burned.

For over three days, from the smoke that darkened the air even in daytime, from the news channels showing nothing but fire, from the constant whirring of ambulance and fire truck sirens but no police in sight, it seemed like the world was ending. The news anchors talked about the national guard, property damage, looting, about a white man being pulled out of his truck and beaten up, but there was only one news report that I really listened to, one that I digested, two lines in the midst of all the chaos.

Tannah Sutton, Jr., a sixteen-year-old African American, was struck in the head by a stray bullet at seven p.m. on the corner of forty-sixth and Vernon. He is the youngest victim so far of today's civil unrest.

And then they had moved on. "Spent more time talking about people taking TVs," my mother had murmured. One of the guys from next door, Butch, brought us a big screen TV he got from a looted store. I think he was trying to be nice because he wasn't even going to charge us. My father took it out in the street and crushed it with a crowbar, beat it into glassy, metal crumbs, while the neighbors stood on their porches and watched. TJ would have insisted we keep that TV. Reasoned that Butch had already stolen it, it wasn't like we could take it back. It might as well go to good use in his room.

Tannah Sutton, Jr., a sixteen-year-old African American, was struck in the head by a stray bullet at seven p.m. on the corner of forty-sixth and Vernon. He is the youngest victim so far of today's civil unrest.

They didn't say anything about him loving football, blowing a kiss to his Janet Jackson poster every night. Nothing about him being able to inhale a pork chop in two bites or listening to a girl named Kiana play her cello or telling his little sister how to act with boys. They didn't say anything about how he knew all Ice Cube's lyrics by heart or stood against the wall at parties trying to look cool because he couldn't dance or never left the track field until he had beaten the time he ran the practice before. They didn't talk about any of that. I told my mother I would write them a letter to tell them all the things they missed. She looked at me with red eyes and told me to please leave her alone.

I had dreams sometimes where I knew with complete certainty that I was dreaming. I read in a book one time that this was called lucid dreaming. It became very useful because my dreams were often nightmares, and I learned to control things. Sometimes I could make myself win the fight, or draw a window in the wall if I was running from a monster, or simply pinch myself and shake my head until I woke up with little bruises on my arms. However, my most frightening dreams were not when people died or I fell out of a window or got turned into a vampire or pursued by a rabid dog. My worst dreams were when I knew I was dreaming, even if nothing particularly strange was happening, and no matter how hard I tried, I couldn't wake up.

There was one dream that I always had. I would be asleep, warm in my bed in my cozy purple room. I'd wake up, sitting straight up like sleepwalkers did in movies. I'd get out of bed, my feet cold on the unfinished wood floor, and walk down the hall towards my parents' room. Their door would be slightly open, and bright yellowish light would slant out into the hallway. There would be complete silence in the room, but I would know somehow that something really horrible was happening in there and that if I reached it, I would never come out again. But I would keep walking forward, as if an invisible cord was attached to TJ's track medal that I wore around my neck. I would realize I was dreaming and start pinching myself furiously, on my arms and sometimes on my pudding-cup breasts, where the sharp pain on my nipple would draw me back to real life in an instant. In this dream, for a long time, the pinching and head shaking wouldn't work, and my panic would rise until, finally, I was in my bed. I would breathe a sigh of relief, and then fear would grip me as I sat straight up, got out of bed, and began walking down the hall again. This happened more times than I could count, and each time I'd come closer to my parents' bedroom door. I never did succeed in waking myself up when I had this dream. I was only saved by my father's stumbling over stuff trying to get ready for work, or police sirens outside my window, or my mother getting me up for school. I wondered sometimes what would happen if I was left alone to dream that dream until I got into the room and everything ended. I had a concrete belief that if I ever reached their room I would never wake up.

That was how the weeks after the phone call about TJ felt to me. Like a horrible lucid dream that I moved through without really being a part of. The dream fog had fallen over the whole city, or at least the part of it that I knew. People wandered, shaken, through ash-clogged air and the burned-out shells of buildings. They limped around like the butterflies I had let out of Yosi's jar. They went home to stolen electronics or emptiness or the space of the people missing or all three. We were all swallowed up in gray dust and the horrible blurry feeling that something was missing, something was wrong, it was never going to be all right again, and things had never been all right before.

My school, which never was in the danger zone, anyway, had reopened, but I simply did not go. I don't think it was ever an official decision that I wouldn't go to school. Everyone just forgot about taking me, and I didn't bother to remind them. Our cable had been turned off because my parents had forgotten about the bill, just as they had forgotten about trips to the grocery store. I would sit, stinking from every pore, eating pickles and cake frosting as I watched soap operas and talk shows after regular programming had come back on, all the faces and voices blending together. My parents came in and out of the house without saying much to me, figures moving slow like they were going through water.

I used to play with a boy in our neighborhood who'd gotten shot a couple of years before, shot in the head. When we heard, we all thought he was gone forever. He came home a few days later with a bandage wrapped around his head. "It was a graze," the boy's father had told mine over our fence, annoyed nonchalance in his face but joyous laughter in his eyes. "Lucky-ass little niggah. So hardheaded, that shit bounced right off." TJ had to be among the most hardheaded people I knew, so I asked my parents, too excitedly, in a shrill voice. "Was it a graze? Was it a graze?" They looked at me blankly, their eyes blood-brushed. My only information came from overhearing phone conversations, as they didn't talk much to each other. I knew my brother was alive, but words like "brain-dead," "life support," "vegetable" floated around through the slow, filmy movements that had become our days. I didn't know what any of it meant. I pictured a stalk of corn lying in a hospital bed with a football in the curl of one leaf.

"But he's going to be better, right?" I would ask cheerfully, eating old peanut butter with a spoon. I think my mother finally sat me down, explained that no, he wasn't going to get better, that it was only the machines keeping him alive, and Daddy and Charlotte were deciding if they should pull the plug. I pictured someone yanking a plug out of the wall, like you did the toaster or the iron when you were done with it. "Can I see him?" I think I asked, and my mother looked skeptical. "I don't think that's a good idea."

"I want to see him," I protested. "I'm twelve, I'm not a baby. Girls my age in some societies are married with kids."

I don't remember her agreeing, but she must have because one night I took a long bath, leaving brown suds in the tub from the dirt of more than a week. I remembered my mother yelling at

TJ for not rinsing out the tub good, I heard his under-the-breath muttering response, and suddenly, I couldn't sit in there anymore. I jumped up, as if cold hands were going to reach out of the drain and grab me, and jumped out. I slipped wildly on the wet floor and grabbed the towel bar just before my head crashed on the side of the tub. I wished for a second, lying on the floor, naked and breathing deeply, that it had. Then I'd be a vegetable, too, a turnip maybe, lying next to a cornstalk, pom-poms on either side of it, no horrible hollowness in the chest, no fuzzy, dreamlike, left-behind feeling.

When we got to the hospital, we saw Charlotte in the waiting room gazing straight ahead and drinking from a Styrofoam cup that had been chewed up on one side. Her hair wasn't done, and her deep, shining skin was dull. She lifted her eyes and mumbled an acknowledgment to my mother.

"How are you doing, Charlotte?" my mother said, surprising me. I'd never heard my mother say Charlotte's name. To me she had always been "that woman," to TJ "your mother," and to my father "that bitch."

"He smiled a little bit today, I think, when I was trimming his hair." She drank some more, and a dribble of liquid came down her cheek. I lifted my hand to point it out to her, and my mother slapped it down.

"I always used to beg him to let me cut his hair. I knew I could do it, and it would save some money. He always wanted a fresh haircut, every week. Worse than a girl in that way. Couldn't let it grow in at all. He wouldn't let me do it, though. Had to go to the barbershop and get it all lined up with that ramp-looking thang on top and those damn designs in the back of his head." She laughed hoarsely.

"Do you want some more coffee, Charlotte?" my mother asked. Charlotte clutched the cup to her like someone was going to steal it, and some sloshed onto her blouse. She looked at my mother with narrowed eyes. Then her eyes shifted over and found me.

"Tanis!" she smiled, a spit bubble forming in the side of her mouth. "You done got so big. So big and pretty." Tears and mucus dripped through her voice. She grabbed me and hugged me, pulled me into her large, soft breasts. Her breath smelled old and mildew wet. I felt smothered, and even though I couldn't see or touch her, I knew my mother was stiffening beside me. I patted Charlotte's back then disengaged myself as delicately as I could.

"He was so crazy about you," Charlotte sniffed. "Sure was."

"We're going in now, Charlotte." My mother clutched my shoulder.

"Y'all look at his face good. They say there ain't nothing happening in his brain, but y'all watch his face. He smiled at me. I know my son."

My father was in the hospital room, sitting beside the bed with his head hanging.

"Hey, baby." He looked up at me with glassy eyes.

"Hey, Daddy." I didn't know what else to say. I felt like we hadn't seen each other in years and I barely knew who he was. I looked at the bed, the cornstalk image still in my mind. But it was just TJ with bandages on the side of his head, looking pretty much the same as he always did when he slept. Except TJ slept curled up with the tip of his thumb in his mouth, which I had always thought was really funny. This person lay flat on his back, his arms stretched out straight on either side of him. TJ would never sleep that way, he'd be uncomfortable. The long eyelashes resting on his cheeks were his, but the gold was gone from his skin. It looked darker, ashen. The line where Charlotte had cut his hair was crooked. I touched that part of his head, pushed the hair with my nail as if I could move it back into place. TJ was obsessive about his haircuts. If he knew it looked like that, he'd get up right that second and beg for a ride to the barbershop and ten dollars to get it fixed. His skin was cool and faintly moist.

I watched his face carefully, but the still expression never changed. I looked for his clenched mouth when he was determined, his crooked, cocky grin. His lips stayed where they were. I wondered what being brain-dead was like. I pictured him locked in a dark room and looking for the door, trying to get out. Hearing our voices from far away and trying to follow them. Panic rose up in me as I saw him running wildly from door to door, like me stuck in a lucid dream, and, suddenly, I was shaking him, ignoring the wires and suction things and IVs plugged up, my voice higher pitched than the beeping of the machines. "We're over here, TJ! Get up! You have a game! Over here!" I shrieked, over and over again.

"Oh, Jesus." My mother closed her eyes. My father came over to me, lifted me up, and took me out of the room. I was much too big for that and felt myself slipping, my legs dangling long to the floor. I kicked against him, screaming tearlessly. My screams excited Charlotte, whom we passed as my father carried me out.

"My baby! My baby! My baby! Why they do that to my baby? Why they do that to my baby? He was supposed to be safe with y'all! I should have never sent him over there! Why they do that to my baby? I should have never sent him over there!" Her relatives crowded around her while my father took me outside. Her screams had quieted mine, but my father sagged down in the parking lot, making rough, strange noises I realized were sobs. Watching him cry was infinitely worse than watching my mother, and made even worse by the fact that I couldn't do it myself. My throat was hoarse from screaming, but my eyes were completely dry. What was wrong with me? That was my brother in that bed and he wasn't ever getting up. I hadn't cried for him. I hadn't cried for Grandmere. Did I only know how to cry for myself? Or was it because I helped kill him? I was full of ifs: if Rodney King never went speeding that night, if the police never beat him, if the stupid jury never made the decision they made, if people never got mad about it, or if they all had done all of that but I never went to TJ's room that night and said what I said.

We had never talked about what happened that night. Everything had happened so quickly, my mother calling my uncle's store, my father coming home, my parents calling Charlotte and all of TJ's friends, my father going out again in the midst of fires to look, the phone call from the hospital. The police insinuated that he had been looting, but the only thing in his gym bag were a few pairs of boxers, his signed game ball, and a beat-up picture of him with his mother and our father. Where he had been headed when the stray bullet hit him—his old neighborhood, USC, some girl's house—we didn't know about, no one knew. He had run away before, no one had focused on why, and my mother and I had stayed quiet. I closed my eyes, tried to squeeze some tears out, but they wouldn't come. I turned away from my father so he couldn't see.

When we got home that day, without saying anything to my parents, I slipped across the street to Kiana Jacobs's house. I wore a thin tank top, but I didn't need a jacket. The air was warm, as if the fires had heated up the temperatures for all of LA. But this was California, we were still in a drought, and April had passed into May while we were all occupied with other things. Summer was coming soon.

Mr. Jacobs answered the door. I didn't see Kiana outside at all while the riots raged on. She had only begun going back to school the week before and she never played her cello on the porch anymore. Mr. Jacobs's face was softer than usual when he looked down on me.

"Need some more help with your homework?" he asked gruffly.

"No. I have a letter for Kiana from my big brother. You don't have to worry about him having sex with her or getting her pregnant or anything because he's a vegetable now and he's not going to wake up." Mr. Jacobs widened his eyes at me for a moment, then stood back and let me pass.

I had done my best to re-read TJ's letter and wrote it over in full, neat cursive, going easy on the curls at the end of letters so it didn't look so girly. I had double-checked every big word in the dictionary, sprinkled music notes and butterflies and hearts throughout it, and even separated the paragraphs with lyrics from LL Cool J's "I Need Love," which I had overheard TJ listening to in his room more than once, though he always tried to act so hard. I had sprayed the envelope with the cologne TJ would sneak from my father's dresser and drench himself in before he went out, making me cough when he passed me in the hall. I placed the envelope in Kiana's hands and she turned it slowly over. She stared at me with her wide eyes. "I don't know what to say," she finally said. I shrugged and turned away, running to the front door. Mr. Jacobs actually met me there and insisted on walking me back across the street.

"You never know, it's still dangerous out here," he said. "People still mad and taking it out on everybody 'cept who they need to be taking it out on. I been meaning to come tell your people how sorry I am to hear about your brother." He glanced back towards his house. "There ain't nothing worse to fear than losing your child."

The Jacobses moved away later that month to Santa Clarita Valley, and some Latinos bought their house. Tejano music pumped out of their windows instead of deep, flowing strains of Bach. I wondered about Kiana sometimes, if she turned out to be everything they wanted her to be, if she ever rebelled, what she really thought about when no one was looking. It must have been romantic to know a dying boy loved you. I would have liked something like that; it would have made me feel like somebody special.

"Where you coming from, Toodle Woodle?" my father asked, absently. He had put in TJ's last game tape and was watching it from his recliner.

"Just outside," I answered. I wanted to go climb onto his lap and put my arms around his neck, but I was too old for that. I sat at his feet. TJ and I had given him new corduroy house shoes for Christmas that lacked the old comforting smell. "Daddy, Miss Charlotte said TJ smiled when she was cutting his hair."

"He didn't do anything, baby. There's nothing going on in his head."

"We don't know that. We don't know that he's not thinking anything, feeling anything."

"Maybe so, baby."

"Are you going to pull out the plug?" He rubbed his hands

over his face.

"Baby, I don't know. Thatta be like giving up on him, and I wouldn't ever want him to know we gave up."

"I don't think he would see it like that," I said, thinking about my image of TJ rushing from door to door of a locked, dark room.

"What you talking about, Tanis?" my father said tiredly.

"I mean, you know how mad TJ was when he hurt his knee. And he could still walk, then." On the tape, which my father kept rewinding, TJ leapt over the rolling of somebody that one of his blockers had taken out, still on rhythm. "I think he'd be really mad at us for leaving him like that. Even if he woke up one day, I think he would still be mad." My father put the flat of his big, deep-lined hand against his face and cried. I leaned over the back of the chair and put my arms around his neck, feeling his hot tears tickle the insides of my elbows.

Chapter Eighteen

I didn't cry at the viewing or the funeral. I almost threw up when I bent to kiss TJ at the viewing and his head, which they fixed up so it looked like nothing ever happened, was so cold and hard. I refused to walk by and look into his coffin at the memorial service. My mother didn't go, either. We sat in the pew staring straight ahead, squeezing each other's hands. I imagined whispers around us observing, muttering.

Look at 'em. Two of a kind, ain't they? They didn't love him. That woman, she was the one let him go out that night, you know that, right? Yeah, just let him go. Probably put him out. She didn't want him there in the first place. She didn't even want Tannah to claim him. Umm hmmm. And that little one, she ain't no better. You seen her cry once, huh? You seen that bright-ass dress she got on? And this her own brother's funeral. It's a shame, ain't it?

My father's mother was too weak to travel and her sister, who my mother couldn't stand, had flown up for the funeral. In a black suit complete with long gloves and a netted veil I had only seen in movies, she had rumbled endlessly about the pale-yellow, lace-edged dress I was wearing to the funeral.

"This ain't Easter," she said as I tried it on for my mother to see how it fit. "You 'sposed to wear black for funerals."

I loved my yellow dress. It was the dress I'd worn to TJ's last football banquet. I'd chosen it because it was what I had been wearing in the last picture we had together. My mother hadn't been sure about it, either, but my great-aunt's disapproval had made her certain it was what I should wear.

"She's a child," my mother snapped, sticking pins in the places where it needed a little taking in, where the hem needed to be let out. "Nobody's looking at her."

"She damn near grown." My great aunt eyed me. We didn't care much for each other, either, maybe because I didn't see her much and wasn't good at faking affection, maybe because to her I was an extension of my mother. "It just ain't right." My mother ignored her, and she shuffled to the kitchen, calling out that she hoped my mother hadn't soaked the chicken in grease this time, it wasn't good for her blood pressure.

"I hope it isn't," my mother muttered, piercing my skin with her nails as she pinched the fabric at my waist. "Can't wait 'til this is over and she takes her old ass back to Alabama."

After the last viewing, the pallbearers, all teenagers and young men, TJ's cousins and closest teammates, lifted the white coffin and carried it down the aisle. We followed the hearse to Inglewood Park Cemetery, which was as bright and pretty and rolling green as a park, a place you'd bring a picnic. We didn't go out to the grass and throw dirt on top of the coffin, like they always did in the movies. Everyone filed into a large, dark, cool room with stairs that went down low. He was being put into a crypt. For the week after they took him off the machine, I had heard people saying crypt and didn't know what they were talking about. They had pronounced it crib, and I had nightmares about TJ curled up in a baby crib, his legs hanging out the bottom, clutching his signed game football and sucking his thumb, a bloody bandage on his head. He turned to look at me when I peered over the railing, took his thumb out of his mouth to say,

"Fuck this, Tiny," and reached to snatch his track medal from around my neck. I had woken up from these dreams sweating and sat up in bed the rest of the night with my back against the headboard to avoid falling back asleep.

Now, though, I understood. He would be put in a locked case underground and his nameplate would be posted next to a green plastic vase on one of the white walls near the entrance. When we went to talk to him or put flowers in the vase, we would be a mile away from where his body actually was. Something about that felt false and pitiful to me. It made it seem less like we would be visiting him and more like what it actually was, a metal nameplate and a rotting body that would never laugh, never push me in the head, never kiss a girl, never run across a field again. I choked on that image and had to run out into the sun, past the white walls, past the flowerbeds, back to the limo's safety. After everything else I had done, I had also forgotten to tell them. I thought I had done everything TJ wanted me to, giving his letter to Kiana, convincing my father to let him out of that locked room, but the nightmares hadn't stopped because I had forgotten. Forgotten to tell them that he had wanted to be cremated, had wanted his ashes spread on the football field at Jefferson High. No decaying body, no being locked into a crypt packed too tight to flirt or dance or run. He would still be pissed at me, and I would never go to see him in that place.

Two days after the repass, my mother enlisted my help in a rigorous, top to bottom cleaning. We scrubbed the walls and doorframes with bleach, most of which bore TJ's handprints from his habit of leaning against them when he came in sweaty and funky from practice. We waxed the floors, cleaned behind the refrigerator and under the beds, swept the broom up in the corners of the ceilings, took newspaper and glass cleaner to the windows, inside and out, all those things that only got done a few times a year. She threw out all the leftovers from the impasse, even though there was plenty of good food: a pot of spaghetti with more hamburger meat than pasta and big chunks of real tomato, a basket of fried chicken, pans of homemade macaroni and cheese and hot water cornbread and bread pudding. It was like Thanksgiving, and like Thanksgiving, I'd expected to live off of that for at least a week. But she threw it out, got me to help her move the furniture around, and opened all the blinds and doors and windows, as if to let light and air push through whatever living-boy smell remained. She made chicken and peas for dinner and my father looked at his plate in confusion.

"What happened to all that food?"

"I made your dinner."

"Yeah, but we already had all that food."

"I made some groceries; I needed to clean out my refrigerator."

"Yeah, but why you have to go grocery shopping when we had all that food?"

"You don't like your dinner? You don't like it, you don't have to eat it."

"Didn't say all that, just don't understand why you would throw out a bunch of good food," he said, his voice dropping to a mumble. "People try to help out—"

"I don't need anybody to cook for me."

My father looked at her with tired eyes, picked up his plate, and moved to the living room. We heard the cheering and whistle sounds, the background chants of young girls' voices, my father's own gruff commentary. He had taken to watching TJ's game tapes in the evenings instead of cable.

It was several weeks before my mother entered TJ's room, and this time she didn't ask me to help. I watched her clean, frantically and methodically, with that feeling you get when you watch a character in a horror movie walking into that fatal mistake. I didn't know why, but it seemed so wrong to move his things; the clothes he left on the floor, the balled-up papers scattered around the thrift-store-salvaged desk where he occasionally did homework. It seemed wrong to dilute the thick, corn-chip musk that clung to the room more than when he lived there, filling the sheets, climbing the walls, and peeking out at us into the hallway. She washed the linens, made the bed that he had left a jumble of covers, and dusted off the trophies. She went through his hamper and armoire, washed and pressed all of his clothes, and put them neatly away. She asked my father, "You think *she* would want TJ's stuff?" Charlotte had ceased to be "that bitch" in my mother's mouth since TJ's death, but you could still sense the edge in her voice when she said "she" or "her."

"What?" my father asked tiredly. He was watching the tape of TJ's last-minute touchdown at the championship game against the Sheriffs.

"I washed all TJ's stuff."

"Why you do that?"

"What am I supposed to do, just leave it?"

"Why you worried about it?"

"I was just wondering if maybe *she* wanted it."

"You in such a hurry to get rid of his shit, ain't you? Just like you wanted to get rid of him!"

My mother's face flushed hard, her coppery skin deepening. She'd finally gotten her hair done again, her nails. She stood up straight and her eyes were clear. It was as if the new pain had cracked her depression over Grandmere, as if she was getting stronger as my father broke down. "I know you're hurting, Tannah," she said softly. "But don't pull that shit on me. I'm a mother, too, and I know she'd want his clothes."

"Just leave it alone."

"It just doesn't seem right, leaving his room all set up like he's coming back to it, and you sitting here, watching these tapes every day—"

"Just leave it alone! Just leave it!" my father roared, standing up and knocking his TV tray over in the process, spilling his ashtray and plate of black-eyed peas across the carpet. "Just leave me the fuck alone!" His hands were balled into fists, his eyes red-veined. My mother had jumped back when he stood but now she put her hands on her hips and spoke quietly. "All right, T, if that's what you want, I'll leave you alone. We can leave everything just like it is. I'll leave you alone." With nowhere else to spew his anger, he sank back into his armchair.

"Are you going to clean this up?" my mother asked, gesturing to the floor. I wished she wouldn't have said that.

"Fuck you, Becky." My father stood up. "You clean it up." He billowed out of the doorway and slammed the door behind him. We heard his motor and music gun up in the driveway.

"Mommy, did you have to say that?" I asked.

"What? If he thinks that because of what happened I'm going to start being some kind of mouse in my own house, tiptoeing around him, he has another thing coming. Go get the broom and dustpan." Cheers rang out loudly on the TV screen as TJ made that last leap over the goal line. My mother stepped over the mess on the floor and slapped at the VCR with shaking hands until TJ stopped moving in mid-flight.

When my father first started fixing things that summer, we thought it was because he was getting better. He had always done work around the house and had seemed to enjoy it, even if he never seemed to be able to keep up with all the things in our house that were breaking down or falling apart. There was a different spirit in the way he did his home improvements now, a jittery restlessness, fervor in his eyes as he jumped from task to task. Sometimes a hammer would wake me up in the middle of the night, banging on the hallway wall. He put new doorknobs on the doors that didn't turn, he put new hardware on the kitchen cabinets that my mother hated, and wouldn't tell her where the old knobs and drawer handles were.

He tried to put crown molding up in the living room but didn't finish. He left half the boards outside and they got ruined by the rain and the stray dogs that were always roaming through the neighborhood. He tried to clean out the fireplace and infuriated my mother by getting ashes all over her carpet, and the fireplace still smelled like burning soot and spewed out dangerous smoke when he tried to light it on a warm day. He decided to try to insulate and drywall the back porch, TJ's old room, by himself. We had left the room alone except for my mother going in and dusting every now and then. It had the door to the backyard, which my dad had locked from the outside to stop TJ from sneaking in and out at night. Though he was gone, we'd never unlocked it and never resumed using the room; we walked through the kitchen door and around to get to the back.

My mother and I got home one day to find my dad covered with dust and wearing goggles, breaking through the slapped-up plaster to get to the framing of the back porch, piles of bubbly foam-wrapped insulation all around him and piled up and down the halls.

"Tannah!" she tried to cry out over the sound of his sledge-hammer. "Tannah, what is all this shit? What the hell are you doing?"

"Ima make this into a real room. You feel how fucking hot it is in here? We should be ashamed of ourselves, having anybody sleeping up in here."

"Nobody's sleeping in here now, Tannah."

He kept swinging away, and my mother jumped back, coughing as dust flew our way. "Nobody's sleeping in here, Tannah," she repeated, fear in her voice.

"Yeah, I know, and that's the way you like it, huh?" he roared. I saw my mother's face go through seven emotions in one moment and finally shift into a scowl that couldn't hide moist, hurt eyes.

"Fuck you!" she screamed. "Fuck you! You think I wanted him to die? You think I wanted anybody's child to get shot in the fucking head? You want to blame me? Go ahead and blame me, I don't care anymore!"

"Look who's talking about blame," my father laughed wildly. "Who always blamed me for not having shit, for not going back to school, for not having a three-bedroom house!" He struck the wall again. "Well, Ima give you a three-bedroom house, Becky, Ima give you a three-bedroom house!" He struck it again, and more dust filled the room, gray and hot as some kind of sandstorm in a nightmare. A large chunk fell loose, and my mother jumped back, knocking into me and trampling my feet. She had forgotten I was there, like they always did. I usually tried to forget, too, but I felt frozen now, watching my father in the gray, hot room, filled with his wild, red eyes and TJ's dust-covered trophies.

"You're crazy," my mother said, almost to herself, shaking her head. "I thought you were back on that stuff but maybe you've just gone crazy."

"I'll show you crazy!" My father rushed towards us. I was suddenly flattened against the wall as my mother pressed away from him, in the one horrible moment when we both thought he was coming for her. He rumbled past us with the sledgehammer. We stood still, my mother's breath loud and heavy, until we heard glass breaking and the whirring ear-stabs of my mother's car alarm. My mother ran outside, and I followed, walking slowly, pinching myself even though I knew this was not a dream. Maybe this was finally it, when one of them would kill the other or they would kill each other and I would go live with Auntie Trish or my great-aunt with the high blood pressure and black funeral veil. I paused at the door, my forehead against the screen, before going outside to see what had happened. My father was gone. My mother's new Honda looked like a jumped kid with cracked glasses, but it wasn't her car that my mother had run to. She knelt over her flowerbed, where the rosebushes, including Grandmere's bush, were all hacked apart. The brilliant, lazy summer blooms lay like burned trash on the dirt.

Chapter Nineteen

By the time I had gotten back into the rhythm of going to school, it was summer. Somehow, I still pulled out good grades, and though I had not made many friends, several eighth graders I had never talked to before asked me to sign their memory books. TJ's funeral had been on the news, and I had been clearly identifiable in the yellow dress that stopped inches above my knees because we never did let out the hem. I now had a certain degree of notoriety. I was an object of the sort of reverent pity that comes with losing a close family member, and losing someone to a gunshot in riots that most people at my school had only seen on TV gave me ghetto credibility. I was right up there with the gangsta rappers that some of my white schoolmates were just starting to discover, that I listened to on the tapes and headphones I swiped from TJ's room before my mother sent the last of his things to Charlotte. I wasn't sure how to feel about this fame; but in the absence of real friends who I could tell how much I missed my brother, I took it. Even as things shut off and fell apart in the house and the bills piled up on the table by the door, my mother had started to shop feverishly, dressing me in clothes so freshly made that their sharp corners scratched at my skin. My legs were long in my new skirts. I was taller than all the boys in my grade, and the crew of black eighth-grade guys always called things out to me when I rounded their corner.

My mother had packed everything that my father owned in boxes and trash bags and pulled it out onto the porch. I was left there to meet him, alone, on the day he came to load up his truck. When I heard the music in the driveway, Stevie Wonder lilting about skies and ribbons, I went outside with dread, expecting some monster version of him like what I saw on the day he tore up the roses. But when he came around the front of the truck he looked fresh, his bald head, white shirt, and clean tennis shoes gleaming in the sun that had no right to shine so hard. As he got closer, the newness stopped at the haircut and the fat white shoelaces. His face looked like a pit bull's, heavy-jawed and unloved. We hugged awkwardly, and I pulled back first. I felt useless, so I picked up a bag of neatly pressed and folded work jeans to have something to do. Their weight strained the plastic, making thin, silvery stretch marks on the bag's bulging sides.

"You don't need to be helping me do this, baby." My father reached for the bag.

"It's not that heavy. And I'm not a baby."

"No, I guess you ain't. But go on, I don't want you helping me with this."

I sat on the porch but could not stay still there for long, still feeling as if there was something else I should be doing. I had not eaten a pollaseed in months; it was a habit I had picked up from TJ, and it had left with him. I went into the kitchen, cut a jagged piece of watermelon with a dirty knife I found sitting on the counter, and carried it, with no plate, out to the porch. I slurped hard in between pushing patent leather-shiny black seeds through my teeth into our empty flowerbed.

"Do you think a watermelon will grow, Daddy?" I asked as he moved back and forth, shouldering boxes and bags.

"No, ba—. No, Tanis, can't just set the seed down there. Gotta plant it in the right weather and work on it. You should know that, you such a big girl." He looked at me and laughed. "You look like the folks down in 'Bama, sitting on the porch sucking watermelon like that." He paused. "You know that's where Daddy's headed, right? Ima go on down to Alabama."

I stood up, and the watermelon tumbled down, leaving pink juice trails on my white shorts. One of the worst fears I had always had was that one day my father would gun up his engine and back down that driveway and not come back. Alabama might as well have been Bosnia to me. I had never been so far from either of my parents in my life.

"Alabama?"

"Tanis, there ain't nothing good for me in this city if I'm not here with you and your mama."

"You could get her new rosebushes." I knew as I said it that this wouldn't happen. I had brought up getting new bushes before, as my mother and I packed up the house. She said she couldn't make the note without my father, and she sure as hell wasn't going to plant something pretty for whoever came after us to fuck up. She had applied for the city's rental assistance program and taken me to see a little white box in a bigger brown box of a building closer to my school. I had heard someone blow their nose on the other side of the wall and seen my mother cry over the kitchen sink as she pretended to test the faucet.

My father looked towards the house. "Can't just get new things when you lose the old things and think it's gonna be okay. My granddaddy in 'Bama used to have a little farm and he always said you gotta let a field lie fallow sometimes, that's the only way new things gonna grow good." He hoisted a box into the back of his truck, took out a bandanna, and wiped it across his head. "Still a little bit of land down there that my mama's house is on. Need to be with her a bit before she go, help her out some. I wanted to go down there when she had first got sick, but your mama said she wasn't gonna be nobody's Alabama hillbilly." He laughed, low and bitter. "You can breathe the air better there. And they got real backyards with no fences, not these little pitiful squares of grass. When I get some money together, I'm gonna send you a ticket to come down for your next school break." I thought about the drill team I wanted to try out for at school, how they were always in a big holiday parade over winter break, and how tight my mother's eyes would narrow if I talked about spending Christmas away from her. I thought about the sleepaway college prep program my English teacher said I could get a scholarship for next summer. I saw the school breaks and the visits in my future, the moments of being my Daddy's little girl again, stretching further and further apart. I ran and fastened myself to him, relieved that my arms still fit comfortably beneath his, that my head still rested comfortably on his chest. When he left, there would be nobody in my life left that I could hug like that. Nobody big enough to make me feel small and safe.

"Did you love TJ more than me?" I asked before I knew I had decided to ask that.

My father looked down at me, took my face tight between his rough hands. "Why you ask me something stupid like that?" he asked roughly.

"It's not stupid. You were always with him, all the time."

"So now you mad at me, just like he was."

"I'm not mad. I just want to know."

"You gotta be mad at me to think I don't love you more than anything in this whole world. I was trying to do right by my son, Tanis. He loved the hell out of you, but he never liked that I was here with you and your mama instead of him and his. But one thing he always listened to me about was his runnin' and ballplayin', so I put everything I had into helping him be good at that. Sometimes I think he might have been good at a lot of other things, too, and we ain't never gonna know what."

"He liked music," I said before putting my face back into his chest.

"Yeah. Always had them headphones on, but you could still hear that shit through them. Boy probably wouldn't have had no hearing left by time he was thirty." He chuckled, and I felt the chuckle choke somewhere in his chest. "What I did, bringing him over here to live, I did it for me, to make me feel like somebody." He pressed me tighter into his chest, to the point where I couldn't breathe, but I took slower, deeper breaths and didn't move. "Daddy's fucked up a lot, baby, losing jobs, messing over women. I wanted to be a big man with my two kids in one house. If TJ woulda been in the Valley that night, he'd still be here."

I popped my head up. In all of the memories, all of the grief, all the replaying, all of the blaming that had been going on, I had never thought that my father was blaming himself. I wondered if my own guilt would make him feel any better. If I had ever brought up what happened that night, my mother probably would have said, "Let sleeping dogs lie." But it seemed to me like the dogs that you left sleep always woke up one day when you weren't paying enough attention to run.

"Daddy." He looked down at me again, brushed the permed hair off my forehead. "What, baby? You got something to tell me?" I stared at his face, his eyebrows that were mine, the lines too deep for his age, the filmy drops of sweat freezing into a sugary crust on his forehead, dark eyes searching my own in a way they never had before. I lowered my eyes back to his shirt. He looked at me like I was a real person, not just his little girl, like I could tell him real person things.

In biology class, I had learned that butterfly wings had a dust that helped them to fly, and once you touched their wings you ruined it forever. I remembered the goldish power that would stain the tips of my fingers after Yosi and I caught butterflies, and how they hadn't burst into the air like I expected when I opened the top and let them go. I had thought I had given them just enough to live with the cherry tomatoes and the small flowers we dropped in. I had watched them stick their long black tongues into the flower centers and prided myself on catching so much beauty in one little space. But then I sent them into the world all broken. We had all gotten broken, my mother and father and I, in our big and our little ways, touched too hard to get back the things we had lost.

"I'll miss you, Daddy," was all I decided to say.

"Daddy'll miss you too, Toodle — I'll miss you, too, Tanis, I'm gonna miss you every day." He squeezed me until I couldn't breathe, and again, I was the one to disengage my arms, to step back. My mouth had left some watermelon juice on his white tee shirt. He brushed at it absently with his bandanna and wiped at his eyes. I watched him finish loading up the truck, and I let him drive away.

Made in the USA
Columbia, SC
21 November 2023

26269399R00150